THE PHARAOH KEY

DOUGLAS PRESTON and LINCOLN CHILD are the number one bestselling co-authors of the celebrated Pendergast novels, as well as the Gideon Crew books. Preston and Child's *Relic* and *The Cabinet of Curiosities* were chosen by readers in a National Public Radio poll as being among the one hundred greatest thrillers ever written, and *Relic* was made into a number one box-office hit movie. Readers can sign up for their monthly newsletter, The Pendergast File, at www.PrestonChild.com and follow them on Facebook.

Also by Douglas Preston and Lincoln Child

Agent Pendergast Novels

Relic*
Reliquary*
The Cabinet of Curiosities
Still Life with Crows
Brimstone**
Dance of Death**
The Book of the Dead**
The Wheel of Darkness
Cemetery Dance
Fever Dream†
Cold Vengeance†
Two Graves†
White Fire
Blue Labyrinth
Crimson Shore
The Obsidian Chamber
City of Endless Night
Verses for the Dead

Gideon Crew Novels

Gideon's Sword
Gideon's Corpse
The Lost Island
Beyond the Ice Limit
The Pharaoh Key

Other Novels

Mount Dragon
Riptide
Thunderhead
The Ice Limit

*Relic and Reliquary are
ideally read in sequence
**The Diogenes Trilogy
†The Helen Trilogy

By Douglas Preston

The Lost City of the Monkey God
The Kraken Project Impact
The Monster of Florence
(with Mario Spezi)
Blasphemy
Tyrannosaur Canyon
The Codex
Ribbons of Time
The Royal Road
Talking to the Ground
Jennie
Cities of Gold
Dinosaurs in the Attic

By Lincoln Child

Full Wolf Moon
The Forgotten Room
The Third Gate
Terminal Freeze
Deep Storm
Death Match
Lethal Velocity(formerly Utopia)
Tales of the Dark 1–3
Dark Banquet
Dark Company

PRESTON & CHILD

THE PHARAOH KEY

HEAD of ZEUS

First published in the USA in 2018 by Grand Central Publishing,
a division of Hachette Book Group, Inc

First published in the UK in 2018 by Head of Zeus, Ltd
This paperback edition published in 2019 by Head of Zeus Ltd

9 7 5 3 1 2 4 6 8

A catalogue record for this book is available from
the British Library.

ISBN (PB): 9781788547727
ISBN (E): 9781788547697

Printed and bound in Great Britain by
CPI Group (UK) Ltd, Croydon CR0 4YY

Head of Zeus Ltd
First Floor East
5–8 Hardwick Street
London EC1R 4RG

WWW.HEADOFZEUS.COM

*Lincoln Child dedicates this book to his
daughter, Veronica*

*Douglas Preston dedicates this book to
Anna and Peyton Forbes*

THE PHARAOH KEY

1

GIDEON CREW SAT in the fourteenth-floor waiting room of Lewis Conrad, MD, restlessly drumming the tips of his left fingers against the back of his right wrist, waiting to find out whether he would live or die. An oversize envelope he'd brought with him, currently empty, lay beside his chair. Despite Dr. Conrad being one of the more expensive neurosurgeons in New York City, the magazines in his well-appointed waiting room had a greasy, well-thumbed look that deterred Gideon from touching them. Besides, they were of a subject matter—*People, Entertainment Weekly, Us*—that held little interest. Why couldn't a doctor's waiting room have copies of *Harper's* or *The New Criterion*, or even a damn *National Geographic*?

A door on the far side of the waiting room opened silently; a nurse with a file in one hand poked her head out, and hope flared within Gideon's breast.

"Ada Kraus?" the nurse said. An elderly woman rose to her feet with difficulty, walked slowly across the waiting room, and disappeared into the hallway beyond the open door, which immediately closed again.

As Gideon settled back into his chair, he realized it wasn't restlessness, exactly, that afflicted him. It was a feeling of unsettledness that had kept him in New York City ever since the completion of his last mission for his employer, Effective Engineering Solutions. Normally he would have made a beeline for his cabin in the Jemez Mountains of New Mexico, gotten out his fly rod, and gone fishing.

It was so strange. His boss, Eli Glinn, had vanished with no word. The company's offices in the old Meatpacking District of Lower Manhattan remained open, but the place seemed to be slowly winding down. Two weeks ago, his automatic salary payment had stopped, with no warning, and last week EES ceased paying for his expensive suite in the Gansevoort Hotel, around the corner from EES headquarters. Even so, Gideon had not left New York. He'd stayed on for over two months as his arm healed from the last mission, wandering the streets, visiting museums, reading novels while lounging at the hotel, and drinking far too much in the many hip bars that dotted the Meatpacking District. Finally, he admitted to himself why he'd been hanging around the city: there was something he had to know. The problem was, it was also the last thing he wanted to know. But in the end his need to know had overcome his fear of knowing, and he had made an appointment with Dr. Conrad. And so two days ago, he had been given a cranial MRI and now he was cooling his heels in the doctor's waiting room, awaiting the results.

No: it wasn't restlessness. It was a powerful combination of hope and fear pulling him in different directions: hope that something might have happened to him during the past ten months that fixed his condition, known as AVM; and fear that it had gotten worse.

And here he was, waiting, hoping, and fearing, all tangled up in his head like the AVM itself.

The door opened again; the nurse stuck out her head. "Gideon Crew?"

Gideon picked up the empty envelope, rose from his chair, and followed the nurse down the corridor and into a well-appointed doctor's consultation room. To his surprise, the doctor was already seated behind a desk. On one side of his desk were the beat-up medical records and MRIs that Gideon had been carrying around with him in the envelope for the better part of a year. On the other side was a fresh set of pictures and scans—the ones taken two days before.

Dr. Conrad was about sixty, with a mild expression, gray eyes, and a sheaf of salt-and-pepper hair. He gazed kindly at Gideon through a pair of black-rimmed glasses. "Hello, Gideon," he said. "May I use your first name?"

"Of course."

"Please sit down."

Gideon sat.

There was a moment of silence while the doctor cleared his throat, then looked briefly from the old MRIs to the new. "I take it that you are already apprised of your condition?"

"Yes. It's known as a vein of Galen malformation. It's an abnormal knot of arteries and veins deep in my brain, in an area known as the Circle of Willis. It's usually congenital, and in my case inoperable. Because the arteriovenous walls are steadily weakening, the AVM is expanding in size and will eventually hemorrhage—which will be instantly fatal."

There was a brief, uncomfortable silence.

"That's as good a summary as I could have made." Dr. Conrad propped his palms on the edge of his desk and interlaced his fingers. "When you first learned of your AVM," he asked, "did the doctor give you a prognosis on how long you might expect to live?"

"Yes."

"And how long was that?"

"About a year."

"When was that?"

"Almost ten months ago."

"I see." The doctor shuffled through the images on his desk, cleared his throat again. "I'm very sorry to have to tell you, Gideon, but from these tests and everything else I've seen, the original prognosis was correct."

Although he had half expected this—indeed, he'd had no real reason to suppose it would be different—for a moment, Gideon found he couldn't speak. "You mean...I've only got two more months to live?"

"Comparing your original MRIs with the ones we just did, the progress of your AVM has been textbook, unfortunately. So yes, I would say that is a likely time frame—give or take a few weeks."

"There aren't any new treatments or surgical options?"

"As you probably have learned, most brain AVMs can be treated with surgery, radiation, or embolization, but the location of your AVM and its size make it impossible to be treated with those methods. Anything we did, either surgical or radiological, would almost certainly cause severe brain damage, if you survived at all."

Gideon leaned back in his chair. All the anxiety and uncertainty that had been hovering around him the last several weeks now settled down like a deadweight. He could hardly breathe.

Dr. Conrad leaned forward. "It's tough, son. There's nothing I can say to make it otherwise. It may not help to hear this, but: you know how much time is allotted you. Most of us don't have that luxury."

"Luxury," Gideon groaned. "Two months, a luxury. *Please.*"

"When Warren Zevon, the rock star, knew he was dying of cancer, someone asked him how he was coping with that knowledge. His reply? *Enjoy every sandwich.* My advice to you is similar: don't become miserable and paralyzed with grief and fear. Instead, do something worthwhile and engaging with the time you have left."

Gideon said nothing; he merely shook his head. He felt sick. *Two months.* But why did he expect anything different?

"You're strong and mobile, and will remain so...until the end. That's the nature of AVM. So I'll tell you what I tell my other patients facing the same situation: live every minute the best way you can."

A long moment passed while Gideon sat in the chair, motionless. Dr. Conrad smiled at him from across the desk with the same kindly expression. When he started gathering together the various reports and scans, Gideon realized the conference was at an end. He stood up.

"Thank you," he said.

The neurosurgeon stood as well, handed him the paperwork, then shook his hand. "God bless you, Gideon. And remember what I said."

2

THE CHILL MARCH sun, streaming down 50th Street, struck Gideon full in the face as he stepped out of the building and into the afternoon rush of Midtown, blaring horns and exhaust mingling with the smell of a street vendor's roasting kebabs. He felt stunned, hardly able to walk. *Two months.* Despite knowing better, he realized he'd held out a crazy hope that his AVM had been cured—or at least arrested.

A feeling of self-pity swept over him as he turned the corner onto Madison Avenue. Glinn had vanished. He was, it seemed, without a friend in the world. While he had more than enough money to last a couple of months, what good would it ultimately do him? Was he really going to go back to New Mexico and live in an isolated cabin all by himself, fishing and running out the clock?

His cell phone dinged and he glanced at it: a text from Manuel Garza, second in command at EES. It read: *Come to the office right away.*

Garza. He had long had a difficult relationship with the man, a brilliant engineer who could be both prickly and cold-blooded.

But the two had developed a rapport of sorts on their most recent assignment; he'd found that Garza wasn't quite the ruthless human being he'd assumed. Underneath that brushed-steel veneer, he did in fact have a heart.

Right away. Gideon decided to walk down the sunny side of the avenue, hoping a brisk, two-mile hike would help clear away the shock of what he had just learned. Two months. Jesus.

Half an hour later, he arrived at the ugly loading dock entrance to EES's corporate headquarters on Little West 12th Street. He hadn't been there since they stopped his salary two weeks before, but he found that his card and key code still worked. As he entered the vast, cavernous space of the company's main working area, he was surprised by what he saw. The huge space, once filled with models of various engineering projects, whiteboards covered with scribbled equations, and people in lab coats scurrying about, was now almost empty. The floor was strewn with papers and other detritus: evidence of a hasty breakdown and removal. The worktables and desks were empty, with dead computer monitors, some draped in plastic, and snakes of cabling leading nowhere.

A dark, muscular figure came out of the gloom, lumpy computer bag slung over his shoulder, and Gideon recognized Garza. The man looked furious.

"It's about time. What did you do, walk?" he said loudly, even before he had reached Gideon. "Can you believe this shit?"

"What shit?"

He swept his hand around. "This!"

"Looks like they're shutting the place down."

"Did they cut you off, too? Last week I didn't get my salary deposit. No note, no explanation, no dismissal notice. Nada."

"Same here."

"And now this. After all those dangerous ops, after risking our lives half a dozen times, after all those years of hard work, this is the thanks I get? What do I have to show for it? Nothing but *this*." And he raised his wristwatch to Gideon—a black-faced Rolex with a gold band—and shook it in his face. "I don't know about you, but I am *pissed*."

"Pissed" seemed like an understatement. As for Gideon, he felt more stunned than anything else. What did it really matter, when he had only two months to live? "He did pay us well."

"For all that I did for him, I should be worth seven figures. As it is, I've hardly saved up anything. Life is expensive, especially here in New York City, and I'd planned on a steady revenue stream for years to come. But it's not just the money—it's the *way* he did it. I haven't been able to reach him in almost six weeks. No response to emails, cell phone messages, nothing. I don't even know where the son of a bitch is. And now we've got until five o'clock to clear out our stuff. That's in ten minutes, in case you hadn't noticed."

"Um, I hadn't noticed."

At this point Garza paused and looked closely at him. "Hey— are you all right?"

Gideon tried to answer, but something seemed to be stopping up his throat, preventing him from talking.

Garza took a step closer, comprehension dawning on his face. He already knew of Gideon's earlier diagnosis, and now he seemed to be putting it together. "You hear some bad news?"

Gideon nodded.

There was a long silence before Gideon finally found his voice. "Two months."

It was Garza's turn to look stunned. "Aw, shit. *Shit*. I'm so sorry. There's no possibility, experimental treatment, something?"

Gideon waved his hand. "Nothing."

Garza took a deep breath. "That pisses me off even more. Glinn knew you only had a year to live when he hired you ... and look how he's treated you since! You should be even angrier than I am. We should have had a big score—a really big score—long ago. That's why I joined EES when we left the military, took all those crazy risks. Eli promised that we'd all have just such a payday. And we did—that's almost the worst part. Because just when we really, finally struck it rich, he went and funneled every dime back into that white-whale project of his! *That* was a success, too, of course—thanks to us—but it cost everything and left us high and dry. And now he's fired us and is shutting down the company!"

It was hard for Gideon to get exercised about Eli Glinn. He mumbled his agreement.

"Well," Garza said, "I've got all my stuff in here—" he raised his computer bag—"so clear out your desk and let's head over to the Spice Market and get ourselves righteously shitfaced."

"Now, that's a good idea. But I don't really have anything to collect."

"So much the better. Let's go."

Gideon paused to take a moment and look out over the vast, dead, silent space of half-completed projects and dark electronics. Garza paused as well, finally shaking his head.

In that moment Gideon heard, from a distant corner, an electronic chime. A small computer screen woke underneath a clear plastic shroud, creating a glow.

Garza saw it, too. "Looks like somebody forgot to turn off their monitor." He walked toward the computer and Gideon followed. Taking the corner of the tarp, Garza jerked it away.

A message stood against a white background:

Phaistos Project
TASK COMPLETED
Time elapsed: 43412 hrs 34.12 minutes
Solution Follows

Garza stared at it. "What the hell?"

"Forty-three thousand hours..." Gideon did a quick calculation. "That's almost five years. You think this computer's been
working on some problem for five years?"

Garza started to laugh, his voice echoing. "It's just the sort
of thing Glinn would do: give a computer some impossible task
and let it grind away, day in, day out, just to see if it could come
up with a solution. And look here—it finally did! A little late, but
what the hell."

Gideon squinted at the screen. The "solution" following the
message was a long listing in hexadecimal. "What's the Phaistos
Project?"

Before Garza could answer, a voice rang out from the far side
of the room. "Five o'clock, gentlemen! Sorry, but it's time to
leave. We're locking the place down."

Gideon turned to see two security guards at the main door.
He glanced back to find Garza bending over the computer, in-
serting a USB stick into the computer.

"What are you doing?"

"Downloading this data."

"What for?"

But Garza was busy tapping on the keyboard.

"Gentlemen?" The guards were starting to walk across the
room.

"We'll be there in a sec, just clearing out our stuff!" Garza shouted from a bent position.

"Sorry, but we're under orders to shut down at five o'clock sharp."

Garza pulled the USB stick out and slipped it in his sock. "Wish I had time to fuck this machine up," he muttered. "That would serve old Eli right."

Now the guards had arrived. "You're not supposed to be using any of the electronics," the taller one said.

"Sorry," said Garza, straightening up. "We'll go."

The guards escorted them to the entrance hall and then paused. "Sir," the taller one said to Garza, "I'm afraid I have to look through your bag."

"Bullshit," said Garza, "this is my stuff."

"We're under orders," said the guard. He reached for the bag and, after hesitating, Garza let him take it.

The guard opened it up, and his blunt fingers sorted through everything. There was no laptop in it, but his busy fingers selected a small hard drive. "I have to take this."

Garza stared at him. "It's *my* data."

"When you leave this company, nothing is yours anymore," said the guard.

"Bullshit."

The guard took the hard drive and dropped it into a slot, where there was a sudden grinding noise from an e-waste shredder.

"Hey! What the *fuck*?"

"Sorry," the guard said in a tone that was anything but sorry as he stepped forward, one hand coming to rest on the butt of a holstered Glock. "Time to leave."

Garza stared at him.

"Let's go," said Gideon.

They turned and left without a word, the two guards following them out. Once they reached the loading dock, the massive steel door to EES slid shut with a clang and Gideon heard the automatic bolts shooting home.

Garza turned to him. "Time for that drink."

3

As they rounded the corner of 13th Street, Garza let out a cry of dismay. "Closed!"

Indeed it was. The Spice Market, where they had occasionally gone for drinks, was padlocked.

"The story of our life," said Garza bitterly. "Shuttered."

They wandered down the street to another watering hole, Catch. At five it hadn't gotten going yet, and they found seats at the bar. Gideon ordered a Hendrick's martini, dirty, while Garza took a pint of craft beer.

The bartender served their drinks, and Garza raised his glass. "To...what the hell, I can't think of a good toast, I'm still too pissed off."

"To being pissed off."

They clinked glasses.

"Okay," said Gideon, "now tell me about this Phaistos Project."

"One of Eli's crazy shots in the dark."

"How so?"

"For the past six years, since the sinking of the *Rolvaag*, he's been desperate for money. He had to raise two billion for his white-whale project, you see: to return to the Ice Limit and finish what he started. All those intervening years, he tried to scrounge up funds wherever he could—and some of those areas involved treasure hunting. The Loot of Lima, the Lost Dutchman Mine, the Victorio Peak gold...shit like that."

"Did he ever find any?"

"Hell, yes! Remind me someday to tell you the story of the Caves of Asphodel. My God, when we entered that antechamber...!" He whistled. "So anyway, Glinn launched a whole bunch of speculative projects that he hoped might lead to a payoff. That included trying to decipher various ancient inscriptions. One of those, in fact, led to your own assignment on the Lost Island. There were others. He had his cryptanalysts and historians trying to crack the Voynich Manuscript, the Shugborough Inscription, the Dispilio Tablet, the Rohonc Codex...and the Phaistos Disk."

He took a long draw on his beer.

"So here's the story." He paused a moment, as if sorting out his thoughts. "The Phaistos Disk was found in 1908 or thereabouts in the ruins of a Minoan palace on the island of Crete. It's three thousand five hundred years old, made of fired clay, and is covered on both sides by a dense spiral of stamped hieroglyphic figures—heads, people, helmets, gloves, arrows, shields, clubs, ships, columns, fish, birds, bees—all tiny little pictures. It seems to be the script of an unknown language. Since its discovery, everyone and their sister has tried to decipher it, to no avail, and today it's the most famous unsolved inscription in existence. Many claimed to have translated it, of course, but all those solutions have been discredited."

"So how is it supposed to lead to a treasure?" Gideon asked.

"We couldn't be sure that it would. Like I said, it was a shot in the dark, one of many. About five years back, Glinn dedicated a single high-powered computer to cracking the code. Over time, the project was basically forgotten as other projects took priority. *I* sure as hell forgot about it. But all that time, the computer must've been cranking away, patiently trying one cryptanalytical approach after another."

"And finally it succeeded?"

Garza retrieved the USB stick and held it in his hand. "It's right here."

"Are you sure?"

"Oh, it's the translation, all right. Eli put his best cryptanalyst, philologist, and coder to work, creating the program for that computer. If that computer says it finished, it finished. We just have to figure out what it's telling us." He took another pull at his beer, draining it.

"What do you think it means?"

"We'll find out. Maybe a thirty-five-century-old message from one Greek king to another, something like, *Give me back my wife Helen or I will kick your ass.*"

Gideon chuckled despite himself. "Why was Glinn interested in it, specifically?"

"Because of its fame. And he was a gambler of sorts, always putting a chip down on one long shot or other."

"If it's such a gamble, why did *you* just bother downloading it?"

"Are you kidding? The gamble wasn't the secret the Phaistos Disk contained—it was thinking he could ever decrypt it at all. But that program succeeded—and the joke's on him." He waggled the USB stick in front of Gideon. "Whatever the message on this tells us, whatever it leads to, there's one thing for sure: it's got to be worth money. Probably a hell of a lot of money.

It might make us famous—and we'll have done it right under Glinn's nose."

"I need another drink."

They ordered a second round. When it came, Garza raised his glass. "My turn for a toast. To fame, glory, and riches." He took a deep swig. "And it's ours, Gideon—yours and mine. Finally: a chance to get some of our own back! We'll take our time, do it right, translate that hexadecimal file, and—"

"No," Gideon interrupted.

"What do you mean, no?"

"We're not going to 'take our time.' If we're going to do this, we're going to do it now. Like, today."

Garza began to object, then suddenly shut up. "Right. I forgot. Two months."

"I've just been given a prescription from a neurologist: enjoy every sandwich. Well, for better or worse, life just served me up this particular sandwich. So let's go up to my suite and put that USB stick into my laptop and see what the Phaistos Disk has to say after all these centuries of silence."

"Fair enough. We'll do it now. But I have a condition of my own."

Gideon, who'd been about to stand up, went still. "Yes?"

"We both agree that whatever this Phaistos Disk leads to, it's worth money. Right? It might be Homer's lost work, *Margites*. It might be the keys to a spaceship. It might be the proverbial diamond as big as the Ritz. But it's going to have value."

"And your point?"

"My point is, I'm sick and tired of finding something and then turning it over to somebody else. When—*if*—we find whatever pot of gold is waiting at the end of this rainbow, we're keeping it. Agreed? We're not giving it to some museum, or donating it to the Library of Congress, or whatever. We're turning it into cash—

whether that means breaking it up and selling it piece by piece, or auctioning the thing off to the highest bidder."

"But..." Gideon began, then fell silent.

"But what?" Garza replied, his tone shading toward the belligerent.

"We don't know what it is. It could be anything. It might be of great historical or cultural value. It might be the patrimony of some civilization that—"

"Now you're sounding like Glinn. I'm not doing this for the good of humanity—I'm doing it for myself. I don't care if it's a centerfold of the *Mona Lisa*—we're selling it for the most dough we possibly can, and then splitting the proceeds. You can always donate your half to—well, to medical research, maybe. I just want to be crystal-clear about this: if it has value, we're gonna *steal* it. Are you with me?"

This was followed by an awkward silence. Then Gideon shrugged. "What the hell. The worst that can happen is I have a few weeks to feel guilty about it."

"Good man." And with that they stood up and shook hands.

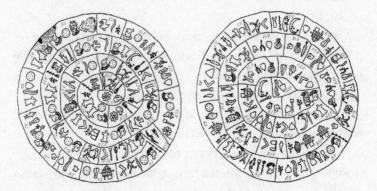

4

THE BAR AT the top of the Gansevoort Hotel was quiet, the rooftop pool still shut down for the winter. Gideon had fetched his laptop from his room, and he and Garza slipped into a leather banquette in one corner.

Garza ordered a round of mojitos while Gideon fired up the computer. The drinks arrived. Garza pulled the USB stick out of his pocket. "Ready?"

"Go for it."

Garza inserted the USB stick, called up a hexadecimal-to-ASCII converter, and fed in the downloaded data. An obviously nonsensical output resulted.

"Okay," said Garza, "that's strange."

Gideon took a long drink of his mojito. "Are you sure the computer successfully decoded the Disk?"

"I told you—I'm sure. Try hex-to-decimal."

Pulling the laptop toward him, Gideon ran the conversion utility again, but another list of apparently random numbers resulted.

"Try Unicode," said Garza.

"How will that help?"

"Just try it."

More garbage.

They tried Base64, octal, HTML numeric, binary, and Windows ALT codes.

Garza sat back. "Okay. What totally obvious thing are we missing?"

"Here's what I don't get. If the computer had really deciphered the Disk, why would yet another decryption step be necessary? Why did the computer output it in hex at all? Why not just in regular plaintext, or ancient Greek, or whatever the original language was?"

Garza didn't answer.

"Maybe we just aren't drunk enough to figure it out." Gideon waved over the waiter, and they ordered another round.

"We've got to go back to the beginning," said Garza, slumped in the banquette, twirling the ice in his empty glass. "There are two possibilities here. Either the Phaistos Disk was written in some sort of ancient ciphertext, or it is, quite simply, in an unknown written language."

"Meaning that one is a real honest-to-God code, and the other a philological mystery."

"Yup."

The fresh drinks arrived as Garza fell into thought. "I dimly recall that the computer attack on the Phaistos Disk assumed, first, that it was in an unknown language. So it was programmed to look at many ancient forms of writing—Linear A, Linear B, cuneiform, Luwian, Egyptian hieroglyphics—and try to find parallels. If that failed, the program would go on to assume it was a ciphertext of some ancient language, and attack it from that assumption."

"So what particular attack finally succeeded?"

"Good question. For that, we'd need the log file."

"The log file?"

"It's similar to that generated by an installer program. It keeps a list of what particular attack algorithm is currently running, and how long it runs, before giving up and moving on to the next. If we had the log file, we could check its last entry and discover exactly what algorithm succeeded."

"So where's the log file?"

"Still in the computer," said Garza. "Back at EES."

"So we break in. Steal it."

"Are you kidding? That's got to be one of the most secure buildings in New York City. It's like breaking into the gold vault at the Federal Reserve."

Gideon took a sip of his drink. "Good point. We won't break in. We'll get in by other means."

"Other means?"

"Social engineering."

"Yeah, right. Who are we going to socially engineer?"

"Glinn."

Garza started to laugh. "That's hilarious. Socially engineer the world's expert on social engineering?"

"Why not? He's just egotistical enough to believe he's too clever. When you think about it, he's a perfect target." He paused. "You really want to get back at Glinn, right? Piss him off? So here's your chance. We just need to find his prime weakness and work up a script."

A long silence, and then Garza drained his drink. A broad grin spread over his flushed face. "Sally Britton."

Gideon searched his memory. "The dead captain of the *Rolvaag*? What about her?"

"*That's* his weakness. That—and the arrogance of always being right."

5

Two days later, Gideon and Garza followed the same two security guards—one in front, one behind—up a dedicated elevator to the top floor of the EES building on Little West 12th Street. This penthouse was Eli Glinn's private quarters, a sleek aerie perched atop the old meatpacking building. Gideon had been inside only once before.

They came to a blank metal door, and one of the guards punched in a code, then stood in front of a device in the wall, which evidently scanned the irises of his eyes. The door whispered open, revealing a small, dim entryway; another door hushed open, and they proceeded down a corridor that eventually opened into a small, exquisite yet austere library with a marble fireplace.

In a chair near the fire sat Eli Glinn. He had been reading. Laying aside the book, he rose from the chair.

Gideon was shocked at his appearance. He was transformed—a far younger man, it seemed, glowing with health. It was almost as if he were aging backward. All signs of his previous infirmity were gone. While always self-assured, he now seemed uncharacteristically cheerful—or, more accurately, self-satisfied. His gray eyes, smooth domed forehead and unlined face, impeccable gray suit, straight bearing, and subtly condescending expression were more intense than ever. *And why not*, thought Gideon with a flush of resentment: the man had succeeded. He was vindicated. He had atoned for the most catastrophic mistake of his life—the sinking of the *Rolvaag*—and done so with great skill and sangfroid. His fine spirits and good health made Gideon feel his own anger grow at the way the man had abandoned those who'd helped him achieve this goal.

Glancing over at Garza, Gideon could see the man was having a much harder time dealing with Glinn's persona than he was. Garza's face was darkening, his black eyes flashing with resentment. And he saw, too, that Glinn was observing Garza's reaction with supercilious amusement.

"Please," said Glinn, "sit down."

They sat down and Glinn resumed his seat. "May I offer you anything? Coffee? Water? A glass of port?"

Garza shook his head and said "No" with ill-concealed disrespect.

Glinn threw one leg across the other and gazed at them with speculative eyes. "Before we begin, let me lay my cards on the table. I'm well aware you two are planning some sort of confidence game. It's astonishing, and rather amusing, that after all our time together you might think I could be taken in."

"I think," Gideon said, "you might be wise to see what cards we're holding before you lay your own on the table."

Glinn gave this a brief, cynical smile.

Gideon went on. "You've agreed to see us because—admit it—you're curious."

"True."

"And despite your suspicious nature, a small part of you

thinks that maybe, just *maybe*, we do in fact—as we implied in our communication—have a message for you from the late Captain Britton."

"Highly unlikely."

Gideon smiled. "Unlikely, yes. Highly unlikely, perhaps—in your opinion. But not impossible."

"I'll be the judge of that."

"Of course you will. Manuel?"

Garza leaned forward, elbows on his knees, his shoulders stretching the fabric of his suit. "You son of a bitch," he said, voice low. "I gave you sixteen years. I almost died on the *Rolvaag* and again down there when we returned to the Ice Limit, just a couple of months ago. I was the one who saved your ass on Phorkys island. You'd be dead many times over if it weren't for me. *And* Gideon. And now that you finally got what you wanted, you threw us away like so much garbage."

Glinn inclined his head. "Your anger is irrational. I paid you extremely well. And it's not just you: I'm disbanding the company, as you know, so everyone has lost their jobs, except for a few guards."

"Without even a note of thanks."

"Manuel. Do you mean to imply that after all these years, you know me so poorly? I am not a man of the empty gesture. You already know how grateful I am to you—and Gideon. You want a piece of paper to that effect? A Hallmark card, perhaps? I would consider that an insult if I were you. Come now—this is not how individuals like us conduct our affairs. Let's stop bandying useless recriminations and get to the real reason you are here. As I understand from your message, you each want a million dollars. And in return you will give me a letter from Captain Britton, addressed to me, which she entrusted to your care shortly before her death."

Garza nodded. "Think of it as severance pay."

"How nice, but it meets the definition of extortion more exactly."

"Call it what you will."

Glinn leaned back in his chair, arms crossed. "Why didn't you give me this letter years ago, after the *Rolvaag* sank?"

"When you see the note, you'll understand. It's the nature of what she wrote to you." Garza paused. "What she had to tell you... is *awful*."

Glinn's smoothly groomed eyebrows rose. "Of course there is no note. What a shabby and ill-conceived plan."

"How can you know it's a con," Gideon said, "without actually seeing the letter?"

"Come now, Gideon. I've built my entire career on quantitative behavioral analysis. This is so clearly a trick that it's painful."

"I see you're just too smart for us," said Gideon abruptly. He turned to Garza. "Let's go."

"Security will let you out." Glinn pressed a button, and the two security guards materialized in the library doorway.

Gideon rose, along with Garza.

"After you, sirs," one guard said, gesturing with his hand.

At the door Gideon paused, turned to Glinn, and said:

There is no love;
There are only the various envies, all of them sad.

"Come on," said the guard as the door whispered open.

"Wait," said Glinn, holding up a long white hand.

Gideon turned.

"Why did you just say that?"

"Just quoting the first two lines in the note. They're from a poem by W. H. Auden, in case you didn't know."

"I know where they're from," Glinn said. A silence hung in the room, and finally Glinn sighed. "I see your game is more sophisticated than I anticipated. Please come back and sit down."

They returned to their chairs, and Eli looked from one to the other. "Now, Manuel. Please tell me the exact circumstances of how you came into possession of this alleged note."

6

Gideon glanced at Garza. The engineer was a lousy liar, and he hoped Garza would continue to be just as poor now. It was important Glinn continued to think their con was, in fact, a con.

"We need to go back to the last moments of the *Rolvaag*," said Garza. "The ship was caught in the grips of the storm, dead in the water, broadside to the sea. If you recall, you, Captain Britton, and I were on the bridge when the captain gave the call to abandon ship. You protested and left the bridge in a rage. Remember?"

"Vividly and most unfortunately. Keep going."

"You went down to the hold to try and secure the giant meteorite in its cradle. The captain followed you down in the hope of convincing you to return to the bridge and trigger the dead man's switch—the one that would release the meteorite and save the ship. But you refused. As I saw for myself, watching that reconstructed video feed of the *Rolvaag*'s final moments several years later, in the forensic lab of the *Batavia*. Do you recall all that?"

"Of course I recall it. Get to the point."

"After that, Britton returned to the bridge. The ship was in its death throes, at a twenty-degree heel from which it was unable to recover. I saw her grab the paper log and scribble something in it. Then she tore out the page, folded it twice. And handed it to me. 'If you and Eli survive,' she said, 'give this to him. I'm going down to electronics to try and trigger the dead man's switch from there.' I stuffed the note into my pocket. The ship sank ten minutes later, carrying Captain Britton down with it."

He paused and waited.

"And?" Glinn finally said.

"When I was rescued, I was unconscious. The rescuers, of course, stripped me of my frozen clothes. It wasn't until a week later that I was in any condition to recall the note. Luckily the rescuers had gone through my pockets and everything was returned to me in a ziplock bag, including the note. I intended to give you the note at the first opportunity, but you were in a coma for almost a month and your recovery was agonizingly slow. The note was hastily folded, and I'm sorry to admit I read it."

"That would be unlike you."

"You try holding a note like that for a month and not reading it. I was astonished. I had no idea you and the captain had fallen in love with each other."

At this Glinn shifted. "I wouldn't put it in those terms."

"Then you aren't being honest with yourself. *Of course* you loved her. And she you."

"Continue, if you please."

"The note said such terrible things that I decided giving it to you would set back your recovery. So I put it away, intending to destroy it but never being quite able to."

"But now," Glinn interrupted, "after feeling ill used by me, you've decided to extort money via this same note."

Garza crossed his arms and sat back defiantly. "You *owe* me. And Gideon."

Glinn did not respond immediately. Gideon took the moment to examine Glinn's face closely, but it had smoothed back into its usual impassive expression.

"Well," said Glinn at last. "it's quite a story. But remember that I *know* you, Manuel. I've studied your psychology. I have a QB Analysis on you a foot thick. You are not a good liar— despite having concocted a rather clever farce."

"It's not a farce," said Gideon, breaking in. "Think about it: her writing a note to you when she realized she was going to die. It's perfectly consistent with her *own* psychology, as far as I understand it. Think back to that moment. Doesn't it seem logical she would write you a last note, a sort of farewell damnation?"

Glinn looked at the floor for a long time, then raised his head. "The transparency of this ploy is rather sad. Even if you showed me the alleged 'note,' I wouldn't believe it. Frankly, I'm surprised the two of you couldn't do better than this."

"But it's the truth," Garza protested. "And this one time, you're just going to have to take it on trust."

Glinn swiveled his gray eyes on him. "You ought to know me better than that, Manuel. I never take anything on trust, especially in this kind of situation." He paused, thinking. "Besides, I don't have to. In fact, I'm sorely tempted to teach you two a lesson. Because in all your supposed cleverness, you seem to have overlooked a small fact."

"Which is?" Garza asked.

"The bridge of the *Rolvaag* was thoroughly covered by CCTV cameras." He looked from Garza to Gideon and back. "And thanks to the two of you, we have those tapes."

Gideon and Garza said nothing.

"Those tapes will show the touching scene you describe on the bridge...or, more likely, *not*. Would anyone care to go down to the computer room and review them with me—before I have you thrown out on your ears?"

At this, Gideon glanced at Garza. He noticed that their exchange of looks did not get past Glinn.

"Well, *shall* we?" Glinn pressed.

"We can't be sure the moment was captured," said Garza. "Not all the tapes were recovered."

"The bridge cameras had overlapping coverage. Since the tapes are indexed and sequenced, it will take all of five minutes to verify your story."

Gideon could see Glinn was absolutely sure they were lying—but instead of leaving it at that and dismissing them, he couldn't resist the triumph of exposing them. That was in keeping with his fatal weakness.

Glinn smacked his hands on the arms of his chair and rose. He pressed the button again, and the two guards returned.

"Please escort us to the central computer room. We'll be watching a bit of video."

Once again, Gideon found himself in the vast, cavernous central space of EES. The place looked even more abandoned than before, their footsteps on the polished concrete floor echoing in the empty vault. Their two escorts, once again in front and behind, stopped them at the security barrier.

"You're going to make us go through security?" Garza asked.

"Naturally," said Glinn.

"We never had to do this before," Garza protested.

"Times have changed."

After more grumbling, Garza emptied his pockets and Gideon did likewise. The guards took away their cell phones.

"What are those two USB sticks?" Glinn asked, pointing to Gideon's tray.

"My private stuff. None of your business."

Glinn motioned to the guards. "Put those aside with the cell phones."

They walked through the metal detector. Glinn led them across the room to a low console of computers, which appeared to be among the last machines still hooked up and running. The machine that had deciphered the Phaistos Disk was now gone. This was a good sign—it suggested to Gideon that the data and log files had been transferred to the central system.

Glinn sat down at the console and booted up its workstation. Gideon watched as the man typed, drilling down through various files and folders.

"Here we are." A huge series of video files appeared, with time stamps and locations. A quick database sort narrowed these to a list of relevant files.

"Five CCTV files from different cameras," said Glinn, "all covering the same ten-minute segment on the bridge, in which you claim the captain wrote the note and handed it to you. I'm going to pull them up and play them simultaneously on these monitors. Do you really want me to proceed?"

"Absolutely," said Garza. "You'll see we're right. Play it." The bravado in his voice sounded hollow.

"If you insist." Glinn pressed a button, and the videos winked into life on five of the monitors.

"There," said Gideon, pointing. "The third one. That's the one to watch."

The monitor's bird's-eye view took in the navigational station and four large flat-panel displays: one with radar, one of the GPS chart plotter, a third a split screen, and the fourth the output from a sonar transducer. To one side stood an old-fashioned chart table, with paper charts, dividers, and parallel rules. Next to it was a series of cubbyholes containing bound logbooks, including the main ship's log.

The video started dramatically, in medias res. The bridge, illuminated as was customary in a dim reddish light, appeared to be in chaos. Hurricane-force wind and rain lashed the windows. The roaring of the storm, the straining of the ship's great engines, and the groaning of the superstructure under the weight of the shifting meteorite filled the speakers. The ship was listing alarmingly, and all personnel were hanging on to rails and handholds to keep from falling. The captain stood at the helm while the chief mate, Howell, stood behind the navigation station.

Captain Britton turned. "Mr. Howell," she said, her reproduced voice crackling slightly as it emerged from a nearby speaker. "Initiate a 406 MHz beacon and get all hands to the boats. If I'm not back in five minutes, you will assume the duties of master."

She vanished through the rear bridge hatch while Howell initiated the beacon. A siren sounded, red lights flashing, and a mechanical voice bellowed over the intercom: *"All hands to abandon stations. All hands to abandon stations,"* over and over again.

Three minutes passed as the ship careened still farther, with a vast metallic groaning; slowly righted; then began to heel again. This time, the slanting did not level out; the ship canted and great wallowing waves broke just below the bridge windows, cascading foam and water. One of the windows blew out with a bang and a howling of wind.

And then Captain Britton returned.

"This is it!" said Gideon excitedly, leaning over Glinn's shoulder and pointing to the middle screen showing the navigation station. "Watch closely—she's coming over. See…here she comes." He leaned closer still, bracing himself on the console with one hand while the other stabbed at the screen.

And Britton did stagger over, speak to the navigator—her words lost in the roar—then turned and said something to Howell.

"Here's the moment!" Gideon said.

Britton made a gesture to Howell, indicating something below, then disappeared again out the rear bridge hatch.

She never touched the paper log. She went nowhere near the logbook.

"Seen enough?" Glinn said acidly.

"Wait," said Gideon, "she might come back."

"Gideon, this farce is over. We *know* she went down to the electronics room, because that's where her body was found!" Glinn's voice was cutting. His face was pale and beads of sweat had appeared on his forehead. The video, still running, had disturbed him—just as Gideon anticipated.

"Wait. Wait until the end."

The slanting of the bridge continued. Howell and the navigator now left their stations, as did everyone else on the bridge, staggering out as the ship continued to heel. The groaning of metal became a shriek; a massive wave blew out an entire row of bridge windows; the sound dissolved into a screaming static—there was a flash of white and then the screen went dead.

Glinn punched off the feed. He turned and rose from the chair. His gray eyes bored into them both. "Not only was this a cruel trick, but it was monumentally stupid—to *think* you could game me like this. I never expected either of you could stoop so low."

Garza mustered his self-presence. "All right, so we didn't succeed. But it's the principle. You *deserved* to see that again—as an example of the same kind of hubris that would prompt you to dissolve EES, threatening the livelihood of hundreds of people. And you still owe us. We're going to get our money, one way or another."

"If either of you two communicate with me again, I'll slap you with a restraining order." Glinn turned to the guards. "Get them out of here."

Gideon felt himself grasped by the shoulders and propelled toward the exit, along with Garza. A moment later they were out on Little West 12th Street, in the cold afternoon sun.

They walked together in silence as far as Greenwich, turned the corner, and stopped.

"Did you do it?" Garza asked.

"Hell, yes." Gideon reached into his pocket and pulled out a tiny USB stick.

Garza's face lit up. "I thought maybe you didn't get the chance. I didn't see you do anything."

"Not seeing is the whole point. That's a magician's first trick—misdirection. If you control where the audience is looking, you can get away with anything. The video was a perfect foil. When I leaned forward and pointed at the screen, and told Glinn to watch closely, that's exactly what everyone did—not only Glinn, but the guards as well. As I pointed, I braced my other hand on the console—where the USB ports are—and inserted this USB stick. When the video ended, I straightened up, plucked it out, and palmed it between my fingers—the same method I used to bring it into the room. You said the search program on the stick needed thirty seconds to auto-start, fetch the Phaistos log file, copy it, then redundantly delete the data from the EES system. But I gave it forty, just to be sure."

"But how did you get it through the metal detector? I freaked when they took away your USB sticks."

"Decoys." Gideon laughed. "A mini USB stick doesn't have enough metal in it to set off a detector."

Garza grinned and mimicked Glinn's cool, astringent voice. *"To think you could game me!"*

They both laughed as they made their way down Greenwich toward Garza's apartment.

7

G ARZA'S PLACE IN SoHo was a fifth-floor loft in an old industrial building. It would have been a cozy, appealing apartment, Gideon thought, if it wasn't so bloody neat. Everything, down to a pen sitting on the desk, was lined up in order, clean, polished, and organized. It was all of a piece with Garza's personality.

The large industrial elevator began creaking its way back down to the lobby. Years ago someone had sprayed FUCK YOU inside the elevator, but the rest of the owners in the building—Garza had explained, irritated—thought it was charming in a chic-gritty sort of way and refused to paint it over. "Drives me crazy to see it every day," he'd observed.

The apartment itself had brick walls and old arched windows with metal frames looking out over Broome Street. It was a classic one-room downtown loft, a sleek kitchen in one corner with a dining table, a bed in another, a living area in the middle, and a work space up against the row of windows, with a brushed-steel table on which was arranged an array of equipment surrounding a gleaming iMac Pro.

Gideon felt a mounting excitement, and he sensed the same in Garza. The success of their trip to EES left him with a glow of pride. It had taken almost two days of planning and rehearsing, but they'd managed to socially engineer the formidable Glinn with a simple, elegant little mise-en-scène. It had come off without a hitch. No doubt they had left Glinn shaking his head at their pathetic attempt to shake him down, with no idea what their real purpose had been or—more important—that they had succeeded.

"Beer?" Garza asked, heading for the fridge.

"Absolutely."

Garza slipped two frosty bottles out of the fridge and headed for the worktable, placing each on a coaster and taking a seat. Gideon sat down beside him and picked up his beer.

"Here's to pretexting the master pretexter," he said.

They clinked bottles and Gideon took a long pull, taking care to place the bottle back on the coaster.

"All right," said Garza, "give me the USB stick."

Gideon handed it over, and Garza inserted it into one of the computer's ports. After a few seconds, an image of the log file appeared on the display. Garza opened it, then quickly scrolled to the end. The last item read:

Stegano-1

"What kind of attack is that?" Garza asked.

"You're asking me?" Gideon shrugged.

"Let's look at the previous strategies logged by the computer."

They went through the log file from the beginning to the end. The computer had tried hundreds of different attacks, starting with various philological, logosyllabic, and linguistic analyses, based on various dead languages and scripts including Old Persian, Mycenaean Greek, Akkadian, Elamite, Linear A and B, Minoan, hieratic, demotic, and hieroglyphic. None of those attacks worked, even though the time stamps indicated the computer had battered away for weeks, even months, at each one. Finally the program had switched approaches, apparently assuming the Disk was incised not with a normal written language but instead a cipher of some kind. Polyalphabetic and brute-force attacks followed, and then more exotic exploits. None of those had worked, either. Until the last one, labeled Stegano-1.

"Stegano-1," Gideon repeated, then suddenly gave a cry and smacked his forehead. "What an idiot I am! Stegano—short for steganography!"

"Which is?"

"It's a form of encryption. Or rather, it isn't really encryption at all—it refers to a message hidden inside another message or an image. It's one of the most ancient of all forms of concealment, going back thousands of years." He paused. "Herodotus, in one of his *Histories*, recalled a king who sent a secret message to another by shaving the head of the messenger and tattooing the message on his scalp. When the man's hair had regrown, he delivered the message, with instructions for the messenger's head to be shaved."

"Not a lot of time pressure to deliver that message, I guess."

"I guess not. During World War Two, steganography was used to send messages in pictures, using microdots. It's even more common today. With computers you can take, say, a photograph of a landscape and hide in it another image, then reveal it by subtracting various data bits from the main image. Or you can hide a message in computer code by writing redundant instructions."

"But how would steganography apply to the Phaistos Disk?"

Gideon shrugged. "That's the problem."

Garza typed a command and pulled up an image of the Disk, and beside it a file showing the glyphs, or images, in a table. "There are two hundred forty-two 'letters' in the message, made from forty-five different glyphs. The information encoded in the Disk can't be very extensive. I mean, how much information could possibly be contained in two hundred forty-two letters?"

"True."

"And here's another problem. If the computer couldn't identify the original language—which apparently it didn't—then how could it claim to have *deciphered* the message coded in that original language?"

Gideon thought about that. It seemed logically impossible. If you didn't know a language, how could you decipher any coded message originating in that language? You *had* to have the original plaintext to decipher the code.

He let out a long breath. "There's only one possible answer. It's not a language at all."

"What do you mean?"

"The Phaistos Disk is not a language. It never was. It can't be. You just proved it."

"Then what the hell is it?" asked Garza.

"It's a picture. A drawing. That's how steganography works."

"But how could it be a picture? It's a bunch of tiny *unconnected* pictures that don't fit together."

"You've seen pictures made of arrays of letters? This could be like that."

"I'm not following you," said Garza.

"Each one of those glyphs," said Gideon, thinking fast now, "could represent a black dot of a certain size. Arrange them in the correct array and you get a crude picture. That's steganography in its purest form. Here was a secret message, made to look like it was written in a language—but there's no language involved at all. Instead a *picture* is hidden in what appears to be undecipherable or nonsensical text."

"I see what you're getting at. Let me think a minute."

Gideon watched as Garza's face turned inward. He had seen this before, when the man was solving a complex mathematical or engineering problem in his head.

"Okay. We have two hundred forty-two glyphs—but look again at the image of the Phaistos Disk. The symbols on the Disk are arranged into eighteen groups. So you take two hundred forty-two divided by eighteen, which yields thirteen with remainder of eight."

"Which means?" asked Gideon.

"We arrange the symbols sequentially in an array of thirteen by eighteen and see what it looks like." Garza typed furiously, and in a moment the desired array appeared. But it was fuzzy and vague, and Gideon could make out no obvious image in it.

"No problem," Garza said, undeterred. "Let's say each symbol stands for a shade of gray scale, going from white to black. We have the data file in hexadecimal code. We simply plug that in, low values to high, with zero zero in hex being white and FF in hex being black, and arrange the rest in graduated shades of gray."

"But the ancients didn't understand assembly language!"

"They didn't need to. We're just applying modern methods to an old riddle. And don't forget, steganography was *your* idea."

More typing. An image appeared on the screen, crisp and clear this time. It showed three dark lines snaking into the center, creating a roughly triangular section in the middle. Along the edges of the image were two ragged, convoluted lines. Off center, near the meeting point of the three lines, was a geometric array of five dots.

Garza breathed out. "There it is. The translation of the Phaistos Disk."

"It's a bunch of squiggles and dots. Still looks like a damn code!"

"Not to me." Garza stared at the image. "It kind of looks like it might be an image looking *down* on something."

"You mean, like a landscape formation?" Gideon took another squint at the image. "You know, with a little imagination that could look like a valley where three canyons came together."

"In order to view a canyon in such a way, you'd need to be at a great distance above it."

"A great distance," muttered Gideon. And then he breathed: "*Yes.* Like standing on the top of a mountain. I think you're right. It's a landscape. Those could be three streams or washes coming together in a valley, and those other squiggles could be the base of mountains on either side."

"Then what's that thing with the five dots?"

"If I had to guess, I'd say that was the X marking the spot. It's an old symbol called a quincunx."

"The spot of what? Treasure?"

Gideon leaned back. "There's only one way to find out: go there. We need to figure out where this canyon or valley is."

Garza snorted. "Sounds like the wild goose chase to end all wild goose chases."

"Maybe. But that location was important enough to be encoded on the Phaistos Disk and stored in the palace of a Minoan king. So it can't be just anything. We simply have to find where on the surface of the earth this place is." He paused. "Have you heard of a search tool called Terrapattern?"

"No."

"It works with Google Earth. It's like facial recognition software, but it recognizes landscapes instead. You start with an aerial view of a geological formation or a map, plug it into Terrapattern, and it finds the exact spot on earth."

"I'm on it." Garza began typing furiously. He accessed the Internet, found the Terrapattern program, and fed their image into the software. He hit a button.

Gideon squinted at the icon that indicated the program was now running. "It says it could take up to thirty hours."

"I'm not surprised. The earth is a big damn place. If I understand how this works, it's got to compare that crude little drawing to the entire surface of the planet, at many different scales."

"Let's get dinner. Maybe when we come back it'll be done."

When they returned at eleven PM the program had found a match. A Google Earth picture was displayed on the screen, with a small yellow rectangle indicating the selected area. It was a view from about ten thousand feet up of spectacularly rugged desert mountains, riddled with barren washes, deep ravines, plains strewn with giant boulders, and patches of crescent sand dunes. The highlighted area was not a river, but rather a confluence of three dry washes that cut through the mountains, creating an isolated valley with only one point of ingress. A natural fortress.

Gideon squinted at the screen. "Where the hell is that?"

"Says here: Hala'ib Triangle, Eastern Desert, Egypt."

"Egypt." Taking the keyboard, Gideon opened a new window on the computer and called up Wikipedia. "The Hala'ib Triangle seems to be a twenty-thousand-square-kilometer region claimed by both Egypt and Sudan. Zero annual rainfall, zero population, zero life, heavily broken country of rugged mountains, sand dunes, and dry washes. It says here that it's one of the most extreme desert environments in the world." He stepped back. "Zoom in to the valley."

Garza complied, creating a split-screen image showing the Phaistos map on one side and the Google Earth image on the other, both at the same scale.

"Could there be a more desolate place on earth?" Gideon asked, staring at the screen.

It took Garza some time to answer. "I doubt it."

8

At six in the morning, Eli Glinn lay in bed, still wide-awake after a long restless night. He was bothered by something, but he wasn't sure exactly what it was, beyond the aggravation caused by the ridiculous visit that afternoon from Garza and Gideon.

It was the damnedest thing. Both of them should have known him well enough to realize he was perhaps the least sentimental person on earth, impervious to the kind of stunt they had tried to pull. Perhaps they did have a legitimate gripe—Garza, anyway—but the fact was they had been compensated fairly, and he had never given the slightest indication he wanted to continue any sort of relationship with any of his employees after his special project was complete. For the first time since the sinking of the *Rolvaag* almost six years before, Glinn felt unburdened. He wanted to enjoy this newfound freedom and not have anyone around to remind him of those terrible years of self-recrimination.

But this ridiculous extortion scheme had proven a shock. It had, to his profound surprise, shaken him. When he looked into the Quantitative Behavioral Analysis programs he'd run on the two of them, he found no indication this was a possibility. Their plan was so badly executed that he wondered how two highly intelligent operatives could have conceived it. Gideon was always impulsive and unpredictable, so perhaps it wasn't so far-fetched for him, but Garza was rock-solid. Although not always...he cast his mind back to Garza's breakdown on the Lost Island, when he had stolen a helicopter and put the mission at risk. Yes, even Garza had his moments of poor judgment.

Still, this confidence trick took the cake. As Garza had essentially admitted, they'd gleaned the information about himself and Britton from the video surveillance tapes recovered from the wreck of the *Rolvaag*. But then to gin up a story of a hastily scribbled note of Sally's, entrusted to Garza at the very moment her ship was foundering...It wasn't in her nature. Even if she'd wanted to write such a note, she would not have had the time. The whole con was transparent. And so easily disproven.

So easily disproven...

Glinn sat up in bed. His heart was suddenly beating fast. This, he began to realize, was the unsettling thought at the back of his mind that had kept him up all night: how Garza and Gideon had not understood how easily their con could be refuted. Maybe they understood—all too well.

Sleep was hopeless. He might as well get up and make coffee. He stood, stretched, and as he did so paused to appreciate the unaccustomed strength once again surging through his legs. Strolling to the nearby floor-to-ceiling window, he gazed over the sweeping views of the Hudson River and the bejeweled skyline of Lower Manhattan. *So easily disproven...*It seemed extraordinary that two such intelligent individuals would not have realized how flimsy their scam was.

They had come up to his apartment, tried to pull their little trick, and acted like damn fools when he exposed their lies.

That was quite a moment, he had to admit: that video segment showing that Sally had never touched the log, never written the note...

Didn't they realize he would check the tapes?

A chill crept up his spine. Maybe they had realized. Maybe they'd anticipated that. Maybe the con was *meant* to be easily disproved.

He felt he was letting his mind run away with speculation. But what if, in fact, they'd had another purpose in mind? What could that purpose have been? Had he been "pretexted," to use a social engineering term? But pretexted to what end? What could they have possibly gained by coming in with that ridiculous story, attempting to extort him, and then getting thrown out?

What had they gained?

For one thing, they had gained access to the highly secure EES computer center. He recalled Gideon leaning over his shoulder, pointing his finger at the screen, demanding that they watch, that the crucial moment was about to occur. When he must have known that moment never would occur. That in itself was strange. He recalled the position of Gideon's body, leaning over his shoulder, his right hand pointing at the screen, his left hand braced on the side of the computer console...

Where there were various input ports, including USB.

A cold, ugly feeling crept outward from his gut. He turned, picked up his secure intercom line, dialed a number.

"O'Bannion? Could you check the EES central computer system and compile a list of all activity that took place between three and three thirty this afternoon? I need to know specifically what files were accessed, from what location, and at what exact time. Thank you."

He hung up the phone and waited, staring out at a sliver

of moon floating above the Freedom Tower. The sky was just starting to change from black to deep blue, the first light of the approaching day.

The phone rang. Glinn picked it up, listened for a moment, and then slowly replaced it in its cradle. Although it was dark and cool in the private aerie, Glinn felt the heat of humiliation invade the capillaries of his face and spread like an infection over his body. All his self-satisfied sense of comfort and triumph vanished in a moment.

He *had* been duped. And with the greatest of ease.

This would not stand.

9

Gideon stepped up to the balcony and slid open the polished doors, letting in a cool, predawn breeze. The din of Cairo was already rising, interwoven with the honking of cars and the shouts of early-morning vendors setting up their wares along the Nile Corniche. Gideon gazed out at the waking city, cup of strong Turkish coffee in hand, breathing in the heady scent—car exhaust, dust, and the richness of the Nile itself, which lay like a sheet of blued steel in the distant light. They had taken a suite at the Ritz-Carlton at Gideon's insistence—he'd banked close to half a million dollars from his work at EES, and whenever he could he would make damn sure he enjoyed the two months that were left him, no matter the cost. Garza, a born cheapskate, had grumbled a little but finally relented. It was just one of many disagreements they'd had in the five days since they'd hatched this plan—and getting to Cairo, Gideon knew, was the easy part.

And now Gideon heard a faint, singsong cry, then another and another, rising over the dawn: a melodious pentatonic chanting. For a moment, he wondered if it was some kind of musical performance, until he recalled it must be the muezzin's call to prayer coming from the many minarets that dotted the city.

He had never been in the Middle East before, and he found Cairo entrancing: a profusion of color, sound, and exotic sights. They had arrived the previous afternoon on a flight from New York. The journey from the airport to the hotel had been wild, plunging them into epic traffic jams, where limousines were crammed cheek-by-jowl beside semi-trucks, lorries, carts being pulled by donkeys, and shabby taxis, all going every which way with no regard for traffic lights or the proper side of the street. The scene had annoyed Garza, with his mania for order, and he'd issued a steady stream of disparagement as their taxi stopped, started, and honked, the driver enthusiastically participating in the mayhem. Gideon, on the other hand, had been energized by the chaotic atmosphere.

He heard a door open and turned to see Garza emerge from his room. He looked drawn.

"I made a pot of Turkish coffee," said Gideon. "It's on the warmer."

"Turkish? Any good old American coffee around here?"

"Sure, but you've got to make it yourself."

Garza went into the kitchen and soon Gideon heard him fussing with the drip machine. Since departing from New York, Garza had put on what Gideon privately called his "game face," an expression of humorless, cautious determination to get the job done. Gideon remembered it well from their previous missions. The engineer, he thought, might prove to be a challenging traveling companion.

As he mused about Garza, he understood that in many ways the man was a lot like Glinn, which perhaps explained the depth of the engineer's resentment. Strange that, after several missions with Garza, Gideon still didn't know much about his background, beyond the fact that Garza and Glinn were in the Rangers together, coming up through Airborne, and that Garza had been Glinn's second in command. The engineer had always presented a taciturn, gruff exterior and openly disapproved of Gideon's way of doing things. In the beginning, he'd even opposed Glinn's hiring of Gideon. This disapproval had slowly ebbed during their ops together, and at times the man seemed capable of surprising acts of independence and rare courage— his commandeering of the chopper during the Lost Island mission, for example.

He heard footsteps and Garza returned from the kitchen carrying a steaming mug of coffee. He held a manila folder in his hand.

"What's that?"

"Couldn't sleep," Garza replied. "Jet lag. So I put the time to good use." He handed Gideon the folder. "Background on our destination, the Hala'ib Triangle. It's going to be quite a trek, and we still have to determine the optimal form of travel."

Gideon opened the folder. There were printed maps, topographic and geological charts, and descriptive text. He flipped through it, impressed. Classic Garza. While there were drawbacks to traveling with him, there were also pluses. The guy was an Eagle Scout, always prepared. "Let's order up some breakfast from room service and go over this."

"Room service? Hotels like this rob you blind. A glass of orange juice is thirty-six Egyptian pounds!"

Gideon frowned. He resisted the idea of pointing out that was only three dollars. "Okay, then, tell me about the Hala'ib Triangle."

They both settled in overstuffed chairs with their coffee. "To summarize," Garza began, "the Hala'ib Triangle lies along

Egypt's border with Sudan. The area has been in dispute between the two countries since the British screwed up while drawing the boundaries in the nineteenth century."

"They screwed up boundaries all over the world."

"That's for sure. Anyway, it's a desert that lies between the Red Sea to the east and the Nile to the west. This is not a Sahara-like desert of endless dunes, though: it's mountainous, cut by steep ravines and maze-like wadis. The temperature often hits a hundred and twenty degrees. Because it's in dispute, travelers into the area are advised to obtain permission from the Egyptian government and travel with a police escort."

"What? We have to hire *police*? That isn't going to work!"

Garza allowed himself a cynical smile. "Of course not. We'll find a way around it. Egypt is a country where much can be accomplished with baksheesh."

"Baksheesh? You mean bribes?"

"Never call it a bribe. It's a monetary favor—a tip, so to speak—to establish goodwill and a sign of respect."

"Gotcha."

"Our ultimate destination lies inside the Proscribed Zone—unfortunately."

"Which is?"

Garza reached over and pulled out a topographic map. "It's this region, here, in the southwestern part of the triangle. As you can see, it's dominated by a great mountain called Gebel Umm, which means in Arabic 'the Mother of Mountains.'"

"Christ." Gideon stared at the region, dense with topographic lines.

"It's incredibly forbidding. There's a maze of serpentine valleys, canyons, and lesser mountains surrounding Gebel Umm. The area features a strange phenomenon called a mist oasis."

"Mist oasis?"

"It's also termed a fog desert, and occurs in only a few places on earth—the Atacama Desert, the Namib in Africa, and here. It's a section of desert with no rainfall but heavy fog. The way it works is, a stream of humid air coming off the Red Sea gets forced upward by the mountains and condenses into heavy mists. These mists gather in high mountain valleys and create specialized, miniature ecosystems living off the dripping fogs. They don't exactly help with aerial or satellite photography, either." He tapped the stack of maps. "The word UNSURVEYED is stamped all over these surrounding valleys."

"So our valley is cloaked in mist?"

"No. As far as I can tell it lies beyond. But we have to pass through a mist oasis to reach it."

Gideon was almost afraid to ask his next question. "Why is it called the Proscribed Zone?"

"During the British era, in 1888, a battle was fought between Egypt and Sudan over the triangle. It ended in a stalemate, but both sides suffered high casualties and took prisoners. They faced off and tortured their respective prisoners to death, in full view of the other side, in a tit-for-tat escalation of brutality. As a result, the British declared the southwest part of the triangle a no-man's-land, a sort of demilitarized zone. This led to a fragile peace in which both sides agreed that neither would enter the Proscribed Zone again. Only the scattering of Bedouin tribesmen who already lived there could stay. But in the past forty years, the Egyptian government has been building modern settlements along the Red Sea coast, trying to encourage the mountain Bedouins to come out and settle down. Most have done so, but it's rumored that a few remain, stubbornly and even violently clinging to their ancient way of life."

"Figures the Phaistos people would choose such a remote spot."

"The ancients clearly picked the most forbidding place they could find in the known world to hide the secret of the Phaistos Disk."

Gideon shook his head. "It really is the ends of the earth."

"We've faced worse, Gideon. We can do this." Garza put his hand out for the manila folder. "What are you going to do?"

"Do?"

"With your half."

It took Gideon a moment to parse the question. "That's assuming we find anything. And that it's worth something."

"Oh, we'll find it, all right. The fact it's so well hidden just shows how valuable it is."

Gideon took a deep breath. "It's not like I have a lot of time left to enjoy anything. I really haven't given it much thought."

"Well, I have."

"Oh yeah? What are you going to do with your half, then?"

Garza was silent for so long Gideon thought he wouldn't answer the question. Then he said: "Duesenberg."

"What?"

"I'd resurrect Duesenberg. They made the most elegant and technologically advanced cars of their day. Individually coach-built to the owner's taste. Hell, they had straight-eights with dual overhead cams as far back as the '20s. No car in America was more powerful, more expensive, or faster. That company was run by engineers—engineers with passion and dreams. If they hadn't been wiped out by the Depression, who knows where they'd be today?"

This was one of the longest and most heartfelt monologues Gideon had ever heard Garza deliver. "Duesenberg. I had no idea."

Garza nodded slowly, his expression far away. "My dad was a mechanic. Liked to tinker with cars. He loved old ones best:

Packards, Pierce-Arrows. There were always a couple, half assembled in the garage. He drove a 1921 Kissel Gold Bug every year in the Independence Day parade. But his true passion was Duesys. We had a supercharged SJ he'd restored to perfect condition, but he couldn't resist messing with it anyway. He'd let me help after I finished my homework. We must have taken that thing apart and put it back together a dozen times. Three tons of elegance, but it went from zero to sixty in eight seconds."

"What happened to it?" Gideon asked.

Garza didn't hear. His gaze was still far away. "Nobody makes driving machines for the love of engineering anymore. It's a damn shame, because there's so much technology kicking around these days, just aching to be put to use. I mean, the internal combustion engine's a dinosaur. People think electric cars are too sluggish, but Christ, look at the Venturi Fétish. Just think: to be able to combine electrical power, performance, *and* real luxury, for owners who appreciate attention to detail and aren't worried about price—that would be Duesenberg today."

There was another long silence. Finally, Gideon cleared his throat and asked: "Do you think Glinn has any idea what we're up to?"

The faraway look left Garza's face. He drained his coffee cup and set it down. "You saw him. He's still coming down off his high of saving the world. Besides, he's too arrogant to ever admit he was bamboozled."

"But what if he finds traces of our data theft in the EES computer network?"

"He won't unless he looks for the intrusion specifically, and he's not going to do that. If anything, he's still congratulating himself on seeing through our ploy."

Gideon didn't answer, but he wondered if Glinn would be so easily fooled. What would the man do if he figured out they'd scammed him? In Gideon's experience, Glinn wasn't vindictive or cruel, but he'd be a seriously formidable opponent if crossed.

"It's not Eli we have to worry about," said Garza with one last shake of the folder. "It's reaching the Proscribed Area without getting executed as infidels along the way. So let's go get breakfast at a café along the Corniche and work out the details of how we're going to get from here to there."

10

THE VESSEL, THE *Egyptian Epiphany RiverShip II*, had disembarked from the gleaming docks of Suez that morning and was now headed down the gulf, the minarets of the great mosque at the mouth of the Suez Canal dwindling to aft in the clear desert air. Gideon and Garza had hoped to find passage on a Nile River cruiser to Aswan, but at this late date everything was booked. So they'd done the next best thing and reserved a stateroom with two double beds on a small cruise ship making a circuit of the Red Sea. This had been followed by a hellish midnight taxi ride from Cairo to the city of Suez. By morning light, Gideon had found that the town was surprisingly modern and clean, not hectic like Cairo, although lacking Cairo's charm and exuberance.

Gideon stood at the stern of the three-hundred-foot vessel, Garza next to him, each holding a warming bottle of Stella Lager, the ship leaving a creamy wake across the turquoise waters of the gulf. Gideon slipped a glance at his partner in crime. Garza was wearing a Hawaiian shirt and cargo shorts, along with Ray-Bans and a cheap Panama hat bought at a Cairo bazaar. Gideon had taken care dressing the both of them, and it wasn't until too late that he realized he'd made a miscalculation. He had assumed all cruise ships were stuffed full of rowdy, tacky, half-drunk yahoos. He hadn't realized that the *Egyptian Epiphany* was on a semi-academic tour of ancient archaeological sites, and that most of its passengers were retired intellectual-minded Europeans who dressed well and kept to themselves. What saved him was a noisy group of ten or so Americans who had somehow won this cruise in a lottery; couldn't care less about the lectures or video presentations; and spent most of their time in the bar, sundeck, or massage salon. Despite their laughing and their bluster, they were basically goodhearted and naive Midwesterners, and Gideon quickly switched his cover story to that of a tractor salesman from Milwaukee who had earned a trip to Egypt with his buddy by winning a sales incentive. The only problem left was Garza himself. He hadn't gotten with the program and stood at the rail, looked distinctly unhappy.

As the boat steamed southward, a guide on the far side of the deck was describing the passing sights on the Sinai and Egyptian coasts to a large group, several of whom were actually taking notes.

"John Deere," Gideon continued to the British couple standing next to him, holding watery gin-and-tonics, "made in America. None of this Chinese factory business."

"Terrible how so many jobs are being sent to the Far East."

"Not John Deere. We just celebrated our hundred and eightieth anniversary."

"That's remarkable."

"I'll say. John Deere was an inventor, and he got his start by inventing the self-scouring steel plow in 1837."

"Is that so?"

"That is so." Gideon had absorbed a raft of information from Wikipedia. "He took a Scottish steel saw blade and re-forged it into a slick-sided plow. The trick was the dirt didn't stick to it, unlike iron or wooden plows—and, by God, that's the plow that conquered the earth of the Midwestern plains! Now, me and my partner Manny here, we're on the agricultural side of sales—"

Already he could see the couple was edging away, rapidly losing whatever enthusiasm they might initially have had for striking up a conversation with him. This was his goal: to mix with the other Americans when necessary, but to quickly establish with the other passengers a reputation as a garrulous tourist to be avoided. The journey on the *Egyptian Epiphany II* to Safaga was thirty-six hours, and there were several Egyptian soldiers on board, apparently to reassure the tourists against a terrorist attack. They could not afford to arouse suspicion.

"I've had about enough of this," said Garza abruptly, turning away and striding down the walking track that circled the deck.

The couple took this as their cue to leave as well. "I think we'll go dress for dinner," the husband said. "Lovely to meet you."

Gideon watched them depart, pleased with his own performance but mightily irritated with Garza. It had been a chore to get Garza to dress like an American tourist to begin with; discovering this hadn't necessarily been the best cover only made things worse. But it wasn't just the clothes: his perpetually suspicious look practically broadcast that this was someone with something to hide. If they were going to succeed, he really needed to straighten Garza out, the sooner the better.

He found Garza in their cabin directly behind the gift shop, already out of his costume and back in a white shirt and pressed khakis. He rose when Gideon came in, his face dark. "Listen,

Gideon, this isn't fun and games. You're the one who keeps saying we shouldn't stand out, and there you are, making a spectacle of yourself right on deck."

Gideon stared at him. "You're the one who stands out, sulking in a corner, not talking to anybody. And that outfit of yours, that white shirt and damn desert boots—it makes you look like an undercover Fed."

"I look like who I am, nothing more. I don't want to be a frigging tractor salesman from Dubuque. What the hell does it matter what people think?"

Gideon took a deep breath and tried to swallow his anger. If this expedition was going to succeed he, the more flexible of the pair, would have to meet Garza more than halfway. "Look. It's true that right now a disguise may not matter all that much. But once we reach Shalateen—the jumping-off point for the Proscribed Zone, where there are Bedouin tribesmen instead of tourists and our very presence might be illegal—we're going to have to look and act totally convincing."

"As what?"

"I don't know yet. We have to scope it out when we get to Shalateen. But we can't just walk into the Hala'ib Triangle without a damn good cover story, dressed to play the part. Think of this as a rehearsal. Because we're going to be lying all the way there. You need to get used to it."

He could see his point was finally sinking in. The engineer ran a hand over his short black hair. "I can't act worth shit and I know nothing about tractors."

"Come on, Manuel! You spent an entire night researching the triangle. Spend another five minutes on John Deere, like I did."

"Tractor salesmen. Why couldn't we be petroleum engineers? I mean, Egypt has some oil production right here in the Suez."

Gideon had to laugh. "And you don't think that would arouse suspicion? I'll leave the expedition logistics to you, but you leave the social engineering to me. Okay?"

A pause. "Okay."

"Speaking of logistics, have you figured out just how we're going to get the stuff out of Egypt? I mean, it's true we don't know what we'll find—maybe a tomb, maybe an ancient library, maybe a fossilized Burger King—but whatever it is, we're betting that there's loot."

"That's exactly the issue: whatever it is. I can't be certain how to smuggle it out of the country until I see what we find. But I've already made provisions. Depending on the size and weight, I'm hoping to pass it off as some type of tourist junk. If necessary, we can paint it in garish washable colors and ship it out as knickknacks or maybe replicas to a nonexistent distributor in the US."

"You see? That's a good plan. And that's how we'll succeed—with each of us playing to our strengths."

They shook hands.

"Now put that damn Hawaiian shirt back on and let's go up for dinner."

11

EIGHTEEN HOURS LATER the *Egyptian Epiphany II* emerged from the Gulf of Suez into the Red Sea, and within a few hours more it had slid into a ferry berth in Safaga. This was a huge south-central Egyptian port packed with great ore ships being loaded with potash. Since the cruise ship was heading across the Red Sea to the Saudi city of Duba, while Gideon and Garza were headed southward, they had to disembark and find transportation on a coastal ferry—the only method of travel.

They strolled along the waterfront with their cheap duffel bags slung over their shoulders, still dressed as Americans but having changed into what Gideon hoped would look more like adventure-tourist garb. They located the ferry ticket office, a wooden shack standing in the middle of a great asphalted pier shimmering in the heat. The Red Sea lay beyond, a sheet of restless dark water ending in a burning horizon. Inside the shack sat a ticket seller wearing a galabeya, sipping tea.

"Let me handle this." Gideon did not think Garza's perpetual scowl would go over well. He approached the man and gave him a big, friendly, dopey American grin.

"Hello, my friend," he said. "Do you speak English?"

The man put down his glass of tea and shook his head, his twin-forked beard shaking.

Gideon glanced around and spied a little boy in dirty shorts and a torn T-shirt, hanging back and watching from a distance with intent bright eyes. "Hey, young fellow!"

The boy came scampering over.

"Do you speak English?"

"Yes, sir."

Gideon pulled a couple of Egyptian pounds from his wallet. "Would you tell the gentleman here we'd like to buy two one-way tickets to Shalateen?"

The boy stared at him. "You want go there?"

"Yes."

The boy shrugged and spoke in Arabic to the ticket seller. The man stared at the two of them with open astonishment and then spoke a torrent of Arabic to the boy.

"He say ferry no good for American. Only for *fellahin*. He ask why you go."

"We're scuba divers." He gave the duffel at his feet a light kick. "Great diving off Shalateen. Tell him we're used to traveling rough."

The boy eyed him, then held out his hand. "Two pound?"

Gideon fished in his waist pouch and brought out a five-pound note. "Will that take care of the rest of the conversation?"

"Yes, *sir*!" The boy snatched the note with a dazzling grin. Soon the transaction was completed, eased along with a few pounds of baksheesh to the ticket seller. The ferry, they learned, would not be departing until the following morning.

Gideon turned to the boy. "What's your name?"

"Asim," the boy said with a toothy grin.

"I am Gideon. This is Manuel."

"Hello, sirs! You need guide?"

"As a matter of fact, we do."

The boy slapped his skinny chest. "I guide!"

"Perfect. We need a place to stay. Something cheap and close by. Got to have air-conditioning, though."

"Follow me!" The boy marched off at a rapid pace, and Gideon and Garza heaved up their duffels and followed. Through the dusty streets they meandered, turning one way and then another, passing goats and a camel and a pair of water buffalo yoked together, being driven along by a five-year-old boy with a long switch. They finally came to a modest hotel, actually more of a guesthouse, made of poured concrete.

"Here is good hotel," Asim said.

They went inside and once again the boy translated. The price was fifty pounds a night—four dollars. Before paying, they inspected the rooms, which were surprisingly clean and fresh. While the A/C unit in the window thumped and shuddered, it did a decent job of cooling the rooms. They dropped off their duffels and met again outside, where Asim was waiting.

"Okay, where now?" the youth asked. "Beach?"

"No, we want to go to the bazaar."

Asim set off, matchstick arms churning, and they followed him through more winding streets, among concrete housing blocks that quite suddenly opened into a wide market, with brightly colored tents and stalls in crowded profusion, surrounded by alleyways going every which way. A heady smell of spices drifted on the desert air, and big sacks and baskets of spice, both ground and whole, were laid out in droves.

"We want to buy some Egyptian clothes," said Gideon.

"Follow me!"

They wound among the stalls until they came to the clothing

area. One row of stalls featured Western garb, but most sold traditional clothing. Gideon sorted through the galabeyas—the long, loose shirts favored by Egyptian men—picked one out, and held it up to himself. It was made of gray cotton with blue pinstriping, long enough to be a dress. He pulled it over his head.

"You like it?" he asked the boy.

"Yes, sir!" cried Asim.

"Now for the thing you wear on your head." He gestured. "What's that turban or headcloth called?"

"*Imma.*"

"Right. *Imma.* Where are they?"

"There." Asim indicated racks with long looped lengths of fabric.

"You mean we have to wind them up ourselves?"

"Yes."

"Can you show us how?"

"Yes."

"We'll take two." He turned to Garza, who had been standing back silently during this exchange. "Come try on a galabeya."

"We're not really going to try to pass ourselves off as Egyptians?"

"We already had this conversation. I'm in charge of our cover. Get over here."

Garza came over reluctantly. Gideon sized him up, pulled a galabeya off the rack. "Try it on."

His scowl deepening, the engineer pulled it over his head and let it fall. "Fits." He pulled it off with alacrity.

"How much?" Gideon asked Asim.

The boy engaged with the vendor, a young man with a big black beard, and a terrific argument ensued, with the boy shouting and gesturing, waving his arms, making a chopping motion with his hands and shaking his head. Finally he turned to them. "He try to overcharge. I get better price. Two hundred five pounds."

Gideon did a quick calculation: eleven dollars. "Good work, Asim."

"Thank you, sir!"

Gideon paid the scowling vendor.

"Now for some dinner."

"You like kebab?"

"Oh yeah."

Another journey through oppressively hot streets among adobe walls led them to a kebab shop with a couple of tables outside, in the shade. The boy sat down with them, and they ordered kebabs and Fanta. Garza tried to order a beer.

"No beer. It is haram. Orange Fanta only."

"That's it? No Coke? Pepsi?"

"Fanta the best!"

"I guess we're in for a dry trip," said Garza, grumpily.

The kebabs came and Gideon found his to be delicious. Asim ate like a dervish and ordered again for himself long before they had finished.

"You've got quite an appetite," said Garza.

"Kebab good!" the boy said, his mouth full. He waved over the waiter for a third order and another Fanta.

"Watch out you don't explode," said Garza. Indeed, Asim's skinny belly already looked distended.

"Never."

After dinner Asim led them back to the hotel. At the door he showed them how to wrap the *imma*. Gideon fished a five-hundred-pound note out of his wallet and gave it to him.

"Thank you, sirs!" He tucked the note in his pocket went running off with a huge grin.

"You overpaid him by about five times," said Garza. He had mostly kept quiet throughout their mini adventure.

"Twenty-eight bucks?" said Gideon. "We can afford it. He was a nice kid."

"Check to see if you still have your wallet."

Despite himself, Gideon felt his back pocket and found it was still there. "You're such a cynic."

"Maybe. But still, you checked!"

12

Despite having been paid off and dismissed, Asim was waiting for them the next morning before dawn, as the calls of the muezzin echoed through loudspeakers placed around the town. "I help!" he cried as they came out of the hotel with their duffels. He grabbed Garza's and swung it onto his skinny shoulders, then set off at a fast pace, ignoring Garza's protests as they followed. The duffel was bigger than he was.

When they came to the waterfront, Gideon stopped dead when he saw the lone vessel that was docked across the asphalt quay.

"Oh my God," said Garza, halting next to him. "We're not going to ride on *that*?"

Gideon turned to Asim. "Is that the ferry?"

"Yes, sir."

A huge mass of people, punctuated by honking cars, braying donkeys, men with live goats slung over their shoulders, a teenager driving a yoked pair of water buffalo, a man with a cart heaped with watermelons, were all crowding forward in a chaotic mass onto the open deck of the ferry. The ship had once been painted white with a red stripe at the waterline, but it was now so streaked with rust and peeling paint it looked like a derelict that had barely survived the apocalypse. Two smokestacks belched black diesel smoke, which mounted into the air, spreading a pall. The wheezy chattering of the ship's engines throbbed in the air. At the far end of the ferry a small bridge rose from the deck, constructed of rusted steel. Gideon could see the captain and a couple of crew moving about.

"It looks like Charon's boat to Hades," said Garza.

"You sure this is the only way to Shalateen?" Gideon asked dubiously.

"It was either this or rent a car and drive five hundred miles on a terrible road known for bandits, kidnappings, and the occasional terrorist beheading, where if you break down you might die of thirst or heatstroke before help arrived."

Asim was looking at them anxiously. "I show you on boat?"

"Fine."

Asim proceeded to push through the crowd, using Garza's duffel as a kind of bolster, swinging his shoulders this way and that, nudging people out of the way and shouting in Arabic. The tactic was remarkably effective, and they soon boarded via a broad boat ramp onto a deck sticky with spilled oil and animal dung.

The ferry gave two blasts of its whistle, signaling imminent departure. Asim had boarded with them and showed no sign of leaving.

"You can't come with us," Gideon said.

"Why not? I guide!"

"We don't want a guide." Gideon fished in his wallet.

"You're paying him again?" Garza asked.

Gideon pulled out a hundred-pound note but held it back. "Here, this is yours—but only if you get off the ship."

The whistles boomed again and the last stragglers were fighting to get on. The ferry was packed alarmingly tight.

"I guide you!" the boy said insistently.

"No!" Gideon waved the bill above him like bait. "You have to get off. Now."

"I stay with you!"

"What about your parents? Your family?"

Asim went suddenly silent. Gideon reached in his wallet and took out another hundred, holding the two bills just out of his reach. "Asim? You can't go with us. It isn't safe. Here—take this and get off the ship."

Out of the corner of his eye, he saw Garza shaking his head.

"Okay, sir."

Gideon lowered his hand and with reluctance Asim took the money, shoved it into a ragged pocket, then turned, shuffling halfheartedly and ineffectually against the flow.

"If you don't make it off the ship, I take back the money!" Gideon warned.

Hearing this, the boy darted into the surging crowd and disappeared. A few minutes later Gideon saw him again, wandering disconsolately across the now empty pier, hands in his pockets, kicking pebbles with his flip-flops.

"Now, there's a kid with talent," said Garza. "He didn't have to pinch the money out of your wallet. He got you to give it to him."

"What the hell, he's probably an orphan. He needs the money a lot more than we do."

"Yeah, sure. That was the sweetest con I've ever seen." Garza snickered.

Gideon shook his head. Garza was really starting to drive him crazy.

Shouting, the crew cast off the rotten hawsers, and with a great coughing roar the ferry's engines revved up. The water churned alongside as the boat inched away from the pier, the deck vibrating with the effort. Slowly, agonizingly, the ferry pulled into the Red Sea, showering soot down on them.

"Isn't there a place with shade or something?" Gideon asked, peering here and there.

But there wasn't. They were all crowded onto a single, barge-like deck—cars, trucks, people, carts, and animals mixed together in the blazing sun, with no shade and no place to sit. Gideon was reminded of a car ferry he'd once taken to Nantucket, only larger, far more decrepit, and ten times as crowded. The other passengers seemed cheerful enough and were settling down on boxes, bales of cotton, and ancient pieces of luggage, many setting up umbrellas and crude pole-and-burlap awnings, breaking out food and conversing over the braying of donkeys and the occasional bellowing of a water buffalo.

"We should have bought some umbrellas," said Gideon, sitting on his duffel.

"Where are the lifeboats?" Garza asked, looking around.

Gideon gave a laugh. "Lifeboats? Are you serious? What I want to know is, where's the damn head?"

"I think it's over there," said Garza, "behind that curtain. Where all the people are waiting. Looks like you just kind of squat out over the water."

"Charming."

Away from shore, the ferry turned southward and settled into cruising speed. Gideon squinted into the sun, looking at the passing shore, and then gazed at the water moving along the gunwales. "I'd say we're making about ten knots at the most. How far to Shalateen?"

"Two hundred and fifty nautical miles," said Garza in a clipped voice. He seemed uncharacteristically on edge.

"This trip is going to take forever. I'm already getting a headache from the sun. I think I'll put on my headcloth."

Gideon took the ten-foot piece of cloth from his duffel and started wrapping it around his head, tucking the end inside his mop of unruly brown hair. He tried once, and again, then a third time, but it kept unraveling. He cursed and pretty soon had attracted the attention of the surrounding people.

"Help?" a teenage boy offered.

"Hell, yes. I mean, please."

The cheerful youth unwrapped his own *imma*, then swiftly wrapped it back up, then repeated more slowly. "You see?"

"Okay, my turn." Gideon managed to do it, with a few corrections. The boy helped tuck it in firmly. "Thank you."

The boy pointed to Garza. "Friend need help?"

"Friend not need help," said Garza sourly. "Friend going to die in sun."

"Sun bad." A chorus of advice and warnings to Garza were proffered in Arabic and broken English by concerned neighbors, along with much gesturing. A man offered him an umbrella.

"Thank you!" said Gideon, seeing that Garza was about to decline. He pulled out his wallet but was met with a firm refusal. The man's neighbor urged a second one on them, gesturing and speaking in Arabic, again refusing all compensation. Garza grudgingly accepted it.

"How long till we reach Shalateen?" Gideon asked the young man with broken English.

The boy squinted, held up two fingers. "Two day."

Garza swore. "No lifeboats, no life vests, and at least five hundred people on board, not to mention animals and cars. What if the boat sinks?"

"Nothing like traveling with an optimist."

The wind shifted and another light shower of soot from the diesel stacks dusted over them.

"Did you bring any food and water?" Gideon asked, suddenly apprehensive. "Or are we going to die of thirst as well as sunstroke?"

Garza reached down and unzipped his duffel, pulling out a plastic bag filled with food. "Help yourself."

"I'm impressed. When did you buy this?"

"While you were napping after dinner. I had a feeling we might not want to eat the haute cuisine served in the ferry cafeteria."

Gideon rummaged through the bag and took out a banana, chips, and a Fanta. He braced the umbrella and settled on his duffel with his makeshift lunch. "This isn't so bad, really," he said.

He wasn't sure who he was trying to reassure more—Garza or himself.

The ancient ferry shuddered and smoked as they crawled southward. In time, the scattered towns gave way to an empty shore of vacant beaches and flat coral reefs, behind which rose the dark mountains of the great Eastern Desert of Egypt. It was the most desolate and fearful coastline Gideon had ever seen. As the heat of the day reached its peak, the ferry subsided into somnolence, no one stirring. It was hot but not brutally so—this was late March, after all—and a warm steady breeze blew across the open deck. Like the others, Gideon fell into a doze mostly as a way to make the time pass. He woke toward sunset, when everyone else began stirring, chattering, and breaking out dinners from burlap sacks and greasy cardboard boxes.

The sun hung low over the sea horizon, a crimson ball that

cast a bloody light over the water. It set so fast it almost seemed to fall into the sea, plunging the world into an orange gloaming.

Garza sat up, rubbing his eyes.

"Dinner?" Gideon asked.

Garza rummaged in the bag and extracted some meat pastries, cheese, dates, and two bottles of warm Fanta, and they sat on their duffels eating and watching the sky darken into green and purple, as clear and empty as infinity itself.

"I must compliment you on your planning," said Gideon, his mouth half full of pastry. "This is tasty."

"If I'd known we'd be on a boat like this, I think I would've risked renting that car."

"It'll be over in another day and a half."

Garza shook his head as he looked around. "This ferry is a bloody disaster waiting to happen."

Their fellow passengers began to haul out battery-powered lights and Coleman lanterns, which glowed as the twilight deepened, lending the deck a festive air. The smell of spices and food wafted past. The stars winked in the deep sky above: a few at first, and then more and more, until a vast dome of stars arched over them, bisected by the Milky Way.

Gideon was amazed at how quickly the air cooled once the sun had set. After a noisy dinnertime, the ship quieted down again as one by one the passengers settled in for the night. The various lights went out and voices dropped to a murmur. Gideon rested his head against the soft end of his duffel and closed his eyes.

13

He woke some hours later—it was hard to tell exactly how many—as a murmur of voices rose around him, shot through with a tone of alarm. He sat up, temporarily puzzled. The engines sounded different than before—ragged, higher-pitched.

Beside him, Garza sprang awake. "What the hell?"

Everyone was awake now, and lights were coming on. Something out of the ordinary was obviously happening. The ferry began to make a labored turn toward the west, the water churning out from underneath the hull. Gideon could see the pilot on the bridge, in the red glow of the dim bridge lights. He was gesturing vigorously at a subordinate, while other crew appeared to be rushing about, silhouettes moving against the dim background.

"That doesn't look good," Gideon said. He could see Garza's face in the faint light, beaded with sweat. "Hey, are you all right?"

"Don't worry about me," said Garza brusquely. "What I want to know is, why is the boat turning so sharply?"

People were now on their feet, and the murmur had become

a clamor of talk. One of the engines was now uttering a high-pitched roar, and then the sound abruptly ceased with a muffled bang, while the other engine continued to chug at a higher pitch.

"Son of a bitch," said Garza, "is it my imagination, or is the deck starting to slant?"

"I believe you're right."

"Do you think...we're *sinking*?"

"We turned toward shore," Gideon said slowly. "I suppose it could be because we're taking on water. If so, maybe the captain is hoping to ground the boat."

Garza was silent.

"All these people..." Gideon looked around. Their fellow passengers were thoroughly alarmed, but as of yet there was no panic. "I wonder how many can swim?"

The boat shuddered as the single working engine struggled to move them forward. The deck was now clearly slanting.

"Those cars and things aren't secured," Gideon said. "That shit's going to slide. We need to get ourselves on the high side."

Garza remained silent.

"Let's go! Hold on to your money and leave the rest."

The canting deck was still only a few degrees from horizontal, and Gideon felt there was a good chance the captain could ground the ferry or seal the bulkheads to halt the taking on of water. They wound their way among excited groups of people on deck until they had reached the starboard rail. Gideon looked over. The bilge pumps were running like mad, dumping powerful streams of water from the hull openings. He could see the boat was taking on water faster than the pumps could empty it. What had happened? They hadn't hit anything. Maybe the rotten hull had just given way. From their vantage point at the rail, he now had a better view of the bridge. He was shocked: it was empty. Where were the captain and crew?

As if on cue, he saw the captain exiting the companionway at deck level, moving in haste, followed by his crew. He watched as they scurried to a hatch that led, most likely, to the lower mechanical deck. They undogged it and disappeared, leaving it open. *Going to work on the engine, perhaps*, Gideon thought grimly, *or to seal the bulkheads.* It must be worse than it seemed. If the scow actually sank, they needed to come up with a plan to deal with that—now, before mob panic set in.

"We must be a couple of miles offshore," he said to Garza. "Not too bad a swim, considering the water is warm and there don't seem to be any currents or tides."

"Right," said Garza, voice tight.

"Of course, there might be sharks."

"Sharks."

Gideon took a deep breath. "Look, Manuel. The obvious thing is to swim away from the boat before it goes down, get clear. Then we swim westward until we reach shore. Just keep the North Star on your right."

"On your right," Garza repeated mechanically.

Gideon suddenly had a suspicion. The captain and crew weren't going below to fix the engine. The captain would leave the bridge for one reason only: to abandon ship. He and the crew were probably headed for a lifeboat—the damn cowards.

He grabbed Garza by the arm. "Follow me."

They pushed through the crowd, which was now fully aroused, milling around and shouting up at the bridge in confused and angry voices. More people were instinctually pressing toward the high side of the sinking boat.

They arrived at the open hatch and descended into diesel-stinking dimness. A few caged bulbs illuminated the companionway to the lower deck. They continued following the passage until they heard voices echoing from ahead. In the lead, Gideon slowed and approached a partly open bulkhead door, which he stopped to peer through. The captain and crew were at a boarding platform in the lower part of the hull, open to the calm sea. They were arguing over a small Zodiac hung on davits next to the platform. Seawater was already slopping into the boarding hatch as the vessel settled in the water. The argument was escalating, and in moments it broke out into a fight. There was the flash of steel, a scream of agony, and the captain fell. The crew swung the davits out and lowered the Zodiac into the water, then surged into it, now fighting against the overcrowding; another man was stabbed and fell overboard, then two more were beaten off and left on the platform as the engine roared to life and the Zodiac shot out into the dark sea.

The water was now pouring in through the open boarding hatch. On the ferry deck above, Gideon could hear serious panic taking hold: muffled screaming, a thunder of running feet, the ululations of women.

"We can't go back up," Gideon said. "We've got to jump into the sea from here and swim for shore."

He turned to Garza. The man's face was pale. "No," he said.

"No what?" Gideon yelled. "We've got no choice!"

"No." The engineer backed away.

Gideon stared at him. "In a minute, maybe less, we're going to be trapped down here!"

Garza continued to back down the passageway, a look of something like horror on his face. Gideon stared. He had never seen Garza so unmanned. Even in the most frightening moments they had spent together, the man had kept a cool head. Now he seemed to have lost it completely.

"You can't swim," said Gideon, simply.

Garza finally managed to nod.

Gideon's mind raced. *The man can't swim?* This messed up everything. "Okay. Okay. We go back on deck. Find something that floats. And launch ourselves on it."

Garza managed to croak his agreement. The water was now swirling down the passageway at ankle level and rising quickly. With a great shuddering boom the second engine blew, and immediately afterward the lights went out.

"Just stay with me." Gideon turned and they retreated down the passageway, feeling their way along the walls, up the companionway, and back out the deck hatch.

The scene that greeted them was one of heartbreaking pandemonium. The deck was now tilting at a steeper angle, and various carts, some with struggling donkeys still in harness, were rolling down the sloping surface, dragging the bellowing animals with them. One cart hit the railing and flipped over, throwing both donkey and cart into the sea. The poor animal screamed as it drowned. People had pressed themselves against the higher gunwales of the ferry, clutching at the railing, crying and wailing and reaching beseechingly toward the now empty bridge. Gideon could just see, headed westward, the running lights of the Zodiac vanishing into the murk.

The boat was dead in the water and sinking fast. Water rose over the port gunwales and began creeping up the deck. The tilt grew worse. And now a car began to move, and then another, sliding down the wooden deck and coming to rest against the rail. A large truck suddenly broke free, skidding sideways; it hit the railing with such force that it tore right through with a screech of steel. More trucks and lorries began rumbling down, bashing through the railing into the sea and sinking with a frenzy of bubbles. Screams rose as people caught in their paths were crushed or swept overboard. Flashlights and lanterns bobbed as panicky cries mounted upward from the darkened deck, the shrill screams of mothers punctuated by the wailing of babies—it was a scene out of hell itself. *All these people*, thought Gideon—*they're going to drown.*

He shook his head, trying to clear his mind. The canting ferry felt like it might slide under at any moment; they had to quickly get well clear of the suction and imminent maelstrom of thrashing, drowning people, who would drag any nearby swimmer down with them. It felt heartless, but there was nothing left for them to do now but save themselves.

What could they use as a float? Lumber. He remembered a cart piled with boards that he'd seen loaded on board earlier. He cast about and spied it, jammed up against the port rail with other broken carts. The donkey pulling it, still harnessed, was lying, drowned, in the deepening water.

The lumber was stacked in tied bundles on the overloaded cart. The water was up to its hubs.

"Come on!" He pulled Garza down the deck toward the wagon.

"No—not into the water!"

"Get your ass moving!" He yanked at Garza, hauling him down the sloping deck. Everyone else had gone to the high side, leaving the flooding end free.

Gideon waded through the swelling water, grabbed the wagon wheel, and hauled himself into the cart. Garza followed gingerly, clearly struggling to master his anxiety. The hemp ropes holding the entire load had ruptured, but the individual bundles of wood were still tied and, he hoped, would be able to float like a sort of paddleboard. Gideon braced himself and grabbed a bundle, heaving it overboard, and then another and another. After a moment, Garza followed his lead. The bundles splashed into the sea, but since the boat had ceased moving they didn't drift away.

"Let's throw them all overboard!" yelled Gideon. He grabbed another and heaved it. "Manuel, get the women and children! They can float on these!"

Garza stared.

"We're going to save some lives here! Get going!"

Comprehension dawned on the engineer's face. He hustled off and a moment later returned leading a stream of women and their children, more following behind and soon generating a stampede. Gideon continued to flip bundles of wood overboard until the entire cartload was bobbing in the calm water next to the sinking boat.

Gideon leapt down from the remains of the cart. "Manuel, listen to me: get in the water and climb onto one of those. Do it now. Paddle away from the boat. Head west. We'll meet up on shore."

"And you?"

"I'm going to help these others. And then I'll swim."

"I'm going to help, too."

"You can't fucking swim!"

"I can do *something*!"

Mothers were screaming, clutching their babies and little ones. To Gideon's amazement, the men did not press forward in panic—they were letting the women and children go first. It was a death sentence for all who couldn't swim: a heartbreaking display of self-sacrifice.

Gideon seized a small child. "Go," he said to the mother. "Into the water." He jabbed his finger. "I hand you child."

Someone who understood English yelled at her in Arabic and she slipped into the water, her arm wrapped around a floating bundle of boards. He passed the child to her. "Next!"

Garza and Gideon worked together, helping the mothers onto the bundles of lumber and then handing over the children. Soon all twenty or so bundles had women and children clinging to or riding atop them.

"Manuel, climb onto that last bundle!" Gideon yelled.

"No—women and children first."

"Son of a bitch, the whole point of this was to get you on a raft!"

"You see any other men getting on?"

This sudden and unexpected display of heroism confounded Gideon. He wondered how the man—clearly terrified of the ocean—had managed to stay sane during the long and dangerous voyages of the *Rolvaag* and the *Batavia*...or, for that matter, how he'd kept his secret from Glinn.

Garza helped several girls onto the last bundle of wood and shoved it away from the railing with his foot. Every bundle was now full of people: perhaps fifty or sixty women and children were clinging to the lumber, drifting in a slow pack away from the boat.

The ferry suddenly lurched, a tremor passing over the deck. All at once it rolled sickeningly and people at the higher sections came tumbling down, screaming, hitting the water and thrashing about. Garza was abruptly thrown into the water and Gideon dove in after him, swimming around and calling his name. But the man didn't surface. Gideon looked around and then realized he had to get some distance from the boat or he'd be sucked under.

With a great roar of air lurching up from below, the ferry slid sideways. Gideon swam as hard as he could away from the boat, away from the screams and heartrending cries—and then, with a great turmoil of water, the prow of the ferry swung straight up into the air, people flung from it into the water on all sides—

and the vessel began sliding straight down with a gigantic, horrible slurp and a boiling eruption of bubbles...and was gone.

Gideon treaded water, clothes weighing him down, observing the scene from a distance. The cries did not last long. Almost nobody, it seemed, could swim. Garza was gone, and the flotilla of women and children on the bundles of lumber had drifted off into the darkness of night. There was nothing more he could do. He looked up, found the North Star, and began to swim through the warm water, slowly and steadily, keeping the star on his right, heading for the unknown shore.

14

THE WATER WAS warm and calm, and Gideon saw no sign of sharks. He kept up a slow pace, alternating among breaststroke, backstroke, and an easy crawl, careful not to tire himself out, moving with a current that was already taking him toward shore. After a while, he could see the mountains of the Eastern Desert rising in the west, their outline blotting out the stars, and an hour later he could make out the sound of light surf on a beach. Soon his feet touched sand and he stood up and waded to shore.

He dragged himself up the strand, exhausted. The moon had set, but the starlight was bright enough to cast a faint illumination over the landscape. It was a desolate place: a long, empty beach that curved like a scimitar between low reefs extending into the sea. The water was calm, the gentle waves hissing up the sand. There was no sign of life—not a bush or blade of grass—just sand and rock.

He coughed and spat out the salty taste in his mouth. The image of Garza going down in the dark water overwhelmed him. He couldn't think about that—somehow, somehow, he told himself, Garza must have survived. How could a man like Garza die: his companion on many missions, a man who had survived again and again, a cat with nine lives? When the ship went down, the deck was covered with items that would have been left floating, from bales of hay to luggage and other things he could cling to. If Garza had managed to claw his way back to the surface, Gideon told himself, surely he would have found something…

Then he remembered the way the doomed ship had slipped so quickly beneath the surface; the boiling eruption of bubbles; the desperate shadows of drowning people calling out for help…

He staggered up the beach, peering into the darkness. "Manuel!" he called. "*Manuel!*" He saw something rolling in the surf and ran toward it, splashing through the water. A body. He grasped it by the clothing and turned it over—an elderly man, obviously drowned. A little farther on he saw other bodies turning gently in the surf.

"Manuel!"

He stumbled toward them, trying to see their faces in the dim light, turning them over—men, women, and a child. All were drowned. None were Garza.

He continued up the beach to the end, where a jagged reef stuck out into the water. All the bodies seemed concentrated in the one place. He turned and jogged back.

"*Manuel!*" he screamed, voice hoarse.

He passed the place where he had dragged himself out of the water, and continued south along the beach. Nothing. No survivors, no more bodies.

Exhausted, he could go no farther. He sank to his knees in the sand, gasping for breath. It seemed nobody had made it to shore alive from the disaster, at least not in this area.

He dragged himself beyond the wet sand and lay back, staring up at the stars: a castaway on an unknown shore. After a while he collected his thoughts and recovered his breath. He remembered his money belt and felt his waist, relieved to find it still there, packed with about twenty thousand Egyptian pounds and his passport. But that was all. He had no food and no water, and the rest of their money had gone down with the ferry. It was, he figured, about two in the morning. When the sun rose, the extreme heat and lack of water would become a problem. He would do well to travel at night. He could not afford to rest much longer.

Still he lay there awhile longer, gathering his willpower, and then heaved himself to his feet, swaying momentarily. His mind slowly cleared. If memory served, Manuel's map had indicated that a road ran along the coastline southward to the town of Shalateen, the last vestige of civilization before the frontier of the Hala'ib Triangle.

He began to walk inland, hoping to intersect the road, the salt water in his clothes drying quickly. The air was almost chilly and he shivered, thinking that he'd better enjoy the cold while it lasted. The ground was flat and sandy, the distant mountains a serrated absence of stars. To his relief, in about a mile he hit the road: a single-lane strip of asphalt running straight as an arrow from north to south.

He paused on the roadway, thinking. If the ferry sank at around one in the morning, they would have traveled about two hundred miles, going at roughly ten knots. That meant Shalateen was another eighty miles to the south, more or less. Too far to walk. But then, he reasoned, he had no other choice but to try.

He headed south, walking down the center of the road. Images crowded into his mind: of the sinking; of Garza being thrown into the water and going under; of all the helpless, screaming, drowning people. That last gesture of Garza's, making the ultimate sacrifice to save others—and the old grouch had done it instinctively, without even thinking twice. It made his own struggles with a terminal disease, his months of existential angst, feel foolish; trivial; self-centered.

Well, all that was over now. The expedition was finished. There was no way he could continue on his own. What he needed was to push away these heavy thoughts and focus on getting to Shalateen alive. Then he could go back to his cabin in the Jemez Mountains and live out his last few weeks in the place he loved most—to hell with the Phaistos location.

After he'd spent three hours walking, the sky began to lighten in the east. It spread across the sea horizon in a brightening pink band, and soon afterward a yellow sun boiled up over the water, casting an oven-like heat into his face. It was amazing how quickly the temperature passed through the comfort zone to unbearable heat. He had lost his head covering, and the sun as it rose quickly began to feel as if it were pressing down on his head like hot iron, turning the salt in his hair to bitter dust. The mountains rising on his right looked black and as sharp as needles.

The road ran across the sandy coastal plains, absorbing the heat of the sun and radiating it back in shimmering patterns. No cars came, and in the areas where sand had blown across the road there were no tire tracks. It looked like nothing had passed down the road in days.

Around what seemed like noon, Gideon began to feel lightheaded. The shore lay about a mile off, and he realized that to stave off heatstroke he should make use of the water. He veered off the road and walked to the shore, arriving at an area of flat reefs and a beach of orange sand. He waded into the water, soaking his clothes and dunking his head, feeling the instant relief of the cool water even if it did little to assuage his rising thirst. As he began walking back toward the road, he heard a distant sound. A car? He began to run. To the north, he could see what looked like two decrepit buses lumbering down the highway, belching diesel smoke.

"Hey!" he cried, stumbling forward. "I'm here! Hey! Wait!" He waved his arms and shouted, running as fast as he could, but the two vehicles passed in the distance and soon dwindled into black dots on the southern horizon.

He reached the road and stood there, cursing at the vanishing buses. Now he bitterly regretted leaving the roadway. But at least this meant the road was traveled—albeit infrequently.

He trudged on. The dip in the water had temporarily assuaged his thirst, but it returned quickly. There was no shade anywhere, and he realized it was dangerous to keep walking—it would only increase his need for water. He sat down on a rock by the side of the highway and waited. Hours passed while the blazing sun inched across the sky and began to descend toward the jagged mountains. And then, in the northern distance, Gideon saw the wavering, uncertain image of what looked like a car at the vanishing point of the road. He stood up. It *was* a vehicle—in fact, several of them. They materialized into a jeep and two olive-drab army vehicles barreling down the roadway at high speed. He rushed to the middle of the road and waved his arms and began shouting as they approached.

The lead jeep saw him and the convoy slowed, then came to a stop in front of him. Gideon staggered up as a military officer in the jeep's passenger seat got out, holding a canteen.

Gideon fumbled the canteen from the man's proffered hand, unscrewed the cap, and gulped down the water, spilling it over himself.

"Easy, friend," said the man in good English, grasping the

canteen and pulling it away. "Wait a bit and then drink more."
He was dressed in desert camo, with a black beret on his head
and two stars on his shoulder.

Gideon nodded, releasing the canteen. He felt better almost
immediately.

"Are you from the ferry accident?" the officer asked.

"Yes," he croaked. "Yes."

The officer explained they were part of a rescue team that had
been looking for survivors along the coast, with the Egyptian
navy picking up survivors in the water.

"Did many survive?" Gideon asked, suddenly hopeful.

"Some." The officer didn't answer further. "We're taking the
survivors to Shalateen for treatment and to take statements. Do
you have your passport?"

"My friend was on the boat," Gideon said as he pulled out his
passport. "Manuel Garza. Did you rescue him?"

The man spoke briefly to someone else in the jeep, then
shook his head. "We have no one by that name. I am sorry."
He examined Gideon's passport, then tucked it into his breast
pocket, extending his hand. "I am Lieutenant al-Nimr," he said.

Gideon shook it. "Gideon Crew."

"I'll keep your passport for now," said the officer. "May I ask
what were you doing on the ferry? It is not a normal method of
tourist travel."

"My friend and I are adventure travelers."

"And your friend, his name is Garza?" He made a note on a
small pad. "Manuel Garza?"

Gideon spelled it for him. "You're sure no one by that name
was rescued?"

"I am sure. Sorry. We will take your statement in Shalateen."

The jeep started up, Gideon climbed into the back, and the
convoy continued south. What seemed like forever, but could

not have been more than two hours later, Gideon saw a lone sign appear in a wasteland of sand, written in English and Arabic, SHALATEEN. Moments later a brown, dusty settlement rose into view, low cement houses mingled with scattered acacia bushes, piles of garbage being picked at by goats, a tethered camel resting in some shade, and the twin minarets of a mosque rising into the sky. The convoy drove into town and pulled through a gate into what looked like an official compound, surrounded by naked cinder-block walls topped with concertina wire. They parked in the dirt lot before a large whitewashed building. The lieutenant and his driver got out and motioned to Gideon to do the same.

"When will I get my passport back?" Gideon asked.

"When we've taken your statement. Follow me."

The lieutenant led him into a large open room with a rumbling air conditioner. Three other officers sat at a table at one end, and adjacent to that a man sat behind a desk. In front of the desk was a molded plastic chair. The lieutenant saluted the man behind the desk, spoke in Arabic, handed him Gideon's passport, and left. The whole setup reminded Gideon of an interrogation room.

The man stood up with a big smile and offered his hand. "I am Captain Farouk. Please sit down."

Gideon sat in the plastic chair proffered him. Pleading stupidity and ignorance was the way to go, he reasoned; if he proved to be a valuable witness, he might be detained for whatever legal proceedings would ensue. He couldn't stay in this place any longer than absolutely necessary. He still felt shaken to the core by Garza's death.

"Please tell us what happened," said the captain, returning to his desk and folding his hands. An old reel-to-reel tape recorder was set up to one side, and he now turned it on.

Gideon gave a brief account of what had happened, omitting the part about seeing the captain stabbed and the crew deserting the vessel. He also omitted mentioning tossing the lumber in the water. He described how his friend was thrown from the deck when the ferry lurched upward in its death throes, adding the fact that he couldn't swim. He'd been so frightened, he said, that he didn't notice anything more.

It seemed all four men were taking notes. "What were you doing on the ferry?"

"We're adventure travelers," Gideon explained once again.

"And what is an adventure traveler?" the captain asked.

"Someone who wants to get off the tourist path. We like to go places where visitors don't normally go, see places that no one else sees, travel by unusual means, mingle with local people."

"I see. Well, I think that is all for now."

Gideon said, "May I ask a question?"

"Certainly."

"How many survivors were there?"

The captain looked at him steadily. "Of the forty or so on board, almost all survived, Allah be praised."

"Um..." Gideon didn't quite know how to respond to this obvious lie. There had been at least five hundred on that ferry. It seemed a cover-up was in progress. Well, he thought, there was nothing he could do about it. With Garza dead, it was none of his business.

"We had rescue boats on the scene almost immediately," the captain said, "and picked up many people in the water. Others made it to shore. Fortunately there were only two or three deaths, your friend being one."

Don't argue, thought Gideon.

"The ferry was illegal," said the captain, "operating without permits or inspections. We picked up the crew north of here and arrested them. They will be punished."

"I see." Gideon just wanted to get the hell out of there. "May I have my passport now?"

"Later."

"When?"

"When we've processed your statement."

"I'm not released now?"

"Not yet."

Gideon cleared his throat. "I haven't had anything to eat since yesterday."

The captain spoke in Arabic, and one of the officers at the table stood up. "Follow me," the man said.

Gideon followed him out of the room, through dusty corridors, to a cafeteria buzzing with flies. A machine dispensed coffee and a cooler held an array of cellophane-wrapped meat pastries, bread, and cheese. "Please help yourself," the officer said.

Gideon got himself a coffee with milk and sugar from the machine and took two pastries from the cooler. He sat at a fly-specked table while the officer waited at the door, watching him. When he was done eating, he rose. "What now?"

"Come this way."

Gideon followed him once again through a maze of stifling concrete passageways to a door with a single meshed window. When the officer opened it, Gideon was surprised to see a large gym beyond with several dozen people in it, mostly women and children—evidently the survivors rescued from the boat. Forty out of five hundred. And most of these people, he noticed, were ones he and Garza had saved.

The door shut behind him and he heard the bolt shoot. He was locked in. The people around him looked frightened, confused, and miserable. And now some of the women recognized him and came over, murmuring in Arabic and pressing his hands in thanks.

"No, no. Don't do that. Please." He shook his head. "You're mistaken, it wasn't me. It was my friend." Gideon knew if word got out that he had helped save them, he'd be drawn into this mess and God knew what might happen. But they couldn't understand what he was saying and continued to cluster around him, pressing his hands, murmuring, some with tears streaming down their faces.

"No, no, really..." He stood up, trying to get away. "I want to be alone. Alone." He looked around and saw, in the corner of the room, a man sitting on the floor, his back to the crowd, curled up, seemingly half dead. Gideon's heart turned over in his chest; the man had no head covering, and even from behind his salt-and-pepper hair looked familiar. He strode over and placed his hand on the man's shoulder. The figure looked up stiffly.

"Manuel! My God!"

With a weak smile Garza staggered to his feet, and they instinctively embraced.

"I thought you were dead!"

"Not dead," Garza said in a weak voice. "Just almost dead. Christ. And I was sure *you'd* drowned..."

"How...how did you survive? I saw you go down."

Holding him up, he led Garza to the wall and they sat down together, leaning against it.

"I did go down," said Garza. "I thought it was over. But that sinking ship belched out a mass of air that must have carried me back up. At least, I think that's what happened. When I broke the surface, there was stuff floating everywhere and the vessel was gone. I grabbed a bale of clothes and held on. About three hours later some fishing boats arrived, collected the survivors, and took us to an army base north of here. Then the army showed up and drove us here in buses. And you? What happened to you?"

"I swam to shore. They picked me up on the highway. Listen, Manuel, I have to tell you how impressed I was with what you did. When push came to shove, you were willing to give up your own life."

Garza shook his head. "How could I have lived with myself if I'd left those children to drown?"

"Don't make light of it. You're a hero."

"Well, I have to tell *you*, the fact you're so surprised is a bit offensive to me."

Here it was: the old, prickly Garza resurfacing. *So much the better*, thought Gideon. "No offense meant. But is it true? That you really can't swim, I mean?"

Garza's face abruptly changed expression. He looked away and down, his face darkening, and didn't respond.

"I only ask because you've been on at least three ships that sank: the *Rolvaag*, the *Batavia*, and now this ferry. For a guy who can't swim, you've had one hell of a run of bad luck. Why didn't you ever learn?"

Garza gazed at him, his eyes narrowed. "None of your business."

"I think it's a legitimate question."

"No, it isn't," Garza said in a low voice. "And don't ask me again."

Now, clearly, was not the time to press the man. "Why didn't they tell me you'd survived?"

"I lost my passport and gave them a fake name. You do realize a cover-up is going on."

"Yeah."

"And they're not going to let us go until the whole thing is officially put straight. They don't want anyone talking."

"They can't just keep us. We're Americans."

"Why not? We don't look like important people. Fact is, we look like bums, confirmed by our traveling on that scow."

"We should demand to speak to the American embassy."

Garza laughed. "Are you crazy? That'll blow everything. We need to stay under the radar."

"What the hell for? The expedition's finished."

Garza leaned in. "Why?"

"How can we continue? We've lost all our gear. Our maps. And a lot of our money."

"How can we *not* continue? You've still got the money in your belt, and I've got mine."

Gideon returned the look. "What about our maps?"

"I've got the exact location in longitude and latitude committed to memory." Garza gripped him by the shoulders. "We're almost there. Why the hell not go the rest of the way?"

Why not? Gideon thought to himself. Being reunited with Garza changed the equation considerably. "Just one thing."

"Shoot."

"We couldn't have expected that ferry to sink. Who knows what's still waiting for us up ahead? I'm on a clock, but *you*..." Gideon took a deep breath. "Anyway, promise me that, if this mission ever falls apart and we get separated for good, you'll find a way of letting me know you're alive."

Garza considered this a moment. "Okay. If you promise to carry both our knapsacks from now on."

"I'm not fooling around! I went through a pretty rough patch just now, thinking you were dead."

"All right, all right. I promise."

"That's better. Now: how the hell are we going to get out of here?"

"Baksheesh," said Garza. "How else?"

Gideon shook his head. "We can't spare the money. And if they see we have money, that might raise even more questions. We'll have to talk our way out."

"Talk our way out," Garza echoed. "Figures. To think I was almost relieved to see you again."

15

THEY REMAINED LOCKED in the gym as the evening lengthened. The food ran out quickly and there was only water to drink, along with a single bathroom whose plugged-up toilet soon became a foul nightmare. Nobody told them anything. The survivors huddled, confused and frightened, on the hard floor.

As the last of the afterglow died in the gym's clerestory windows, Garza said, "I don't know about you, but I'm damn hungry. No one is being fed. God knows what's going to happen to them. I still think we ought to bribe our way out."

Gideon shook his head. "Bribing them only puts us more in their control."

"Maybe we should just escape."

"Shalateen's a small town. We need to operate openly here to outfit our expedition. We can't do that if we escape."

"What's it to be, then, Einstein?"

"Bullshit. I've been thinking about it over the last hour or two."

Gideon laid out his plan. When he was done, Garza said: "I don't think it's going to work. The risk is too great."

"Got a better idea?"

Garza hesitated. "No."

"Then trust me. Bullshit is my area of expertise. This will work."

Gideon went to the locked door of the gym and shook its crash bar, peering out the grimy meshed-glass window. "Hey!" he cried. "Hey! Someone! *Hey!*" He pounded the door with his fist, but no one arrived.

He glanced around the gym and saw some stanchions propped up in a far corner. He went over, picked one up, carried it to the door, braced himself, then drove it through the window with a crash.

He cupped his hands and yelled out the shattered window: "Hey, come here! *Now!*"

A moment later two guards arrived at a run. They unlocked the door and, yelling in Arabic, seized Gideon. Garza rushed up to them. "We want to see Captain Farouk!" he demanded. "Captain Farouk!"

The guards seized him, too. He struggled, ramming one guard with his shoulder and sending him sprawling. More soldiers came running up, and the two were quickly immobilized. They were frog-marched down one hall after another until they came to a closed door. A soldier knocked and a voice called them in.

They were back in the interrogation room, with Captain Farouk still seated at the table. He rose, face red. A loud conversation in Arabic ensued and then Captain Farouk turned angrily from the soldiers to them. "What is the meaning of this?"

Gideon made himself look and sound as calm as possible. "I'll tell you the meaning of this, Captain. I lied to you earlier."

"What lie? You will be punished for perjury!"

"You asked why we were riding that ferry. We're not adventure travelers."

"What are you, then?"

"Undercover CIA operatives. Working for the highest levels of your government."

There was a short silence. Then the captain began to laugh. "CIA! That is rich! Where are your credentials? Why haven't I been informed?"

Gideon began to laugh along with him. "You're only a captain. You're not high enough in rank to have been told. Your superiors are keeping you in ignorance."

The captain lost his smile.

"If you don't believe me, contact your superiors. Send an inquiry up the chain of command."

Captain Farouk hesitated. "So what were you doing on that ferry?"

"Following a cadre of terrorists. We're fairly sure they sabotaged the ferry—as a reprisal against the government."

The captain said nothing, his face slowly draining of color. He then nodded at the soldiers to release their grip and dismissed them, leaving Garza and Gideon alone with him and a single aide-de-camp.

"You are saying the sinking was a terrorist act?"

"Yes. And by keeping us here you're interfering with our mission. I wonder how your superiors will react to that?" Gideon pointed to the phone on the captain's desk. "Call them. Go ahead—call your commanding general."

"Let us not be hasty," said the captain. His face reflected insecurity and doubt. Gideon could see the captain was weighing his claim to be CIA: it could be true, but then again it might not be. The entire scheme depended on the captain being careful and pragmatic; a man who took no chances. Sending a query up the chain of command would be very risky; the request itself would raise questions and could create far more trouble for the captain than simply going along with Gideon's story. At least, that's what Gideon hoped.

"Why didn't you give me this information earlier?" the captain asked.

"Why do you think? We were maintaining our cover. And for obvious reasons, we carry no credentials; as you're probably aware, CIA operatives never carry them while working undercover."

"I cannot be held responsible for what I did not know."

Gideon softened his tone. "True. But from this moment on, Captain, you *are* responsible."

No response.

"This, by the way, is my colleague Manuel Garza. I believe he gave you a false name earlier."

The captain, Gideon could see, was wavering. Now was the moment to be aggressive. He walked up to the desk and placed his hands on it, leaning forward into the man's space, the soft tone vanishing. "My colleague and I must continue our mission, undisturbed. May we count on you for help? Your cooperation now will be noted at the highest levels later."

"What kind of help do you mean?"

"You'll release us and lose all evidence of our presence on the ferry. This is to protect you as well as us. You'll overlook our activities in Shalateen, which will be brief and not cause any trouble. We will be gone within days, maybe less."

"And the sinking of the ferry? If this was a terrorist act, what am I supposed to do?"

"Proceed with your investigation as normal. Although I would strongly advise you to treat the survivors well, feed them, and release them to their homes. Continued detention could become a scandal and a propaganda issue exploited by the terrorists."

Captain Farouk nodded. "I understand."

"We will naturally overlook your ill treatment of us, which is understandable given the fact we didn't identify ourselves as CIA. But going forward, I hope we can be friends, Captain."

The captain was sweating despite the air-conditioning. "May I ask what activities you intend in Shalateen?"

"We're going to outfit a trip into the Hala'ib Triangle."

"For what purpose? That is very dangerous country."

Gideon smiled but did not answer.

"I would be glad to supply you with a military escort."

"Thank you, but that won't be necessary. We prefer to continue with as little notice as possible."

The captain removed a white kerchief and dabbed at his brow. "Very well. You will be released immediately." He barked an order to his aide, who went off and returned with Gideon's passport.

"Thank you, Captain."

"I hope," said the captain, "that your activities will be as discreet as you claim."

"You have my assurance that they will."

They stiffly shook hands.

Outside, the sun had set over the purple peaks of the Gebel Mountains. There was a fragrant smell of smoke in the air, and the call of the muezzin echoed through the dusty byways.

"That was a pretty piece of work," said Garza.

"I gambled that a mere captain wasn't going to run inquiries up the chain of command about CIA activities in his area—that would open a can of worms, expose the ferry disaster, and lead to all kinds of trouble."

"Clever."

"I'm dying of hunger. You?"

"The same."

"Let's find some grub."

Gideon looked down the dirt street, lined on either side with a jumble of mud-brick houses with doorways and roofs painted turquoise. The street they were on led into a commercial area, with vegetable and fruit sellers and cafés, their tables spread out under rickety awnings, some festooned with strings of light-bulbs. Men in galabeyas sat around in groups of two and three, drinking tea or coffee out of small glass cups and eating from plates of dates, fruit, and chickpeas in front of them. Now that the air was cooling off, the town seemed to be coming alive, the street busy with people, camels, and the occasional overloaded delivery truck belching and honking its way along. While a few people glanced at them curiously, they were mostly ignored. Gideon was aware that, after what they'd been through, they did indeed look like bums.

"One's as good as another," said Garza. "Let's try this one."

They entered a café with a cheerful porch illuminated by small lightbulbs. A waiter rushed over and, speaking Arabic in a piping voice, led them with elaborate gestures to a good outside table. They took their seats. The waiter stood next to them with a big smile, nodding.

"He wants a tip before he brings us the menu," said Gideon, reaching into his pocket and removing a coin.

"Will this robbery never end?"

"I never knew you were such a cheap bastard."

The waiter went into the café and came out a moment later, laying menus in front of them, written entirely in Arabic.

"Food," said Garza. He pointed to an adjacent table laid with many plates of unknown dishes. "Bring us that. And tea. Tea." He pantomimed the act of drinking.

The waiter swept up the menus and soon returned with cups

and a pot of tea, followed by a series of plates at irregular intervals—chickpeas, lentils, macaroni, boiled okra, fava beans, lamb kebabs, and flatbreads. They stuffed themselves in silence. Gideon felt like he had never been so hungry in his life, and their prodigious appetites brought wonder and joy to the face of their waiter as they consumed dish after dish. The meal ended with honey-drenched baklava.

The waiter started clearing their loaded table.

Gideon said, "Hotel?"

The waiter scrunched up his face in incomprehension.

"Hotel." Gideon made the universal gesture of laying his head down on his hands.

"*Alfunduq*," the waiter said, nodding in comprehension, and disappeared into the café. He returned with a much-soiled color photocopy of a brochure for what was presumably a hotel, with a map showing its location.

Gideon paid for the meal—six dollars—and they set off, map in hand.

"You see?" he said to Manuel. "That tip is now paying off."

After a few twists and turns they arrived at the adobe building pictured in the flyer, with a faded doorway, a portico, and a mud façade covered in round blobs that appeared to have been thrown against the wall, where they had subsequently stuck. A sign in Arabic was affixed above the door, with the English words below: TOURIST HOTEL.

"You realize," said Garza as they paused in front of the hotel, "that those things stuck to the wall are pats of shit. Drying, it seems. I guess that's what they cook with around here."

Gideon peered at them. They were indeed balls of dung, fresh blobs at one end, drier ones at the other, and marks on the wall where some had been recently removed. "Welcome to the Shit Hotel."

They went inside, entering a lobby of faux-marble tiles, many cracked, exposing mud brick behind. A man behind a wooden counter greeted them warmly, gesturing them over and pushing a guest register toward them. With many noddings and signs they managed to book a room on the third floor, with two beds, at eight dollars a night. They immediately went up to the room and, without further ado, lay down on the beds. The window was open and a blessedly cool breeze wafted in, stirring the faded curtains. Beyond a jumble of roofs and mud chimneys lay the dark flat waters of the Red Sea.

"Tomorrow," Gideon said, "we start outfitting the expedition, find a guide, and work out our cover story."

But Garza, he saw, was already asleep.

16

THE FOLLOWING DAY, Gideon exited the hotel, returning a short time later with a bundle slung over his shoulders. He found Garza lying on his bed, dressed only in underwear and T-shirt, can of beer in hand. He rose when Gideon entered.

"Have a cold beer," he said.

"Where the hell did you get beer?"

"Baksheesh."

He rose and handed Gideon a can from a weeping six-pack, stored in a shady corner. Gideon cracked it. "Ahh, the hiss of paradise." He took a deep swig and settled in the lone rickety chair. "So. Find out anything while I was gone?"

"Pretty much what we already know. The Hala'ib Triangle is a no-man's-land, few roads, and certainly none leading where we want to go. Still, there's a lot of smuggling across the Egypt-Sudan border along the eastern edge of the triangle, so people do get through. The western side where we're headed is avoided by the smugglers, though. Anyway, that's the rumor as far as I could comprehend it. I finally found a smuggler who seemed to have an idea of the conditions in the western part of the triangle."

"So what's the deal?"

"The only way to get in there is by camel."

"What about dirt bikes? Or those dune buggies like they use in the Sahara?"

"You saw the satellite images. The Eastern Desert is nothing like the Sahara. It's far more rugged. Dirt bikes are no good in deep sand, and dune buggies or Land Rovers can't climb mountains. Even if we could find them, we can't afford them. As you may have noticed, this town is full of camels and pretty much nothing else."

"Okay. So we go by camel."

"That's what I figured. Given all the trading here—smuggling and legitimate—there are a lot of camel dealers around. Half a dozen, maybe, all set up on the western side of the town. My thinking is that we hire a small caravan, with a guide and camel drivers, take it about ninety miles to the foothills of the mountains. There we'll dismiss the caravan and travel the rest of the way on foot, maybe fifteen miles, to ensure our final destination remains a secret."

"Fifteen miles across the mountains? On foot? Sounds like suicide in this heat."

"We'll travel at night," Garza said. "The key is to make those fifteen miles in a single night, carrying our water and supplies. There are valleys in the mountains we have to go through, the mist oases I told you about, and I'm hoping they'll be cooler, with vegetation and perhaps water."

"What about maps?"

"I scrounged up a couple of maps when I was looking for the beer."

"And what if we get there and find nothing? How do we get back out?"

"We'll cache water along the way and meet the caravan at a prearranged time and location later."

Gideon shook his head. "Camels. Don't they spit on you?"

"They bite, too," Garza said.

"What joy."

"And you. How well did you handle your morning assignments?"

"I've worked out our cover." Gideon opened his bundle, took out a battered Nikon camera, and tossed it on the bed.

"What's that for?"

"You're a *National Geographic* magazine photographer. I'm a writer. We're doing a story on Egypt's most remote desert. The camera is old and doesn't work, but it makes a nice clicking sound when you depress the shutter."

"I'd rather be the writer and have you lug that piece of crap around."

"Sorry." Gideon reached into the sack and took out a bundle of clothes. "And here's a new galabeya and headcloth for you."

Garza looked at the clothes without reaching for them. "Looks like they have lice."

"They're freshly washed, I made sure of that."

Garza gathered up the clothes, smelled them, and made a face.

"Go ahead. Put them on. Beats being a John Deere salesman."

The camel dealers were located in a series of sandy paddocks amid a scattering of acacia trees, on either side of a bustling dirt road that headed out into the desert. A motley assortment of the beasts were staked out, seated and chewing their cuds. The camel traders occupied elaborate tents, with air-conditioning; hoses snaked from the grumbling external units into the interior.

"That one looks good," Gideon said, pointing. "Big and prosperous."

They approached the tent and a boy, evidently an employee of the camel dealer, hustled over. "You want camel?"

"Yes."

"Come!"

They followed him into the tent, which was remarkably sumptuous inside, the floor carpeted in Persian rugs, with leather cushions for seats around low brass tables. A large man rose from a cushion in the rear and came striding over, hand outstretched.

"Please sit, my dear friends," he said, in halting but more-than-passable English.

They sat around one of the low tables. Glass cups appeared, and the boy poured them all tea.

"Where you from?" the man asked.

"The States," said Gideon.

"Wonderful!" He said something to the boy, who came back with a plate of dates. "You need camel?"

"Yes, for packing and riding, plus a handler and guide." Gideon removed one of the maps Garza had purchased and spread it on the table. "We're going to the base of Gebel Umm, here. It's about ninety miles away."

The man leaned over the map, scowling. "That is in the Hala'ib. Why you go there? Eastern Desert much better."

"Because that's where we want to go. Gebel Umm is what we want to photograph." He gestured with the camera.

"I take you much better place, up here." The large man pressed his finger on the mountains to the northwest of Shalateen. "There are caves, paintings on rock, big dunes, mountains, famous ruined mosque. Nothing in Hala'ib. Many snake. Khazraj Bedouin, maybe. You go *here*." He stubbornly tapped his finger again to the north. "Famous Umayyad mosque ruins. Make good photograph!"

Gideon realized this was going nowhere. "Will you take us to Gebel Umm or not?"

After a long hesitation the man shook his head. "I am sorry. Too dangerous."

Back out in the hot sun, Gideon squinted down the avenue that led among the camel dealers. "Try the next one?"

The same thing happened at that one, and the next, and the next. It was always the same story: Too dangerous. Snake. Sandstorm. No water.

They finally ended up at the far end of the camel market, beside the road headed into the desert. This establishment had the shabbiest tent of the lot and six scruffy camels tethered nearby. The tent was the only one without air-conditioning, and unlike the other dealerships, there was no boy to rush out and greet them as they approached.

Gideon grasped the opening of the tent. "Anyone home?"

A moment later a skinny man with a long beard came bursting through the flap. It looked as if he had just woken up. A few strands of hay were caught in his beard, and his smile revealed a row of red-stained teeth and lips. The other camel dealers had been friendly, but this man was positively voluble. After a brief hesitation, Gideon offered his hand. "Gideon Crew. This is Manuel Garza. We're looking for camels."

"Ibrahim Mekky at your service!" The man seized Gideon's hand and began shaking it endlessly.

"Nice to meet you," Gideon finally said, extracting his hand.

"We have the best camels here. They are not pretty, but they are tough!" Gideon was startled to hear the man speak excellent English with what sounded like the trace of a New York accent.

Mekky gave his beard a little shake to get the hay out. "Come, come have tea!" He gestured toward his dark and no doubt hellishly hot tent. After he issued the invite, he leaned over and spat a stream of red juice and fiber into the sand. He had evidently been chewing something.

"No, thank you," said Gideon, "we've had too much tea already. We can deal out here."

"Very good."

"You speak English well, Mr. Mekky."

"That's because I lived in Queens. Astoria. Very nice there! I love America!" Another red-stained smile.

Gideon was roasting in the sun and didn't want to waste more time chitchatting. He pulled out his map. "We want to go here. To the base of Gebel Umm."

Mekky took the map and squinted at it. "Why there? If you go north—"

"No!" Garza interrupted. "We're going to Gebel Umm. We don't want to hear about rock paintings and ruined mosques."

"Fine," said Mekky, backing down with a smile, once again exposing his startling beet-red teeth. "No problem. We will go to Gebel Umm. I will guide you."

"You'll take us there and leave us. And then you'll come back to get us in—" Gideon looked at Garza, made a quick estimation. "Two weeks. How well do you know the area?"

"Very well! We will need three camels for riding, two camels for packing. It will take four days, maybe five. What is the purpose of your trip?"

"I'm a writer," said Gideon. "He's a photographer. We work for *National Geographic*."

"Ah! *National Geographic*! Wonderful! For you, I have special friend *National Geographic* price—"

"Just tell us the damn amount," said Garza.

Mekky reached into a leather bag dangling inside his galabeya and removed a green nut. "May I offer you betel nut? It is always good to share betel nut before doing business."

"No, thank you," said Garza.

Mekky placed the nut in his mouth, cracked it with his teeth, tossed away the shells, and began chewing. He took a pinch of powder from a jar in his robes, inserted the pinch into the wad of nut, and began chewing that as well. He finished this complex operation by spitting out a vile stream of red fluid and, with his tongue, parking the wad in his cheek. "Forty thousand pounds."

Gideon stared at him. "Forty thousand? Why, that's... twenty-two hundred dollars! We don't have that kind of money."

"Mr. Gideon," Mekky said, "you are talking about not one trip for me, but two! And dangerous. Very few who go in there ever return—"

"We know about the danger," said Gideon. "And the snakes and heat and lack of water."

"Then you know why it costs forty thousand pounds. But because it is *National Geographic*, I can do it for thirty-five."

"Ten thousand," said Gideon.

"Ten thousand? My friend, this is not right."

"Twelve thousand."

"Thirty thousand."

"Eleven thousand."

"Eleven?" the dealer said. "But that is less than your last offer!"

"I'm hot. The longer this takes, the lower my price goes. Think of it as a surcharge for suffering."

"Twenty-five thousand."

"Ten thousand."

"Twenty-two thousand."

"Nine thousand."

"My friend, this is not how it's done! You won't find a camel guide like me in all of Egypt! We will need to carry feed for the camels, water, and food for us. My final rock-bottom price is twenty thousand—in advance, of course."

Gideon was about to reply when a feminine voice rang out from the bustling street beyond. "Twenty thousand it is!"

Gideon turned to see a woman emerge from a battered Land Rover parked beside the thoroughfare. She looked Egyptian, wearing a headscarf and an Egyptian-patterned blue-and-black brocaded dress, but her face was sunburnt and her eyes blue. Her accent sounded vaguely English.

Mekky turned. "Twenty thousand pounds, madam?"

"That's right. Twenty thousand. I need five camels, and I hear you're the best guide in Egypt. I'm heading into the western Hala'ib."

"Well, then! I am your man. It is done!" Mekky clapped his hands and turned to Gideon. "I am very sorry, my friend." He underscored this with a stream of red juice spat into the sand.

"Hold on, here!" Garza said to the woman. "We were in the midst of a negotiation. You can't cut in like that!"

The woman turned to him with a smile. "I just did."

17

THE WOMAN, GLANCING at them with a look of both pity and triumph, strode up to the camel dealer. "I'm ready to pay immediately. We leave tonight."

"Excellent!" Mekky said, rubbing his hands together.

"Wait a minute," said Garza. "We were here first and haven't finished bidding." He turned to the dealer. "We'll pay twenty-two thousand pounds."

"Twenty-four," said the woman.

"Twenty-six," said Garza.

"Thirty," said the woman.

"Thirty-five."

"Thirty-six."

"Forty."

When Garza didn't counter, the camel dealer turned to the two men with a hopeful expression on his face, gesturing as if to solicit another bid. "Forty-two?" he asked hopefully.

"We just don't have the money," said Gideon to the man.

Mekky rubbed his chin, then looked pointedly at Garza's Rolex.

"No way," Garza said immediately.

Mekky shrugged. Then he turned to the woman with a big smile. "Well, madam, it seems the camels are yours. For forty thousand pounds."

The woman nodded. "Very well."

"Don't you have other camels we can hire?" asked Gideon.

"I'm sorry, I have only six. She will take five."

Garza rounded on Gideon. "You just had to be too clever with your bidding, didn't you?" he whispered furiously. "We could have had this deal buttoned up by now."

"Who knew we'd have competition? You're the one who refused to trade him your watch. We'll find camels from someone else."

"We already got rejected by everyone else, remember?"

The woman went back to her Land Rover and drove it into the dirt lot beside the dealer's tent. She began removing luggage from the back. It was a crazy collection of baggage: a steamer trunk, a Louis Vuitton suitcase, some duffel bags, a backpack.

Gideon watched, his annoyance turning to something like amusement. This woman, despite her native dress, was clearly far from being a seasoned traveler. After unloading, she handed the camel driver a wad of money and he counted it. Once it was safely in his pocket, Mekky began examining the luggage, asking questions, and then he engaged in a private discussion with the woman, frequently shaking his head.

"Why do you think she's going to the Hala'ib Triangle?" asked Gideon. "I thought no one went in there."

"Apparently there's at least one woman crazy enough to do it."

"I'm going to talk to her."

Garza rolled his eyes.

Gideon strolled over to where the intense discussion was taking place. The woman had opened the steamer trunk, exposing some heavy rock hammers, chisels, and scientific equipment of unknown function.

"Madam, we cannot take all this," the camel driver was saying. "We must consider the weight."

"Excuse me for interrupting," Gideon interjected.

The woman looked up.

Gideon extended his hand. "May I introduce myself? Gideon Crew."

The woman looked irritated at the interruption. "The deal's done. I've already paid."

"No problem. I just wanted to make sure there are no hard feelings."

She straightened up and reluctantly extended her hand, but did not give her name in return. Garza hung back, scowling.

"So you're going into the Hala'ib?" said Gideon.

"What business is that of yours?"

"I ask because that's where we happen to be going."

"How lovely for you." She turned away and admonished Mekky for pulling out and setting aside a sledgehammer and iron crowbar. "I need those."

"They are too heavy, madam!"

"But I'm a geologist. I need to collect samples."

Mekky shook his head doubtfully. "I will need an assistant for all this. Plus the other camel." The discussion promised to go on for some time.

"May I interrupt again?" Gideon ventured.

The woman looked up again, now thoroughly exasperated. "What now?"

"It occurs to me that, since we are all going into the Hala'ib, we might temporarily join forces."

"No." She looked back to Mekky. "I *need* that sledgehammer."

"I cannot take sledgehammers into the desert!"

"We can help," said Gideon.

"Bugger off." She brusquely turned away and continued arguing with Mekky.

"We could help unpack and pack your gear," Gideon said. "Also, there's safety in numbers."

"Can't you tell these people to leave?" she asked Mekky.

He ignored the directive. "Madam, I told you, I will have to hire an assistant if we take all this." He glanced over the sprawl of luggage. "*Two* assistants. That will cost more!"

Gideon said, "We could be your assistants."

She paused and looked back at him. "Why are you here, and why are *you* so anxious to go into the Hala'ib?"

"I'm a writer for *National Geographic* and my friend Manuel here is a photographer. It's said to be one of the most remote places on earth. The *Geographic* loves stuff like that. Do you read the magazine?"

She stared at him. "Of course I read it."

"Well then, you must be familiar with my writing."

"I can't say I am."

Mekky said, "Perhaps, madam, they should come along. It would be useful. I am old. I need strong men to help."

She looked Gideon up and down. "Strong men? Where?"

"It is a good idea, madam. I am in favor." Mekky spat again.

"Excuse me, I hate to interrupt," said Garza, coming over. "But since no one's asked my opinion, I'd like to offer it—if I may?" He bestowed on everyone an exaggerated grin.

"And what's your opinion?" asked the woman.

"*Fuck this.* That's my opinion."

The woman merely smirked.

"Let me just have a chat with my partner." Gideon touched Garza's elbow and steered him aside, out of earshot.

"I'm not going as anyone's assistant," Garza said angrily. "I don't like that woman."

"First, these are the only camels to be had. Second, having a geologist along is a *perfect* cover for us."

"And third, she happens to be pretty—as far as I can tell with that headscarf—and you're no doubt hoping for some midnight-at-the-oasis action."

"It has nothing to do with that."

"It has everything to do with that. Besides, how are we going to keep her from our discovery?"

"We go with her as far as the foothills of Gebel Umm, as planned, and then strike out on our own. We won't take her, and she won't want to go anyway—she said she's heading west of our destination. She goes wherever she's going and picks us up on her return."

"Did you see all that gear she wants to bring?" Garza asked. "It's obvious she's in over her head. She's going to be a drag on us."

"We can let Mekky sort that out. We aren't bringing much more than the clothes on our backs."

Garza scowled. "You really think she's a geologist? Why is she by herself? Why isn't she better prepared? Christ, we don't even know her name! There are a ton of unanswered questions here."

"It's our only option. Either this . . . or go home."

Garza stared at the ground. "I don't like it."

"Neither do I. But you're willing to give it a shot. Right? *You* were the one so gung-ho to continue."

Garza hesitated and then finally nodded.

They returned to where the woman was standing, hands on her hips, scowling.

"We'd like to team up with you," Gideon said. "We will travel together as far as Gebel Umm. You will leave us there, do what you're going to do, then come back and get us later. We can work out the details along the way. And on top of that, we'll contribute half the cost of the expedition—twenty thousand pounds."

She looked at them, then at Mekky, who was nodding hopefully.

Then she shook her head. "Christ. Very well, then."

18

ONCE MEKKY WAS paid off, he roused up a boy to buy supplies, who returned a short while later with a handcart full of food and water. Mekky saddled and packed the camels as the sun lowered in the western sky. After a tedious argument he got the woman—who seemed uninterested, despite various over-tures by Gideon, in introducing herself—to leave behind the sledgehammer, crowbar, and a set of heavy chisels. They set off at sunset, riding toward the boiling orb just as it sank behind the purple mountains. Mekky led the caravan, trailing the two packed camels, and the three of them followed single file in an order Mekky had established: first the woman, then Garza, with Gideon bringing up the rear. Gideon had heard stories about how uncomfortable it was to ride a camel, but he found it wasn't terribly awkward, especially if he rode with one leg draped over the post. The camel's walk was herky-jerky, but after a while he got the rhythm of it and even began to enjoy the rocking sensation. The camels, despite being ugly and ragged, seemed steady enough and they did not spit or bite—at least, not yet—

although there had been plenty of roaring as they were saddled and loaded.

Garza, on the other hand, did not get into the spirit of it. Gideon could hear the engineer muttering and sometimes cursing at his beast. Clearly the man had no affinity for animals. The woman in front was also having periodic struggles with her camel. Mekky, on the other hand, rode his own mount as placidly as if he were sitting in a Barcalounger.

For five hours they rode across a monotonously flat plain, the air cooling as the light drained from the sky and the stars came out. Never had Gideon seen so many stars, not even in the remote mountains of New Mexico. It was like a vast glowing cauldron, striped by the Milky Way. Mekky broke out singing: a mysterious, repetitive song in a minor key that seemed to have a calming effect on the camels. With no moon, the beasts and their riders soon became black outlines moving in a sea of darkness.

At midnight, Mekky halted. "We rest now!"

"For how long?" Gideon asked.

"Four hours. We start up before dawn."

"Thank God," said Garza. "Get me off this bloody beast."

Mekky came around with his little camel stick and held the woman's animal by the halter while giving the creature a few light taps. The camel dropped to its knees and the woman was nearly thrown forward on to its neck.

"Hey, give me some warning!"

"You must always remember to lean back when getting on and off," said Mekky.

Garza also flopped around like a rag doll when the camel dropped to its knees, losing his footing as he dismounted and falling hard into the sand. Gideon, last to dismount, anticipated the move and leaned back, dismounting smartly. He watched with smug, self-congratulatory amusement as Garza slapped the sand off his ass. "Stupid beasts."

"You ride horses?" Mekky asked Gideon.

"Sometimes."

"It is helpful to have horse experience! With camels, we must be patient. Mr. Manuel, when you talk to your camel, be soothing and friendly. Do not curse."

"I'll curse when I want to."

Mekky shook his head. "We take care of the camels before we take care of ourselves. That is the rule of the desert. First we unpack." He lit a small candle lantern and hung it on a tripod of sticks, which threw out just enough light to work by. Gideon and Garza, with Mekky giving polite directions, unstrapped the panniers from the camels, slid them off their backs, and lined them up in the sand. Mekky then led the camels to one side and staked them on ropes. They gratefully sank to their knees to rest and began noisily chewing their cuds.

"And now we take tea!" said Mekky, returning and clapping his hands. He opened one of the panniers and removed a thin but surprisingly large rug, which he unrolled over the sand. Out came some small leather ottomans and a battered wooden box containing a chipped tea set, along with a tiny brass stove with a kerosene wick and two more collapsible lanterns. In a few minutes, a surprisingly intimate tea spread had been created in the desert sands. As Mekky fussed over the setup, boiling the water, the woman unwound her head covering and wraps and set them aside. A mane of blond hair spilled out, which she shook loose. Gideon could see, even in the dim candlelight, that she was very attractive, with a straight aristocratic nose, slender back, and strongly muscled arms. He wasn't sure what a geologist should look like, but to him she looked more like one of those wealthy, eccentric British travelers who go off into the craziest places, have adventures, and then write books about them.

He cast a quick glance at Garza, who gave him a warning look in return. He was more suspicious than ever.

In a few minutes the tea was ready, heavily sweetened, and poured into glass cups. The night was chilly and Gideon accepted his tea with pleasure. The woman eased down on a cushion and took a glass from Mekky, who then produced a platter of dates and sweet cookies and placed them in the middle of the rug.

"So," said Gideon, "are we ever going to learn your name? Or do you intend to remain a mystery?"

"Imogen," the woman said.

"Imogen what?" Garza asked rudely.

She looked at him. "Blackburn. And you are...?"

"Manuel Garza."

"Pleased to meet you, Mr. Garza." She did not sound pleased at all.

"And I'm Gideon Crew, in case you missed it," Gideon said, trying to inject a friendly note.

They shook hands.

"So you're a geologist?" Garza asked.

"That's right."

"Who do you work for?"

"Well, right now I'm working for myself—on my doctoral thesis, in fact."

"For what university?"

"Oxford."

"Why the Hala'ib Triangle?"

The woman paused, looking from Garza to Gideon and back again. "Is this an interrogation?"

"It is, in fact," said Garza.

"What my partner's getting at," Gideon hastily broke in, "is that if we're going to get along in this harsh environment, we should probably get to know each other a little better."

She looked at him appraisingly. "Really? And here I was hoping *not* to have to get to know anyone."

"Why the Hala'ib?" Garza repeated.

"No geologist has ever explored the triangle," Imogen said after a moment. "I'll be the first. Geology is one of those sciences still dominated by men, and so I have to be twice as inventive to get ahead. Bloody typical. That's why I picked this place. Specifically, there's an unusual—actually, unique—geological formation I want to examine. It's called a diatreme."

"What's that?" Gideon asked.

"It's a volcanic formation in which magma deep in the earth rises toward the surface, encounters an underground body of water, and essentially explodes. It creates a crater connected to a volcanic pipe below of highly fractured rock."

"So where exactly is this diatreme?"

"As I told Mekky: west of Gebel Umm. Now, since we're exchanging information, I'm curious about what *you* hope to find in the mountains."

"Just a good story with photos," said Gideon. "We're going to photograph the high valleys around the peak."

"The fog oases?"

"You know about them?" Gideon asked. "Yes, we're hoping to get some unique pictures up there."

Imogen tipped back her tea glass. "Enough chat. I'm knackered." She wrapped her galabeya up around herself and turned on her side, balling up the head covering to use as a pillow.

"Yes," said Mekky, who had been silent up to this point, his eyes sliding back and forth, listening intently to the conversation. "I go stay with camels. You get sleep!"

Gideon lay back with his hands behind his head and stared up at the immense bowl of stars. It somehow reminded him that roughly six weeks was all the time he had left to look at them. After that ... well, after that came the great mystery.

He closed his eyes.

19

It seemed like only a moment had passed when Gideon woke to the sound of prayers drifting through the air. He sat up. It was still night, but a sliver of moon stood above the eastern horizon, bathing the desert in a silvery light. Below it, the horizon was turning a faint blue. Mekky was some distance away in the sand, kneeling on a small prayer rug, chanting in Arabic and bowing in the direction of Mecca.

Finishing his dawn prayer, Mekky rose and rolled up the rug, tucking it under his arm, then approached, calling out cheerfully. "Ding-a-ling goes the alarm! Breakfast!"

In almost no time he prepared a light repast of hot sweet tea, flatbread, and cheese. They ate quickly. Mekky stuffed a betel nut into his mouth and went to fetch the camels. Gideon and Garza helped him pack up and load the beasts. They departed the campsite as the sky in the east turned red.

"Today," Mekky said as they started off, "we enter the Proscribed Area."

The mountains still seemed impossibly far away, five hours of riding having scarcely brought them closer. The rising sun tinged their summits pink. Between them and the mountains, a range of sharp hills rose into view. Somehow the great silence of the desert imposed itself on them, and nobody spoke as they rode, the only sound the soft crunch of camel feet on the gravelly floor of the plain. Soon, in the distance, Gideon spied something unnatural: a white rectangle. As they approached, it revealed itself as a sign, faded and scoured with sand. A message had been written in five languages.

تدخل لا ـ محظورة !

ZONE PROSCRIT—NE PAS ENTRER!

PROSCRIBED AREA—DO NOT ENTER!

VERBOTENEN BEREICH—KEIN ENTRITT!

ZONA PROIBITA—NON ENTRARE!

The sign stood alone in battered isolation, the level sands stretching away in all directions almost as far as the eye could see. But as if placed in warning, the skeleton of an animal with massive horns lay at its base, upturned eye sockets staring at the sky. The sun cast a long, grim shadow over the sand.

"Barbary sheep," said Mekky.

Gideon could feel the heat of the sun on his back. The strange black hills loomed closer. They rode on toward them.

"*Musaeadat!*" Imogen cried out suddenly in Arabic. Her camel shied to one side. Gideon turned and saw what she had seen— a human skeleton lying partially exposed in the sand, a small rill of sand encircling it downwind. A few tatters of clothes clung to the pelvis, and a brass button lay nearby. A bit of hair remained by the skull, and the jaws stood wide open as if frozen in a scream. An ancient army helmet rested nearby, half filled with sand.

"This is where the battle was," Mekky said. As they rode past he related the story of the famous battle, in which the two sides fought to a draw and then killed their prisoners of war in view of the other. The bodies, he said, were given good Muslim burials in the sand; but they'd had nothing to make coffins with, and now with the passage of years the wind was exposing them.

As they rode on, Gideon saw another skeleton to his right, which almost appeared to be crawling out of the sand, the legs buried, the arms thrown forward, skull facedown. Another skeleton lay behind it, and another. As they progressed, the sandy flat was soon dotted with skulls and rib cages and bones.

"Miss Imogen, may I offer you advice?" Mekky said. "With camels, remain calm. Do not shout again."

"Sorry," said Imogen. "That skeleton startled me."

Garza turned to her. "Interesting how fluent your Arabic sounds."

"I've picked up a few words here and there since arriving in Egypt a few weeks ago."

"A few weeks," said Garza. "So what have you been doing? Organizing your expedition?"

"I spent some time in Cairo, playing the tourist. And then it took a while to get to Shalateen. It's like taking a journey to the edge of the world—as I'm sure you know."

"I see," said Garza. "Did you take the ferry?"

"No, I came by bus and rental car."

"Of course."

She turned in the saddle to stare at Garza. "What's your problem, exactly?"

"I just like to know who I'm traveling with."

"Would you care to check my passport?"

"As a matter of fact, I would. The date of your entry visa stamp would interest me."

"I'm the one who should be suspicious. I know much less about you lot than you do about me. For example, you've been lugging around that camera, but you haven't yet taken a single picture."

"We're not where we're going yet."

It sounded lame. Gideon winced; as Glinn had observed, Garza was a terrible liar.

"The photographers I've known are always taking snaps."

"Hey," said Gideon. "Let's cut the inquisition all around, shall we? It's too damn hot."

The woman laughed. "Tossers," she murmured. Garza fell silent.

The heat was climbing along with the sun. On the backs of the camels they were fully exposed. Gideon felt his thirst rising, his lips drying out. They passed a row of abandoned army trucks half buried in sand, canvas tops shredded and hanging, door panels riddled with bullet holes.

"Say, Mr. Mekky?" Gideon called out. "How about a halt for a drink of water?"

"We drink at Bir Qidmid when we stop for heat of the day."

"What is Bir Qidmid?"

"An old well."

"A well? You mean a well with water?"

"No water now. Just forage for camels. And a ruined mosque where we have shade." He turned to Garza. "The mosque makes very good photos." His eyes rolled around in an amused way.

"Right," said Garza.

They entered the hills. Mekky steered them up an alluvial fan into a dry wash. It wound among gigantic piles of split boulders, pockmarked with holes.

"Interesting geology," said Gideon to Imogen, trying to be

friendly. "Very dramatic, these black hills against the pale-yellow sand."

"Indeed," said Garza, looking at Imogen. "Do you know how these hills formed—geologically speaking, I mean?"

"Well," she said, "I would guess we're looking at the remnants of an ancient volcanic field. These hills are the eroded remains of lava flows."

"Why the black color?"

"Basalt is dark to begin with, and it has a lot of iron in it. In the desert environment it weathers into an even blacker desert varnish."

"And the pale sand? Why isn't it black, too?"

"The sand is invasive, blown in here from the shores of the Red Sea."

Garza frowned and fell silent. Gideon hoped he was satisfied; in his opinion the woman not only was beautiful, but was also obviously who she said she was.

They continued on, the hills mounting higher. The ravine, or wadi, they were riding up was now an oven with black walls radiating heat, the temperature inching upward until it was almost unbearable. Gideon's thirst mounted.

"Mr. Mekky, I really need to get at least a sip of water. It's not good to get dehydrated in this environment."

"I second that," said Imogen.

"When we get to Bir Qidmid," said Mekky. "Not far! We must ration water. You must get used to thirst!"

But it was far. Finally, they came around a bend in the wadi only to pause at a picturesque sight: in a round valley, at the base of a black ridge of lava, stood a dramatic minaret rising from the sand. Nearby, a maze of adobe walls rose above drifts of sand, amid a scattering of thorny acacia and tamarisk trees.

"Here is where we stop for the rest of day," said Mekky, bring-

ing the camels around in a circle. "We start again at sunset."
They all drank deeply, then unloaded and unsaddled the camels.
They retreated into the shade of the acacia trees, while Mekky
hobbled the camels so they could browse, then he spread out his
rug and made a lunch of tea, flatbread, and dates.

"Anything else to eat?" Garza asked, squinting unhappily at
the simple fare.

"Cheese."

"We had that for breakfast. Anything else?"

"Chickpeas. But they need to be soaked and cooked. We have
chickpeas for dinner. This is very good diet! You can live for
months on chickpeas, dates, bread, and cheese."

Garza sat down, saying nothing.

They remained in the grove of trees all day, dozing fitfully in
the extreme heat. No one had the energy to talk. As the sun began to sink toward the horizon, they had dinner—chickpeas and
cheese, as Mekky had promised—then saddled and packed the
camels for the evening ride.

They rode and rode, the days and nights blending together. The
black hills and the winding dry washes never seemed to end,
with heat rising off the sand, the camels endlessly plodding.
Once in a while a bizarre mirage would appear—shimmering
lakes with waving grass; trembling ridges and mountains that
vanished as one rode toward them. Mekky rationed their water,
their tea, and even their bread and cheese, keeping them in a
constant state of hunger and thirst. The water, carried in the
packs, sometimes became too hot to drink and had to be set
out in an open bowl to cool by evaporation before it could be
consumed. This was far worse, Gideon mused, than any trip he
had taken in his life. Even when he'd been at sea with Amiko
a few months earlier, searching for the Lost Island, they had

booze, good food, and beds to sleep in. Garza had fallen completely silent, no longer giving Imogen the third degree, while Imogen, too, remained quiet. It was too hot; conversation took too much energy. The songs Mekky sang periodically to the camels—mournful, wailing tunes that rose and fell—were the only diversion amid the endless black hills.

On the third day of the journey Gideon saw, rising over the tops of the hills, a triple-peaked mountain the color of mahogany, surrounded by lesser peaks, Soon, layer after layer of other mountains came into view, mounting to the horizon. The central peak, Mekky told them, was Gebel Umm. They would reach its foothills on the fifth morning, after sunrise. Finally, Gideon thought, they were approaching their proximate goal. What lay after was beyond imagining.

On the fourth day, they stopped at midnight to camp in a place where four wadis came together. It was a place Mekky identified as Bir Rabdeit. It consisted primarily of a dense stand of tamarisk trees surrounding an ancient stone well, now drifted full of sand. Nearby was a stone corral. Under a sandstone overhang, Mekky—after warning the three to beware of vipers—showed them a panel of rock art of men with spears riding camels, along with faded paintings of antelope and Barbary sheep. The images were decorated with mysterious geometric designs. After a subtle nudge from Gideon, Garza got out his camera and took a series of pretend photos. They went to sleep as usual, rolled up in their galabeyas.

Gideon woke with a start at dawn, torn from a rapidly receding dream of swimming with a naked woman in the pool atop the Gansevoort Hotel. He sat up, blinking. The sun was already close to rising; it was very late. He glanced at Garza, still sleeping, and then all around—and then he realized something was terribly wrong. The two of them were alone. Again he looked around in a panic; he saw nothing but sand beyond the rug they were sleeping on and some items scattered on the ground. The camel jockey and the woman were gone, along with the camels, supplies...and their water.

Everything was gone.

20

Garza rose abruptly at Gideon's shout and looked around wildly. "What the hell?"

"We've been robbed."

Garza exploded. "It's Imogen," he said. "I knew something was wrong with her from the start. The way she arrived so conveniently. The way she bid up the price of the camels. The way she insinuated herself into our expedition."

Gideon didn't answer, but he had to admit to himself that Garza was probably right. "They took all the water," he said.

"Sons of *bitches*."

As Gideon looked around at the landscape of sand and rock stretching to the horizon, the gravity of their situation began to sink in.

"This was carefully planned," Garza said. "They must have conspired to dump us in the worst possible place: eighty miles from Shalateen, thirty miles from the mist oasis. They left us where they were sure we'd die. And they took our water."

Gideon shook his head. "It seems like a lot of work just to steal our money and a few hundred dollars' worth of stuff."

He felt sudden heat on his face as the sun peeked over the eastern foothills, casting long shadows.

"We'd better get the hell out of here," Garza said.

"We can't travel without water. We should dig out the well."

"Water could be twenty feet down, if it's there at all."

Gideon looked at Garza, saw incipient panic in his eyes. "The only sure water is eighty miles back. We'd never get there alive. Our only option is to dig—unless you've got a better idea?"

Garza shook his head.

Gideon walked over to the stand of tamarisks beside the old stone well. A circular wall encased the well, and a stone staircase had been built in the side, spiraling downward. The sand had drifted into the well to within about five feet of the top.

"We need to rig some kind of system," said Garza, coming up beside him. "We can make buckets from that rug."

It took them half an hour to cut up the thin rug and fashion two buckets from it, stitching the pieces into containers. They tore their headcloths into strips and braided them to make ropes. Even as they worked, the sun was rising and the heat building.

"I'll fill the bucket with sand," Gideon said. "You haul and dump."

He climbed down the short staircase and began scooping sand into the bucket with his hands. When it was full Garza dragged it up and dumped it, while Gideon filled up the second bucket; and while Garza hauled that up, he filled the first bucket again.

The sand was loose and dry, and it refilled the hole even as Gideon scooped it out. He soon realized he couldn't just dig a hole in the sand—they would have to clear out the entire well, wall-to-wall. It was backbreaking work, and as the heat of the day mounted it became almost intolerable. Gideon's thirst grew rapidly.

By noon, they had brought the level of sand down only four feet, with no sign of moisture. They were both nearly dead from exhaustion, heat, and thirst. They switched jobs several times, and their hands were now raw from scooping the hot sand.

"We can't keep this up," said Gideon. "We need to knock off for a while."

Garza agreed silently, dumping the last bucket while Gideon dragged himself up the staircase a little dizzily. He felt close to hyperthermia. The well had been like an oven, the air dead and unmoving and full of dust. Silently they shuffled over to a large tamarisk and flopped down in the shade.

Gideon looked at his partner. He was like a zombie, his face mottled with dust and sand that had caked onto his perspiration. His eyes were bloodshot. Gideon figured he probably looked as bad himself.

As he sat with his back against the tree, he closed his eyes and tried to clear his head. His lips were cracked and his tongue was a hunk of dry plaster in his mouth. It was frightening how quickly they had become dehydrated. His thirst was all-consuming. He could hardly think of anything else.

"What now?" Garza managed to say.

"We wait for dusk and resume digging."

In silent response Garza held up his hands, which were swollen, the skin cracking. Gideon glanced down and saw his own hands were in a similar state.

"Maybe we should make a dash for the mist oasis," Garza said. "There must be water there."

"Thirty miles in these mountains? That would kill us for sure."

The sun was directly overhead now and the temperature in the shade was at least a hundred and twenty degrees. No matter what they did, Gideon thought, they were probably going to die.

It would be wonderful to go to sleep, to lose consciousness, but the raging thirst made that impossible. It was obvious they weren't going to find water in the well; nor could they go forward to the mist oasis or back to Shalateen. There were no other options.

He roused himself, looking eastward down the broad wadi. The black hills on either side widened to reveal a horizon of pale sand. It was the time of day when mirages began, and he saw one materialize now: a lush oasis, a sheet of sparkling water, and rising from it something that looked like a city of minarets. He could hardly believe that, after all he'd been through—after brooding about the death sentence hanging over him for nearly a year—he'd be leaving the world in such a totally unexpected and pointless way.

The sun passed the meridian and continued on. Soon he would have to move to stay in the shade, but when the sun crept around he felt it wasn't worth bothering. Something was going wrong with his head; it was as if he was becoming detached from reality and drifting into another world. *So this is how it ends.* He watched the play of mirages on the distant horizon. It was something to do, he thought: the television of the desert. The mirage of the city changed into a row of palm trees, swaying in unison and catching fire, the flames flickering back and forth. As the sun continued to move, stranger mirages came and went: cities, sheets of water, a great ship, mountains rising and falling, a caravan moving like a row of ants across the sands.

The idea of waiting until dark to resume work was now a joke, as it became clear that by the time the sun had set and the cool night returned, neither one of them would be able to function. *I'm dying a month and a half ahead of schedule*, he thought with bitter irony, *in this godforsaken place*. But now that death had in fact arrived, a month and a half seemed like a long time indeed, and he fervently wished he could have it back.

His thoughts became feverish and unbearable. He was not going to put up with it any more. He glanced over at Garza, who seemed lost in his own hellish world.

"Manuel?"

Garza slowly turned in his direction.

"Your knife."

"Why?" Garza stared at him for a moment, then Gideon saw understanding in his eyes. The man reached into his galabeya and slid out the fixed-blade he carried on his belt, offering it to Gideon.

"I'll use it after," he said.

Gideon took the knife and tested the blade—razor-sharp, as he knew any knife of Garza's would be. He took the point of it and pressed it slightly into his left wrist, knowing the cut should be longitudinal. He would just go to sleep—simple as that.

"Sorry about everything," Gideon said.

Garza shook his head. "Me too. No hard feelings."

A tiny drop of blood welled up around the knife tip. Gideon raised his eyes to look at the horizon one last time, and once again the mirages flickered about; yet another caravan distorted and dancing in the heat waves. The realism of the mirage enraged him. He was about to plunge the knife into his flesh when he felt Garza's arm grasp his.

"Wait."

"For what?"

Garza nodded at the horizon. "That one's real."

Gideon stared. He blinked, blinked again. The mirage *did* look real—but then, they all did. They eventually dissipated... but this one was getting clearer; as he gazed it solidified into a woman, riding a camel and leading three others, two with packs.

It wasn't just any woman—it was Imogen. This wasn't a mirage; it was a hallucination brought on by heatstroke and thirst. But it loomed ever closer, and finally, when he could hear the wheezing and grumbling of the camels and the crunch of their footfalls on the gravelly surface of the wadi, he accepted that it was real.

Gently, Garza removed the knife from his hand and slipped it back into its sheath. Imogen led the camels into camp, dismounted, and walked up to them carrying a canvas water bag. She leaned down and offered it to Gideon.

He seized it with a muffled cry, sucking and gulping down the warm water.

"Easy," she said, working it out of his grasp and giving it to Garza.

They both drank in turns before she cut them off. Gideon shut his eyes tightly, counted to ten, opened them again. Imogen was still there. "How did you—?"

She interrupted sharply. "I'm going to unpack and couch these camels. Then I'll join you and we can talk."

Gideon watched as Imogen expertly unsaddled her camel, unpacked the others, couched them in the shade of the tamarisks, and came back over with the water bag. It still seemed unreal.

She let them drink again. When they were done, Gideon found her looking at him with a degree of amusement and satisfaction on her face.

"I know," she said. "You've got a lot of questions. So save your breath while I explain. I sensed that crooked camel driver was planning to do this all along. He was never going to bring his camels into the Gebel territory—he'd lose them all, and probably his life as well." She opened up her haversack, and inside Gideon could see wads of Egyptian pounds. "Here's the money we paid him. I got it back along with the four camels, the supplies, and most of the water. I had to leave him two camels and some water so he wouldn't die on his way back to Shalateen, poor sod."

"But how did you do it? I mean, relieve the man of his camels, money, and supplies?"

"It's a long story, better left for later. A night around the fire, perhaps."

"I watched you handle those camels," said Garza. "You're no newbie. And you speak fluent Arabic. Guess it's not only Mekky who's been lying."

She nodded. "I'm afraid that's true."

"So what's your game?"

"Your gratitude for my saving your life is overwhelming."

"I don't like being lied to," Garza replied.

"Reasonable enough," said Imogen. "Right. I'm not really a geologist. Although for a layman, I suppose that term is close enough. Technically, I'm a geoarchaeologist."

"What's that?"

"An archaeologist who specializes in geology and geography. In my case, I study ancient mining. I'm looking for the gold mines of the Middle Kingdom. The source of the vast gold resources of the pharaohs has never been found. I'm going to find it."

"So why lie to us?" said Garza.

"Sorry," she said, not sounding sorry at all. "I'd been knocking about Shalateen trying to figure out how to get into these mountains without attracting attention when you two bumbling Yanks showed up. I realized you'd make perfect cover for my search."

"Gold mines?" asked Gideon. "You looking to get rich?"

She laughed. "I'm a scholar. That wasn't a lie. I want to make a name for myself by solving one of the great mysteries of the ancient world. If I solve this one, I'll have my choice of tenure-track positions. Oxford is lovely—ever been there?"

"No," said Gideon.

"How do you know the mine's out here in the Proscribed Area?" asked Garza.

"Many reasons. Ancient records, satellite imagery, geology. I'm pretty sure I've pinpointed it."

"So where is it, then?"

"Let us just say it's a two-day ride past Gebel Umm—where you're going. I'll drop you off with supplies and two camels, go on to my site, and then pick you up on my return—just as we'd originally planned." She paused. "Any more questions?"

Garza said nothing. The sun was dropping low on the horizon, casting a golden light across the sands.

She gave him a penetrating look. "I'm not the only liar here."

"What do you mean?" Garza asked.

"You haven't fooled me for a moment," She flashed him a cynical smile. "Photographer, my arse. There's no film in that camera of yours."

"I haven't needed to take any photos yet."

"Good try. But after retrieving the supplies, I searched them and found no film anywhere. Besides, what photographer these days isn't working in digital?"

There was a silence.

"Well?"

Gideon was about to speak when Garza stopped him with a gesture. "No."

"No?" She raised her eyebrows.

"While it's true we're not working for *Nat Geo*, we're not going to tell you what we're doing."

She shook her head. "Here I've saved your hides. *And* I leveled with you."

"Sorry, but that's the way it has to be." Garza said with finality.

Imogen gave him a long, cool stare. Then she said, "Care to mount up? We've still got a long way to go. And I hate to break the news to you, but in that little contretemps with our camel driver we lost a third of our remaining water—maybe more."

21

THEY RODE ALL night, without stopping for the usual four hours of rest. At dawn they paused at a thicket of thorny scrub to rest the camels and let them eat. A blood-red light broke over the eastern horizon as the sun rose.

Imogen unpacked one camel and Gideon helped her boil water. With their rug shredded to make improvised buckets, they used one of the camel blankets instead. Breakfast was coffee and a bone-dry piece of flatbread. They ate in silence. Gideon noticed Imogen glancing repeatedly at the eastern horizon.

"What are you looking at?"

She shook her head. "Probably nothing."

Garza brought out the paper maps and spread them on the blanket, weighing them down with stones. He examined them for a while and, with his compass, triangulated their position using the peak of Gebel Umm, which now rose high above them, along with a secondary peak to one side. He drew two lines on the map from each of the bearings he'd sighted. The lines crossed at a narrow wadi.

"That's where we are," he said, tapping the crossing point. Beyond, the map was almost entirely blank—an expanse of paper with just a few wandering contour lines and the word UN-SURVEYED liberally applied. Only the main peak of Gebel Umm itself was marked.

"I thought we'd be a lot farther than that." Gideon said. "We rode all night and we're barely any closer."

Imogen came over and knelt, looking at the map. "All the winding back and forth in these wadis eats up a lot of distance without much progress."

"Where on the map are your mines?" Garza asked.

Her hand swept vaguely over a large blank spot north of Gebel Umm. "Up in there." Once again Gideon noticed Imogen scrutinizing the eastern horizon. The sun had come up, but the horizon had a thin brown line along it.

"Unsaddle the camels," she said.

"I think we'd better keep going," said Garza. "We're nowhere near where we're supposed to be by now."

Imogen ignored him as she couched her camel and began unsaddling it.

"What is it?" Gideon asked. "Is there a problem?"

Still not replying, she pulled off the saddle and blankets, then carried the saddle over to the edge of the wadi, where a pile of black rocks mounted up.

"Couch your camel next to mine and unsaddle her," she ordered Gideon.

Gideon went to his camel, which was grazing on what looked like the thorniest bush in Egypt, its prehensile lips navigating the thorns as it plucked off what little greenery the plant had. He took the camel's halter in hand and, using the stick, tried to get it to move away from the bush. After roaring in complaint, the camel grudgingly followed. He tapped it and the camel eased itself down. Gideon fumbled with the cinch.

"What the hell are you doing?" Garza asked, coming over. "We can get in at least a few more hours before it heats up."

Imogen came over and, with expert efficiency, untied his saddle and slung it down next to hers, alongside the rock pile. "Look over there," she said.

Garza and Gideon both looked in the direction she was pointing.

"Where?" asked Garza.

"That line on the horizon."

"What of it?"

"It may be a *haboob*."

"What the hell's a *haboob*?"

"Also called a brown roller. It's the worst kind of dust storm."

Gideon squinted at the horizon. "I already noticed it. But I can't see much of anything."

"By the time you do, it'll be too late."

Garza, frowning, rummaged in the pack and pulled out a pair of binoculars. He glassed the horizon with an expression of annoyance, which quickly disappeared into a look of concern. Wordlessly he handed them to Gideon.

A dark reddish wall, a thousand feet high, seemed to lie across the horizon. As Gideon watched he could see it boiling and churning and getting bigger, closing in on them at an almost surreal speed. It did indeed look like a giant roller, approaching as if to flatten them.

"What do we do?" he asked quickly.

"Try to survive." Imogen pointed to the saddles. "Manuel, you make a breastworks out of those saddles that we can use for shelter. Dig the supplies in behind them and weigh them down with the water bags. Gideon, you scoop out a depression for us to lie down in behind it. When the storm comes, we'll pull the camel blankets over ourselves. I'm going to try to find a sheltered place for the animals."

Gideon and Garza did as she said, once again scooping away sand with their sore hands. Sudden apprehension gave their limbs renewed strength. They laid the blankets in the depression and stacked the saddles, water bags, and Imogen's now half-crushed Vuitton case in front of them. Imogen moved the camels down the wadi and couched them, staking their halter ropes into the sand. As they worked, the dark wall approached, higher and higher, yet strangely silent. It was almost black at the bottom, where it appeared to be boiling, pulling up ropes of sand from the ground and threading them into great streamers. The air around them was dead calm and unnaturally cool.

"Jesus," said Garza, staring at it.

"Before it hits," said Imogen, "we lie facedown, as close to each other as possible. We pull the camel blankets over us and hang on tight. If we start getting buried in sand, try to shift it off—don't let it accumulate or you'll suffocate."

"How long will it last?"

"Ten minutes."

"Is that all?"

"It'll be the longest ten minutes of your life."

The wall was now approaching swiftly, like the leading edge of a mushroom cloud, mounting ever higher, churning up bushes and scrub and shredding them to pieces in its powerful turbulence. In another moment the sun was blotted out, casting them into gloomy shadow.

"Get down," Imogen said. "Now!"

They lay facedown, squeezed together in the depression behind the saddles, and drew the rugs and blankets over them.

Gideon felt himself pressed against Imogen, the scent of soap and perspiration mingling with the smell of camels.

"For God's sake, don't let go of the blankets," she said.

Now a sound filled the air: a deep vibration, almost like the low notes of an organ, rising in volume and power until the ground itself seemed to vibrate.

And then it hit. A thunderous roar was followed by a blast of wind, which seized the blanket Gideon was gripping and tried to tear it out of his hands. He could feel the force pulling on the saddles, and then suddenly they were gone, sucked upward in a great stream of sand, spinning away over their heads. A dense soup of airborne sand burst into their makeshift shelter. Gideon tried to breathe but got a mouthful of sand instead. He coughed and buried his mouth and nose into the crook of his arm. The screaming wind was flapping and jerking the blanket so violently that finally one gust wrenched it out of their collective grip. Now the full force of the sandstorm fell down on them: a torrent of sand and gravel, driven by the wind at a hundred miles an hour. Gideon felt the scouring blast of it rake his back, literally shredding the loose folds of his galabeya. He tried to raise himself slightly to take a breath and suddenly felt his body sucked upward by the blast. He was almost carried off before he felt an arm wrap around his back and yank him down. Choking, gasping, face buried, he desperately tried to breathe something other than sand. The screaming of the wind was so intense it sent a searing pain through his eardrums.

And then the wind abated. For a moment, he felt enormous relief that the storm was passing, until he realized he was mistaken: a weight was settling down on him, blocking out the scouring blast. It quickly grew heavier. They were being buried alive.

"Keep the sand off!" Imogen screamed in his ear.

Gideon struggled to push himself up even as the mass pressed down. A terror of being buried seized him and he gave his body a violent shake; another twist and he was able to force himself up through a waterfall of sand, straining, muscles popping. But it was a losing battle: more sand was falling than he could keep on top of. Finally, exhausted and defeated, he stopped fighting it and curled up, cupping his hands over his nose and mouth, his entire universe shrunken to a fetal ball in the midst of a wrathful power beyond all imagining. It went on, and on, and on, as a dreadful half night fell and everything grew blacker until he felt like a speck, a fragile disintegrating atom, buried in massive, impenetrable darkness.

22

And then suddenly there was silence again. Gideon swam back into consciousness from far away, wondering where he was for a moment. He couldn't budge. He tried to move his arms but they were frozen. With a muffled scream he struggled, twisting and squirming ferociously in claustrophobic terror—and the sand began to give. With a heroic effort he threw his entire body into a rotational motion and felt more sand slipping around him. With a third, desperate attempt he managed to sit up, the sand cascading away.

An eerie calm had settled. A thin rain of dust was falling, forming a kind of fog. He tried to speak and found that his mouth was packed with sticky sand, which he did his best to cough out. Around him, in the dim light, he could see nothing but mountainous drifts of sand. His companions had vanished.

He realized with a thrill of horror that they must be still buried in the sand. He began digging, scooping like mad and drawing the sand back, and very quickly he exposed a swatch of blue cloth—Imogen's galabeya. Frantically he cleared the sand away toward where her head would be, uncovering first a thick strand of golden hair and then her face.

"Imogen!"

He cleared sand from around her nose and mouth and then, frantically scooping, from the rest of her face. Her mouth was partly open, packed with sand, and she was not breathing. He cleared away the sand with his fingers, managed to raise her head a bit, and put his mouth on hers, breathing in. He waited; the air came back out; and then suddenly she was coughing like mad, rising up and doubling over, gasping and choking.

And struggling up next to her was Garza, writhing and spluttering as he wrestled out of the sand.

At last all three had freed themselves from their sandy graves. Imogen's face was covered with powdery dust, her eyes wet and bloodshot, mouth ringed with mud. The air around them was slowly turning from a dark orange to a brighter yellow.

"The camels," gasped Imogen.

"The camels can wait," Garza spluttered, still shaking sand out of his hair.

"If we lose the camels, we die."

They rose to their feet, shaking out their galabeyas. Gideon could feel the sticky wetness of blood where flying sand had scored the flesh of his back.

Imogen stumbled away in the direction where she had couched the camels, beside the rock pile. There was nothing but sand.

"Are they buried?" Garza asked.

"No. They must have stampeded."

As they stood there, a hot breeze swept through and the air cleared. Gideon looked around. The landscape had become unrecognizable. All trace of tracks and landmarks were gone. The

thornbushes had been stripped of their few leaves and many up-
rooted. Most of their meager supplies had disappeared. There
were no tracks of the fleeing camels. The wind had scoured the
land clean.

"In dust storms, camels go downwind," Imogen said.
"Gideon, you come with me. Manuel, see if you can dig up our
water bags and supplies. We need to hurry." She set off at a
trudge, moving westward down the broad wadi, Gideon hurrying to catch up.

The wash twisted and turned among black lava flows before
coming to an open basin, surrounded by sandy hills. They
peered in every direction, but saw no camels.

"We need to get higher," Imogen said.

With much difficulty, they climbed a pile of volcanic rubble
forming a loose hill. It was a hand-and-foot climb, and Gideon's
hands, already cracked, began to bleed from the sharp lava. He
said nothing and, after a grueling half hour they reached the
top. The view was extensive and it revealed, beyond the sandy
basin, hundreds of volcanic hills cut by canyons and serpentine
washes—a labyrinth of sand and stone—with range after range
of mountains beyond.

"Jesus," said Gideon. "How are we ever going to find the
camels in there?"

After a long silence, Imogen said: "We're not."

"Surely they must be somewhere."

"A camel can run thirty miles an hour. Even if we knew where
they were, they've already gone too far away for us to catch
them." She turned and started back down the hill.

Gideon hustled to follow her. "So what are we going to do?"

"I'm thinking," she said. "Stop asking questions."

By the time they got back to camp, Garza had managed to
uncover one water bag. The rest had ruptured. Most of their

other supplies were gone. He'd found two panniers with maps and some food, but that was it. He was in a dark mood.

They passed around the water bag and all had a drink. Finally Imogen spoke. "Going back isn't an option. We've got one two-gallon bag of water. In this desert, a person should have a gallon a day. A quart a day would be the minimum to keep you alive—if you're willing to go half crazy with thirst. Eight quarts divided by three people . . . it's not nearly enough to get us back to Shalateen."

"There's got to be water in the fog oases," said Gideon. "What do you know about them?" he asked Imogen.

Imogen glanced up toward Gebel Umm, visible in the hazy distance peeking between two lesser peaks. "Well, very little. On the eastern side of the mountain there are supposed to be some high-altitude valleys where prevailing winds off the Red Sea condense into perpetual fogs. It creates a kind of microclimate. Or so it's said—nothing I read indicated anyone had ever been there and seen the phenomenon firsthand."

"And how far away are these valleys?" Gideon asked.

"Gebel Umm is maybe twenty miles as the crow flies."

"That's where we go, then. And pray to God there's water."

At this, Garza spoke abruptly. "Excuse me, but Gideon and I need to talk. Alone."

Gideon followed Garza off a short distance. "What's the problem now?" he asked.

Garza turned on him. "No way is she coming with us."

"We can't just abandon her."

"She's lied to us once already. How can we trust her?"

"In case you hadn't noticed, we're lying to her as well. And she brought back the camels, didn't she? She saved our lives."

"Look, Gideon, if she comes with us, that means sharing our secret. Do you want that?"

"We don't know what the hell we're going to find," Gideon said angrily. "Maybe nothing."

Garza opened his mouth to reply and then shut it. "I don't trust her."

"Manuel, what exactly is your problem? Do you feel threatened by this woman because she's so capable and intelligent? Think: if we leave her, she dies—and then we die, too. Because she obviously knows a hell of a lot more about this desert than we do."

After a moment of silence, Garza spat out some sand. "We tell her nothing. We'll make her wait at a mist oasis while we go on to the Phaistos location and then pick her up on the way back."

"Agreed."

They came back to find Imogen hauling a camel blanket out of the sand. "I guess you two wankers got it through your thick heads that we're stuck with each other, whether we like it or not," she said without glancing at them. "I've saved your hides twice now, and I expect I'll have to do it again before this is over."

23

Using the camel panniers and straps, Garza cleverly rigged up three backpacks. They decided to leave everything but food, water, and a few basic necessities for the overland journey. They started up the wadi, trying to keep to the main course as it branched, then branched again, as Gebel Umm rose above them like a black needle in the shimmering light. Even though the packs were light, hiking in the soft sand, with their feet sinking deep at every step, was brutally hard. Imogen had taken on the role of water-rationing. Every hour they would stop and she would pour half a cup for each person. As the day wore on, Gideon felt his thirst once again mount dreadfully.

The hills grew higher and the wadis narrower, and a dead heat settled over them like a wool blanket. The washes were endless, turn after turn, punctuated by an occasional dead thornbush. Finally, as they rounded yet another curve in the wash, they saw, not far ahead, the mouth of a cave.

No discussion was necessary. Imogen, in the lead, headed for the cave and the others followed. Gideon entered the shady mouth with relief. It was a surprisingly pretty cave, with a floor of pale-yellow sand and walls of smooth lava. Gideon heaved off his pack and collapsed to the ground, leaning his back against the rock wall. Once again he watched Imogen pour out half a cup for Garza with irritating exactness, then half a cup for him, and finally half a cup for herself. Gideon downed his in two gulps. She sipped the water like tea, which irritated him further.

"Let's take a walk on the wild side," Gideon said, "and have another round of that firewater."

"No. Take a nap. We're going to be hiking all night."

"I can't sleep with this thirst," said Gideon.

Imogen looked at him. "Funny, I didn't take you for a whiner."

"Well, I *am* a whiner. An expert, in fact." He closed his eyes and tried to relax, but against his will an image came into his head: the bubbling spring he drank from while fly fishing in the Jemez Mountains of New Mexico. The water gushed from a fissure at the side of a boulder and spilled over mossy rocks into a clear pool surrounded by ferns. It was ice-cold and delicious, with a fresh, clean taste. He opened his eyes and tried to think of something else. As he glanced about the cave in a desperate search for distraction, he saw, with a start, a strange thin red man standing on the opposite side of the cave, holding a tall spear. It took him a moment to realize it was a painting.

He pointed vaguely in its direction. "You see that?"

Imogen nodded, brushing a limp strand of hair out of her eyes. "They're all over the walls."

And now other images materialized: primitive figures, horned buffalo, camels, antelope, giraffes, and an elephant.

"Cave art," Imogen said.

"Amazing that people once lived in this godforsaken place."

"In Neolithic times it was a lot wetter. The Eastern Desert

and the Sahara were grasslands until about ten thousand years ago."

"Maybe that means there's water around here somewhere," said Gideon.

"The water's long gone. Stop thinking about it."

"Easier said than done." He closed his eyes again and tried not to think of that spring, which of course only made him think of it more. His mouth tasted of copper. Eating was out of the question: he had no appetite and the idea of putting dry food into his already dry mouth was disgusting.

The afternoon wore on, the shadows outside the cave slowly getting longer. Gideon dozed fitfully, but woke up every time he dreamed of water. He glanced over at Garza, who had been resolutely silent. The man was sitting up, back propped against the rock, staring out the cave entrance with a grim expression. Imogen, on the other hand, had fallen asleep, her head on her pack, tangled blond hair spilling all over.

When the light became orange, she woke, rose, stretched. "Water, anyone?"

"Hell, yes."

They each got a full cup this time, which did little to slake Gideon's thirst. As the sun slipped below the horizon, they hoisted their packs and left the cave. They soon reached an area where half a dozen tiny washes came together. They picked one that seemed likely to take them in the direction of the mountain and started up it. The landscape began to change, the rocky foothills with their winding wadis giving way to rough slopes and pitches. They were climbing the flanks of the Gebel mountain range, following boulder-choked ravines leading into the secret fastnesses of Gebel Umm.

Imogen led the way, keeping a steady pace. She had been, Gideon thought, uncomplaining, resourceful—and mysterious.

He watched her climb, picking out the route, sometimes through great boulderfalls, rimrock, and volcanic rubble. She had tied up her galabeya, exposing lean muscular legs. He couldn't help but admire her steady resilience. Garza remained silent and stern.

For the first part of the night they had a crescent moon to see by, which cast a fine silvery light over the otherworldly landscape. It set after midnight, and the outline of Gebel Umm, which they had been able to see from time to time as they came over ridges and passes, disappeared into the darkness. But Imogen continued on, picking the way up one steep slope after another, or else working their way down terrifying inclines. Every two hours they rested a few minutes, downing half a cup of water.

When dawn broke in the east, red morning light touched the top of Gebel Umm, turning it into a spear of fire. This time when they stopped, they only got a quarter cup each. "We're running out," said Imogen.

"We've been going all night and the mountain doesn't look any closer," said Gideon.

"This landscape is more deceptive than I figured," she replied. "For every mile forward, we're going two up, down, or sideways."

As the light rose, a lunar terrain of knuckles and talons of stone became visible around them. Looking eastward from where they had come, Gideon could see past layers of peaks and hills to where the flat desert vanished into the horizon. Ahead lay a maze of interconnected canyons, ravines, and needles of stone.

"We don't have enough water to wait out the day," said Imogen. "I think we'd better keep going."

When there were no objections, she shouldered her pack and

carried on. Now they were out of the sand entirely, picking their way over slopes of volcanic rock, which wound back and forth in endless switchbacks. As the sun climbed, the rock became so hot that Gideon could feel it through the soles of his boots. His thirst was intense and he could feel his legs growing shaky, his strength failing. He glanced back at Garza, who hadn't spoken a word in twenty-four hours. The man looked like a walking corpse, his skin gray. Even Imogen appeared bedraggled and exhausted.

They came to the top of yet another stony ridge, which ended in a cliff. They were now high in the mountains. Gebel Umm finally seemed to be getting closer, its ramparts of basalt towering across the middle distance. But between them and the peak still lay a devil's garden of slot canyons and rock formations.

Imogen paused, looking ahead. She contemplated the landscape for several minutes.

"It doesn't look passable," said Gideon.

"Manuel?" Imogen asked. "You see a way through?"

Garza shook his head.

She turned to the left and they followed the cliff's edge. There seemed to be no way down, and—even if they could descend—no apparent way up the far side. A mile finally brought them to a scree slope plunging down the depths. Imogen paused at its top. It offered a perilous, but not impossible, route.

"Do we?" she asked.

"I don't see any other way," Gideon replied.

Imogen started down, picking her way among the razor-sharp rocks. Gideon's cracked hands started to bleed again. His arms trembled uncontrollably, and waves of dizziness swept over him.

The canyon bottom was hot as an oven and filled with split boulders that had fallen from above. They rock-scrambled their way up the ravine on the far side, making only a few hundred yards over the next hour. At last they came to a pour-over, a lip of stone fifteen feet overhead that they could neither see beyond nor apparently get over.

There was a silence. Imogen finally said, "We have to back-track."

Wearily they descended the few hundred yards they had spent the past hour climbing. From there they ascended another scree slope to traverse a narrow layer of rock above the ravine, forming a kind of shelf. Around a turn in the canyon, the shelf led toward the upper part of the ravine, forming what almost looked like a natural trail. The canyon tightened dramatically at the far end, narrowing to a crack from which a dim green light came.

They inched forward on the trail, the canyon so narrow they could brace themselves against both sides with their arms. Imogen went through the narrow crack and Gideon followed, suddenly overwhelmed by the scent of water. The valley opened up into a belly-like hollow of stone, a hundred yards long and perhaps fifty wide. A mass of vines hung down a section of cliff.

"Water!" he croaked.

A dark rivulet came running out of the greenery and into a pool no bigger than a sink, which itself overflowed and disappeared into the valley floor. A thin layer of mist lingered at the surface of the water.

They fell upon the pool in silent desperation, cupping their hands and sucking up the clear liquid. After the initial scramble, they took turns with the cup. As Gideon felt his thirst begin to dissipate, an irresistible exhaustion fell upon him. Clearly, Garza and Imogen felt the same. They stretched out upon the shady ground and fell into a deep sleep.

*   *   *

Gideon woke and sat up in darkness. At first, he thought evening had fallen, but then he realized that they had all slept straight through the night and that dawn was just breaking. Imogen was awake as well and looking at the map, hair hanging down in a tangle. Garza was still sleeping. The upper rim of the canyon glowed gold with the rising sun, and a cool, delicious flow of air was washing over them. He looked around, taking in their surroundings for the first time. While there was water, he had to admit the valley itself was a disappointment. The single rivulet ran just a dozen feet from the watering hole before sinking into the sand. Except for the hanging greenery, a few mounds of moss, a group of overgrown thornbushes, and an ancient tamarisk with a screw-like trunk were the only signs of life.

He seated himself next to Imogen. "So this is the mist oasis?" she asked.

"It isn't quite what it was stacked up to be."

Garza now woke, sitting up. He looked around, not bothering to conceal the expression of disappointment on his face.

"Maybe there's more canyon farther on," said Gideon. Anticipation was overcoming his hunger.

Garza held out his hand. "Be my guest. Looks like a dead end to me."

Gideon set off along the sandy bottom of the little valley, still cloaked in the shade of dawn. Imogen jumped up to walk with him. Garza watched them wordlessly. He made no complaint about Imogen exploring further. *Guess he's given up*, Gideon thought.

The upper end of the valley narrowed once again, then made a turn. They came around it only to be blocked by a blank face of stone.

Imogen gazed up at it. "Looks like this is as far as we go. This miserable little watering hole must've gotten talked about and talked about until it grew into the legend of the mist oases."

Gideon looked around. There was no apparent way out of the dead-end valley. They would have to backtrack through all that awful terrain. He gazed around at the basalt cliffs rising on all sides. The rising sun was gilding the mountaintops.

"Wait. Is that a trail?"

Imogen squinted up. "Probably made by Barbary sheep coming down to the watering hole."

"Don't waste your time," said Garza, coming up behind.

Ignoring him, Imogen started climbing, and after a hesitation Gideon followed.

"If you find the gold mines of the pharaohs, let me know," Garza called up in a sarcastic voice.

"Is he always this pissy?" Imogen muttered.

"You're not exactly seeing him at his best."

They clambered up the rocky slope until the animal track skirted a precarious boulder and came out above the pour-over that had stopped their progress before. Now they found themselves looking into another dry ravine that cut steeply up a great volcanic ridge. The ravine narrowed at its far end to a mere crack in the earth. They climbed toward the crack, through which—as they approached—a strange orange glow emerged. Imogen, reaching the crack first, stopped abruptly. Gideon came up behind her, then did the same. They walked into it.

The crevice was like a doorway into another world. It suddenly opened up, and below them lay a valley, sunken in a deep mist that glowed gold in the early-morning sun. Gideon saw mysterious plants hanging from the walls and flower-dotted grasslands punctuated by mounds of deep moss. Ancient fig trees graced the landscape, mingled with sycamores and clusters of date palms. He could hear, coming from somewhere, the echo of burbling water. As the sun cleared the rim of encircling mountains, the glow brightened, and as the shadows grew shorter he saw ruins take shape on the far side of the valley. A row of toppled stone columns led to a pair of gigantic statues, shattered and broken. Only the feet remained on pedestals of stone.

"Oh my God," breathed Imogen. "A *real* mist oasis."

Then she fell silent and the two stared wordlessly at the ruins, wreathed in swirling mists.

"Jesus," said a voice from behind as Garza came up. "I take back what I said."

Now they walked down a trail that led into the center of the valley, where it fell in alongside the embankment of a stream. A trickle of water ran across a bed of fine sand, overhung with convolvuluses. The air smelled of damp earth and flowers. Larks, butterflies, and swallows flitted about.

They walked alongside the stream, the mist collecting on their clothes. Not far ahead a massive fig tree jutted out of the ground like a muscled torso, its branches heavy with fruit. They stepped up to it and Gideon picked a fig from the nearest branch, soft and round and still warm from the previous day. He bit into it, the juice gushing. Imogen and Garza followed his example. They were all ravenous.

Suddenly Imogen stopped eating and froze. For a moment, Gideon didn't understand. But then, catching movement out of the corner of his eye, he turned to see a dozen figures materialize out of the mist, surrounding them with daggers drawn.

24

THE MEN SILENTLY closed in on them. They were bareheaded, with long, unkempt black hair falling to their shoulders in curls. One of them, evidently the leader, was gigantic: well over six and a half feet tall, with a broad black beard and a massive neck and chest. They were dressed alike, in a long piece of deep-orange cloth wound around their waists with one end draped over the shoulder. The orange dye had come off in places, giving their skin a bronze appearance. The huge barbarian had an elaborate bracelet of what looked like human molars fastened to one of his wrists. Each man wore a leather belt around the middle, with the sheath of a copper-bladed dagger snugged tight against the stomach. Those daggers were all out, in their hands.

"We're friends," said Gideon. "Friends!"

"*As-salamu alaykum,*" Imogen said in Arabic. "Peace be with you."

Both greetings were ignored. The heavily bearded man and two others stepped forward, moving in absolute silence, like ghosts. The bearded man seized Gideon's upraised hand, pulled it behind him, and in one efficient movement threw him facedown on the ground. Gideon struggled but the man quickly tied Gideon's wrists together with a leather thong, then pulled him back to his feet. In seconds the three of them had been seized and tied, then leashed to each other in a line. It was done so swiftly Gideon barely had time to think, let alone resist.

The huge bearded man took the end of the leash and gave it a jerk, pointing down the trail.

Garza yanked back. "No one's going to lead me around like a dog!"

The man stepped toward Garza, waving his crude dagger. Garza charged him, intent on butting him with his head, but the man was too fast and dodged the blow, neatly stepping aside and slamming Garza across the face with the back of his fist. Then the man spun Garza and held a dagger to his throat.

"Son of a bitch!" Garza said as struggled.

"Don't—!" Gideon cried as the blackbeard cut him across the neck, Garza crying out in pain as he did so. It took Gideon a moment of horror to realize the cut was superficial, just deep enough to draw blood.

Blackbeard released Garza, gave a loud order, and the other warriors closed in on them. Imogen tried to speak Arabic again but was quickly muffled by a hairy goatskin that was stuffed in her mouth, then tied with a gag. Gideon and Garza got the same treatment. The skin in Gideon's mouth was horribly rank.

Blackbeard now gestured at them again to walk down the trail. Gideon glanced at Garza. He was pale and shaken, a rivulet of blood running down his neck. For a few moments at least, Garza must also have thought he'd been about to die.

In silence they hiked along the trail, emerging from the misty valley at the far end into higher mountain country, the land rising in a series of ridges, surrounded by peaks. Topping the highest ridge they turned sharply westward, then came to a pass. Below, a second, even more remarkable valley opened up: a vast, mysterious world hidden within the mountains, carpeted in grass and dotted with groves of trees. Gideon could see tiny goatherds driving their flocks and several herds of camels grazing. The tinkling of bells reached his ears. In the middle of the great valley, at least a mile or more away, stood an encampment of tents arranged around a grassy plaza. It was as if they had fallen through a time warp: there was not the slightest evidence of the modern world visible anywhere.

With a shouted command, Blackbeard prodded them down the trail. At length, they entered the encampment and were led to a large tent that stood on a promontory of rock in the middle of the settlement, dyed deep yellow, with an elaborate geometric design in black along its border—the residence, Gideon surmised, of whatever chief ruled that land. As they approached, the flap of the tent was thrown aside and an old man emerged. He wore a long saffron-colored robe with a leather belt in which was tucked a dagger with a handle trimmed in precious metal. He carried a tall staff. The man's wizened face was small and dark, with two eyes under bushy eyebrows peeping out from under a headcloth. Those pinpoint eyes, glittering with suspicion, rested on each of them in turn. As the eyes fell on Gideon, he had a crawling sensation of doom.

The flap of the tent moved again and out stepped a most extraordinary-looking old hag, so bent her body was practically the shape of a question mark, dressed in greasy goatskins. She was using two canes to support herself, and they looked to Gideon as if they were made of human long bones. A veil, draped over her head, trailed on the ground behind her. She slowly worked her way around until she was standing just behind the old man. Lastly, a young woman materialized out of the darkness of the tent. Unlike the others, she was dressed in a soft, gauzy material that no doubt passed for finery. Gideon saw a long swirl of dark, mahogany hair and equally dark eyes. She came up to stand beside the chief, looking at them with the same suspicious gaze as the other two.

A crowd began to gather.

Imogen bowed to the man and tried to speak, gesturing vigorously for the gag to be removed. After a few moments, the old man said something to Blackbeard, who stepped forward and removed her gag. Imogen spat out the disgusting goatskin. The old man waited for her to speak, leaning on his staff.

Collecting herself, Imogen began again in Arabic. The old man listened briefly and then interrupted her angrily. Imogen tried to continue, but Blackbeard made a cutting motion across his throat with the dagger, making it clear she should stop talking. She fell silent.

Now the crone began to speak, in a language that to Gideon did not sound at all like Arabic. What she said caused a stir in the crowd; a wave of suppressed excitement. In response, Blackbeard began prodding the three forward with his dagger, herding them along a faint trail that led out the far end of the valley. Meanwhile, the young woman and old crone were lifted and placed together in a rudely fashioned sedan chair, hoisted up by four men, in preparation for the journey. The crowd gathered behind, chattering excitedly, as if in anticipation of a sporting event.

25

As they were herded along a faint trail, Imogen tried to speak again, but Blackbeard silenced her with a blow from the flat of his dagger. At length, they entered a ravine at the end of the valley and continued along a trail that skirted a cliff, with a drop on one side and a sheer wall on the other. A hot wind blew up from the depths of the ravine and a pair of ravens rode on the air, cawing at them before sweeping away.

Around the side of the cliff a small barren area came into sight, surrounded by scree slopes. A hideous spectacle revealed itself: a rough pit dug into the hard ground, surrounded by a semicircle of twisted wooden spikes on which human heads had been impaled. The heads were mummified, mouths agape, lips shrunken and drawn back from rotten teeth, with only hollow sockets for eyes. Some were clearly far older than others. Several ravens sitting on the spiked heads now rose into the sky, screeching their displeasure at being disturbed.

The crowd following them spread out and fell quiet, kneeling, heads bowed, waiting for the show to commence.

They were led to the edge of the pit. The ends of the leather ropes they were tied with were drawn tight, then staked into the ground on either side of the pit. Blackbeard took up a position behind them.

It was becoming all too clear to Gideon what was about to happen.

He began to mumble desperately, trying to speak through the foul gag, but nobody paid any attention. Imogen began speaking Arabic again, in a soft, pleading tone, but was also ignored.

The four men carrying the young woman and old crone now lowered the sedan chair to the ground, helping the crone out of it. Taking up her gruesome walking sticks, she shuffled forward with the presumed chief and came to a stop on the opposite side of the pit. She was joined by four old men in white robes, each with a long, forked beard. They looked like priests, it seemed to Gideon.

The crone, flanked by the old men, gave them what looked like a series of instructions or—perhaps—commands. Then she raised her withered arms to the sky, tilted her head back, and broke out in a strange, high-pitched wail that then turned into a sort of chant. The crowd dropped to their knees, heads bowed as the crone's cracked voice echoed among the surrounding cliffs. Gideon tried not to look into the pit, but found that he could not help himself. In the gloom below, he could make out numerous corpses sprawled at the bottom, in various states of mummification. A few retained the rotting vestiges of Western clothing, but most wore Arab garb. All were missing their heads. Gideon took a shuddering breath. They were transgressors—and now they were going to be ritually beheaded, their bodies thrown into the pit, and their heads placed on stakes. *What an end.*

Three men appeared, each carrying a fresh wooden pole with sharpened ends. They drove the poles into the ground, following the same gruesome semicircular arc as the other decapitated heads. Meanwhile, two young women carried a long, wooden inlaid box up to Blackbeard. They opened it with great ceremony, and the bearded man reached in and removed a huge broadsword—the first sword Gideon had seen in the camp, and the first sign that these people had steel rather than just the copper and bronze of the daggers they carried. A murmur rose from the crowd. The man held the sword out, examined it this way and that, and gave it a few test swings. The blade was encrusted with dried blood, but its edge nevertheless glittered ominously.

At length, the man began walking toward them with great solemnity, holding the sword high.

Gideon couldn't take his gaze off its edge. He frantically tried to think of a way to escape such an unexpected and dreadful fate, but to no avail. He'd tried to come to terms with his impending death, but he'd never imagined anything like this: at the hands of an executioner's ax. Imogen again renewed her pleading, but Gideon doubted the tribe could even understand her. This pit was clearly the reason this place had remained so untouched by the outside world—any visitors unlucky enough to happen upon it were quickly and brutally dispatched. He recalled the camel drivers who said that those who ventured this way never returned. At the time, he'd dismissed this as rumor and superstition, but now it appeared to be all too true.

The crone went on chanting, her voice high-pitched and grating. Imogen had fallen silent. Gideon glanced at her face, and their eyes met. She was calm now, seemingly resigned.

The crone suddenly stopped her wailing and a hush fell. The crowd remained kneeling, but their heads were no longer bowed; they were looking on avidly.

Blackbeard stepped forward and gestured at Garza. Two

guards came over and cut the thongs attaching him to the others. Gideon could see Garza trying to protest, but he could make little noise and no one paid any attention. The guards, with a violent but efficient gesture, forced him to his knees at the edge of the pit. A third came up and grasped Garza's hair tightly in his hands, while Blackbeard positioned himself, legs apart. The man lifted Garza's head, exposing his neck, and the big bearded man touched it with the edge of the sword, as if calculating the best position for his strike. Then he raised the weapon. The edge of the blade flashed once in the sunlight.

Gideon began to feel strangely detached, as if this terrible thing were happening to someone else, someplace far, far away. Distantly, he hoped it would be quick. Judging by the fearsome muscles on the executioner, his determined expression, and the massive sword, it would be.

The man clutched tightly at Garza's hair, so he wouldn't lose his grip at the moment the head was struck off. It was obviously a practiced motion. Gideon could see Blackbeard bracing himself for the swing. The silence was now absolute. He closed his eyes.

Then he heard Imogen shout in English: "Don't do this! For God's sake, *stop!*"

26

In the silence that followed, the crone let out an astonished gasp, followed by a rapid-fire jumble of words. Gideon opened his eyes to see her yammering at the old chief, who was listening with a surprised expression. The crone gestured animatedly with her veined hands.

A terrible moment of stasis ensued, Blackbeard with his sword still poised. A restless murmur rose in the audience. The chief now held up his hand. When Blackbeard didn't move, the chief pointed a finger at him and said something like a sharp order. This time the man lowered the sword, visibly disappointed. The murmur of the crowd rose in volume. The chief turned and gestured again; he seemed to be ordering everyone to leave. Garza was hauled back to his feet by the guards and tied once again to Gideon and Imogen, still gagged. His face was pale, covered by a sheen of sweat.

More shouted orders from the chief, and the three were pulled back from the edge of the pit, then led along the trail in the direction of the encampment. Gideon stumbled along, dazed, barely believing that he was still alive. His legs were so shaky he could hardly walk.

At the closer edge of the camp, next to a cluster of goat pens, stood a large cage made from green tree trunks lashed together. Its door was removed and—with shouts and gestures—they were pushed inside; the door was fitted back in place, then lashed shut with leather thongs. Two guards took up position outside.

Inside, the three sank to the sand, emotionally exhausted. For a long moment, there was silence. Finally, Imogen swore softly. "Why are we still alive?" she asked.

But neither Gideon nor Garza could answer; they were both still gagged.

"I don't know about yours, but my bindings are loose. I think I can work my way out." She began twisting at her wrists.

Gideon also tested his bonds and noticed that the leather thongs, although tight, did in fact allow some give. By slowly pulling and twisting, they could be loosened, bit by bit. He glanced around, but the guards had their backs turned.

"Keep at it," Imogen whispered. "Mine are coming loose."

Gideon continued to twist and turn his wrists, and then with his loose fingers he managed to grasp the end of the leather thong. He found the knot and started prying it open with his fingertips. Soon it was untied and he had freed his hands. He quickly removed his gag and spat out the goatskin. Turning his back to the guards, he finished untying Imogen's and Garza's hands. Garza removed his gag and also spat out the goatskin muffle. He wiped his mouth with the back of one trembling hand, still in shock from his close brush with death.

Gideon took in their surroundings. The cage was not wholly unpleasant; it had a sandy floor and was large enough to stand in. Air flowed through it, creating a welcome coolness. It was empty except for a wooden bucket in one corner. Looking out, he could see much of the camp, gilded by the morning sun. There was a great deal of activity. Several children came by, stared at them, then went their way. The guards seemed almost lackadaisical and paid little attention to their prisoners.

"What the hell just happened?" Gideon said in a low tone.

"I wish I knew," Imogen whispered back.

Garza massaged his neck. "Getting your throat almost cut twice in one day is a bit much," he said. Although he tried to sound calm, his voice quavered slightly nevertheless.

"Are you all right?" asked Imogen.

"I still have my head."

"You think they were testing us?" Gideon asked.

"No," said Imogen. "They were definitely about to kill us. Until I called out."

"Any idea what language they're speaking? Some form of Arabic?"

Imogen shook her head. "The village looks Bedouin, as do their clothes, but they don't speak Arabic. The women aren't covered and I don't see any signs of Islam: no calls to prayer or any of the traditional symbols or customs."

"If not Arabic, what could it be?"

"If I had to guess, I'd say they're speaking the language ancient Egyptians spoke before the Arab invasion. Which would be Coptic. I think these people are pre-Islamic."

Gideon moved toward the door, one eye on the guards, and cautiously inspected the lashings. "When it gets dark and people go to bed, I'm pretty sure we could cut through these."

"And then what?" Imogen asked.

"We'll steal some camels and waterskins and ride like hell until we get out of their territory."

"I agree," said Garza. "The sooner we get out of this hellhole, the better."

"That makes three of us," she said.

As they were speaking, Gideon noticed the same group of four old men with white beards walking in single file up the ridge toward the chief's tent. As they entered, the chief held the flap aside for them in a welcoming manner. It looked like a meeting of the elders—probably to decide their fate.

All day they waited for the men to reappear. The sun crept down between the mountains and the valley filled with purple twilight. Cooking fires were lit and twinkling lights began to dot the surrounding landscape, the fragrance of smoke mingling with the murmuring of voices and the tinkling of bells as the goats were driven back into their pens for the night. A delicious smell of roasting meat drifted through the air.

"If these people weren't so damn bloodthirsty," Garza said, gazing out, "that scene might almost be beautiful."

As darkness fell, the flap of the chief's tent finally opened, throwing a bar of yellow light over the grass. The priests began filing out.

"Looks like the powwow with the grand mufti is finally over," said Gideon.

"They're pre-Islamic, remember?" Imogen said. "He's not a mufti or sheikh. He's a chieftain."

A group of guards, about half a dozen, now approached their cage, two carrying torches and the others long wooden spears with bronze tips and tails.

"When they see we've worked off our bonds, we're going to be in trouble," Gideon said.

"Screw 'em," replied Garza.

They stopped and one of the men shouted an order to the

two guards. They unlashed the cage door and pulled it aside, gesturing for Gideon and the others to come out. Strangely, they did not seem concerned that the three had untied and ungagged themselves. As they emerged, the guards pushed them forward at spearpoint, propelling them in the direction of the chieftain's tent. They were led up the small promontory, then prodded inside and forced to kneel, the points of the spears pricking their backs.

Despite their dire situation, Gideon could not help but be amazed at the tent's relative opulence. It was spacious and well lit, with oil lanterns casting a warm glow over a sumptuous array of woven rugs, leather cushions, and hanging fabrics. The chief sat on a leather ottoman, as if on a throne. A jostling crowd of people filed up and stood near the entrance, waiting. There was no sign of the young woman who had been standing beside the chief earlier.

Silence fell as the old chieftain gazed at the three. Everyone seemed to be waiting for something. A few moments later, Gideon heard a cracked voice outside, raised in argument—the crone. A flap at the rear of the tent opened and she was ushered in, moving forward with those same macabre walking sticks. She was still dressed in coarse goatskins and a filthy headscarf, from which escaped strands of white hair. The chieftain rose with deference and helped her ease her ancient body onto a pile of cushions. She muttered in displeasure as she adjusted her skins. Once everything was in place, she folded her hands in her lap and turned a pair of beady eyes on them. Her face was creased with suspicion. And yet there was something else there, Gideon thought: an expression that, perhaps, was more curious than suspicious.

The crone spoke to them briefly in a cracked voice. She stopped, waited, then began again. It took Gideon a few moments to realize she was speaking English—with what sounded like a travesty of a British accent.

All three were struck dumb with astonishment.

Into the silence, the crone asked, for the third time: "You speak English?"

"Yes, yes, we speak English," they stumbled over themselves, suddenly all answering at once.

The crone, annoyed, gestured with her hand for silence. Then she pointed at Gideon. "*You* speak. Others, quiet!"

Gideon nodded.

"Why you here?"

"We're...adventurers," Gideon began. He had no idea how this old woman had learned English, and no way of knowing just how many words she understood. But this had to be the reason why they'd been spared—it was when Imogen had finally spoken English that the crone stopped the execution. "Adventurers," he repeated. "Explorers." While he spoke, he was acutely aware of a spearpoint pricking him between his shoulder blades.

"Explorers," the woman repeated, mimicking the word.

"Yes. Explorers."

"What that mean?"

Gideon tried to focus. "We—we travel, looking for new lands. New people."

"Your land no good?"

"Our land is fine. We travel because we are curious. Not to conquer, but to learn new wisdom." He swallowed as she frowned with incomprehension. "We come in peace. Peace. As you see, we are poor people with nothing, and we want nothing from you...except knowledge."

Gideon watched the old woman carefully while he spoke, but her expression was impassive and unreadable until his final words. Then she held up her hand for silence and turned to the chieftain, apparently translating. The chieftain said something in response and she turned back to them.

"Why?" she asked.

"Why do we seek knowledge? Because knowledge is good."

More confabulation with the chieftain.

"We have knowledge you seek?"

"We do not know. That is the reason for being an explorer. You look. You learn."

"You look for...treasure?" Her expression grew guarded again.

"No, no. We do not want treasure. As you can see, we are very poor." He spread his hands. "We care nothing for riches."

Gideon couldn't tell if she and the chieftain were buying this or not.

"You are English?" the crone continued.

"Yes," said Gideon. It would be too complicated to explain the details.

"You crazy?"

Gideon hesitated. "Yes."

When this was translated, the chieftain showed sudden alarm. There was a murmur from the crowd just outside the open tent flap as well.

"Why you say this?" the crone asked.

"Because only crazy people would come here."

The chieftain found this hilarious when it was translated, and the listening crowd dutifully laughed along with him. This was starting to go well, Gideon thought.

"The Father still want to know *why* you come here."

"It was an accident."

"Accident?"

"Yes. We were robbed, and then our camels ran off in a storm. We lost everything. We had no choice. If we did not find water, we would die."

"Who rob you?"

"An Arab camel driver."

At this, the crone perked up. "Arab? Rob *you*?"

The chieftain broke into a tirade on hearing this translated, gesturing, his beard wagging. An answering murmur of anger swelled in the crowd. Gideon had a sudden fear he had offended them, and that their execution was being ordered afresh. When the chief was done yelling and gesturing, the crone did not translate.

"What did he say?" Gideon asked timidly.

"The Father no like Arab."

"But..." Gideon hesitated. "Aren't you Arabs?"

"No," said the crone, sharply.

"Who are you?"

"We *Egyptian*." She spoke the word precisely. "Arab is invader."

Gideon nodded. Apparently, it was as Imogen had guessed.

"Where you go next?" the woman asked.

Gideon felt relief at this question, as it implied they were going to ultimately be freed. "We...will go home."

This answer caused the chieftain to have another fit, speaking loudly and gesturing at them. And again the crowd responded with loud chatter. The crone spoke as well in her high, cracked voice. The entire tent seemed to be arguing. Finally, the crone staggered to her feet, propping herself up with the canes, and tottered over to Garza. She grabbed his wrist in her bony hand and held it up, displaying both the wrist and the watch on it. She shook the wrist, then—with some effort—disengaged the watch and dangled it in the chieftain's face, as if to make some obscure point.

The chieftain took the watch and examined it, turning it over with great interest while the crone talked on.

"Please, accept this as a gift from us," said Gideon quickly.

"Hey!" Garza protested. "That's mine!"

"Just shut the hell up."

The old crone translated and the chieftain fumbled with it, trying to put it on his wrist.

"Let me help," said Gideon.

The chieftain motioned him up, and Gideon demonstrated how to snap the watch's bracelet onto his wrist. Close up, he could see that the man was even older than he'd realized, and frailer. When the timepiece was secure, the chief held it up with a smile.

Gideon sat back down.

"You owe me a solid gold Submariner," Garza muttered.

"The Father say thank you for watcher of hours. It is gold—gold is skin of the gods!"

Now the chieftain rose to his own feet and turned to them. He gave a booming speech, with many hand gestures, and the crowd murmured its approval. When he was done, he turned to the crone and gestured for her to translate to them.

"The Father say..." She slowly raised her withered arm and pointed a crooked finger at Gideon. "...maybe you tell truth. Or maybe you lie."

"I'm telling the truth," Gideon said quickly. "I swear!"

"We find out."

"How?"

The crone was silent for a moment, as if trying to recall a word. "A trial."

"A trial? What kind of trial? You mean, by a council or something?"

"No. Trial by fire."

27

At the chief's pronouncement, a roar of excitement and approval had arisen from the audience that was listening just outside. The guards pulled the three back to their feet and marched them out of the tent through the crowd, which parted as they passed. They were quickly led back to the cage and lashed inside. Various villagers passed by in twos and threes, peering at them with curious faces, as everyone started gathering in the central plaza of the encampment, just below the rise of rock on which the chief's tent stood. The same two guards took up positions on either side of the cage.

"Trial by fire," said Gideon, sinking to the sand, head in his hands. "Oh God. First a beheading—and now this."

"It's actually an ancient Bedouin tradition," said Imogen. "They use it to tell if someone is lying."

Gideon looked up. "You know about it?"

"Yes."

"So what do they do? Make me walk over a bed of coals?"

"No. They heat up a rock, or a piece of metal, until it's red-hot. Then they place it on your tongue. If it burns your tongue, you're lying. If not, you're telling the truth."

Gideon stared at her. "How does it *not* burn your tongue?"

"My understanding is that everyone is found a liar."

"Great. And then what?"

"The liar is beheaded."

"Of course!" He groaned. "What if I say no?"

"If you refuse to undergo the trial, you're presumed a liar and are beheaded."

Suddenly Garza said: "Here we go."

Gideon followed his gaze. A fire was being built in the middle of the plaza, and the assembled crowd was chattering excitedly, faces reflected in the flickering light, clearly awaiting this fresh spectacle. Nearby, Blackbeard oversaw the activity, holding the sword. Beside him was a wooden chopping block.

As Gideon stared, two of the priests brought over a small basket and set it down by the fire, removed a dozen or so round white stones, and—chanting loudly—carefully dropped several of them, one by one, into the center of the flames.

Now the chieftain came striding out of his tent, still decked in his finery, with the crone hobbling behind him. He descended the path with great dignity and entered the center of the encampment, the crowd once again parting for him; there he turned and gave a loud command. The two guards at their cage undid the lashings and hauled Gideon out, leaving the others inside.

"I'm sorry, Gideon," said Imogen.

Gideon couldn't bring himself to answer. He was manhandled into the center of the plaza and held by the guards near the fire, one on each side. The chieftain now gave yet another long speech, with much gesturing, pointing first at the fire and then at Gideon. Blackbeard stood next to the beheading block, grinning with anticipation.

There has to be a way out of this, Gideon thought. But he couldn't seem to gather his wits. Things were too strange, and they were all happening too fast. Now—under the watchful gaze of the crone—one of the white-bearded, yellow-robed priests was bending over the fire, clearing away the burning logs to expose a bed of coals, mingled with pebbles that were already glowing from the heat. The other, with a crude bellows, blew on the coals, heating them up to a bright red. The sun had long since set, the valley was dark, and a scattering of sparks rose into a black, star-filled sky.

Gideon's guards pushed him forward. The first priest leaned over with a pair of tongs and plucked a pebble from the fire—the hottest one—and held it in front of Gideon. He indicated with a series of gestures that Gideon was to take it and put it in his mouth.

"No!" said Gideon, wrenching free from the guards' grasp, knocking the tongs aside in his struggle. One of the guards elbowed him in the face and he fell to the ground, sprawling in the dirt, dazed. The guard gave him a vicious kick before hauling him back to his feet. The crowd whistled and yelled their disapproval. Blackbeard readied his sword.

The chieftain shouted for silence.

Now a priest applied the bellows again, blowing until the bed of coals went from red to orange. The thick smell of smoke filled the air. Again, with persnickety care the first priest selected the hottest pebble with his tongs and held it out, gesturing for Gideon to take it and put it in his mouth. After a moment, Gideon held out his hand. The priest dropped the glowing rock into it and—after a grunt of pain and a brief, dreadful hesitation—Gideon popped the pebble into his mouth.

A long silence ensued. The crowd was transfixed. Every pair of eyes was on him. Gideon remained unmoving, mouth closed, fists clenched, eyes staring straight ahead. A murmur of admiration at his stoicism rose from the crowd. A minute passed, then two, and then three. Finally the priest said something and held out his hand. Gideon leaned over and spat the pebble into the outstretched palm. The priest stared at it for a moment. Then he held it up for the crowd to see: proof that Gideon had indeed kept it in his mouth until it was cool. Meanwhile the chieftain came over and gave an order. The priest pantomimed that Gideon was to open his mouth for inspection.

He complied. The chieftain leaned closer and stared, shoving his fingers into Gideon's mouth, grasping his tongue and moving it roughly from side to side, inspecting it for burns.

The lengthening silence turned into a growing murmur of wonder. There were no scorch marks, no blisters—no signs of burning anywhere on his tongue or in his mouth.

The chief, clearly astonished, spoke loudly to the crowd, eliciting a collective gasp. He stared at Gideon with something close to admiration, then made a brief pronouncement.

The crone said: "The Father decree you telling truth!"

Gideon caught a glimpse of Blackbeard at his chopping block, face dark with discontent.

So glad to disappoint you again, asshole, he thought with satisfaction as he was led back to the cage.

He staggered in and sank down onto the sandy floor of the cell. Garza and Imogen bent over him.

"How in the world did you do it?" Imogen asked.

Gideon lay back, legs stretched out, exhausted and in pain. Both of his fists had been clenched throughout the ordeal, and they remained clenched now. He looked outside the cage for a moment and then, keeping one hand obscured at his side, he slowly opened it. The smell of burnt flesh rose up: and there was a pebble, blackened and bloody, enclosed in the charred palm of his hand. He dropped the pebble, then balled his hand once again into a fist.

"How did—?" Imogen began.

"When I fell to the ground I palmed a fresh pebble from the basket and concealed it between thumb and palm. When they dropped the hot pebble in my hand, I left it there and put the cold one in my mouth instead."

"That must've hurt like hell," Garza said.

"It burned the shit out of my hand, but when I thought of that bastard waiting with his sword . . . well, let's just say it made the pain more bearable."

"Let me see your hand," Imogen said. "I should tend to that burn."

"No," Gideon said, pulling his hand away. "We've got to keep it out of sight. Get rid of that pebble, too."

"How did you pull it off with everyone watching?" Garza asked, tossing the small stone into the darkness.

"A simple combination of legerdemain and misdirection," said Gideon. "As you well know, I used to be a magician."

28

Y<small>ET AGAIN, THEY</small> were roused in what seemed the middle of the night. Yet again, they were led off to begin a long day of forced toil while stars still glittered hard in the sky. As he adjusted the rough garment he'd been given and tried to shake himself awake, Manuel Garza thought back to Gideon's trial by fire. Had that really only been a week ago? It seemed far longer.

Garza wasn't sure if they'd become slaves, or manual laborers, or what, but it was growing all too clear that—whatever their status—the tribe had no intention of allowing them to leave the valley. Things had quickly fallen into a routine: roused before dawn, sent out to dig irrigation ditches, collect bundles of wood, or repair corrals with a chain gang of half a dozen others, led by the hateful Blackbeard. They were given little food and water, and were yelled at or struck with sticks if they slacked off. Imogen's attempts at communication with their fellow workers had met with little enthusiasm: all they'd learned was that the others were all native to the tribe, of the lowest caste in a small but clearly stratified society. Garza hadn't bothered. The only thing that kept him focused was a fixed determination to learn the language, unbeknownst to his captors. Knowledge was power. He listened intently to every order, watched every gesture, and tried to memorize the responses. He had always been good at languages, having been raised in a bilingual family, and he'd already begun to pick up several words and phrases. Imogen, with her previous experience with ancient languages, had a significant head start. Gideon, on the other hand, was either a dunce when it came to learning new languages or else simply couldn't be bothered.

At night, after the brutal days of labor, they talked about plans for escape. The only possible method hadn't changed: steal camels and waterskins and make a break for it. Waterskins were easy to come by—every tent had one hanging next to the front flap. The problem was the camels. Camels were obviously how wealth was measured in this primitive culture, but everyone seemed to know which camels belonged to whom and so there was no theft. As a result they were loosely guarded, and then only at night, apparently due to some beast or beasts feared by all. Garza had overheard his workmates talking about it more than once. From what he could make out, it seemed to be a huge, one-eyed leopard. Apparently, the tribesmen believed it wasn't a mortal animal, but some kind of demon that lived with others of its kind in a labyrinth of canyons beyond the valley. On numerous occasions it had crept into the encampment and dragged off a goat, causing consternation. They said it had taken more than one tribesman, too, and had a taste for human flesh.

These thoughts ran through his head as the work gang proceeded away from the main camp along a narrow mountain trail, with the obligatory escort of guards armed with spears and daggers. Blackbeard brought up the rear, carrying a whip coiled up and tied to his leather belt. The trail branched, and they headed off in a direction they had not gone before. Garza wondered with little interest what new form of arduous work lay in store for them now.

As they left the confines of the broad valley, the guards became watchful, even nervous. They walked for what seemed a long time but could not have been over half an hour. On reaching a high mountain pass, they stopped briefly to rest.

"Take a look down there," said Gideon, coming up to him and speaking in a low voice. The sun was just rising over the rim of mountains, and the landscape below was emerging from the shadows. It was a peculiar-looking valley, narrow and sinuous, with steep cliffs and groves of trees among lush meadows of grass. There were no visible pockets of heavy fog: it seemed that, at least as far as this mountain was concerned, mist oases—an important source of water for the tribe—were confined to the eastern slopes. Here and there on the floor of the valley, curious stone structures about fifteen feet high peeped out of the vegetation. Garza squinted, trying to make them out. Imogen came over, staring as well.

"Pyramids?" said Gideon.

"Looks like it," he said. "Miniature ones."

Blackbeard yelled at them to rise and move on. Garza felt his pulse quicken. *Pyramids*. What else could they be but tombs? He had long harbored a secret hope that the Phaistos location might be the tomb of an ancient king.

As they descended into the valley, they passed the first few structures. These were built from carved sandstone blocks, and each pyramid had an inscription in Egyptian hieroglyphics. He exchanged a significant glance with Gideon. This was more proof, if they needed it, that Imogen was right: this was a pre-Islamic tribe, perhaps dating back as far as the time of the pharaohs.

Around a bend in the trail and past a large, raised stone table of very curious composition, they arrived at a worksite. A pyramid, similar to the others, was under construction. Massive sandstone blocks were laid out in rows at the base of the half-built structure. A long, sloping ramp of dirt led up one side, paved with wooden rollers. As Garza looked over the site, he quickly realized this was a primitive system for moving the massive blocks into position—dragging them up the earthen ramp using ropes and harnesses.

And they, no doubt, were to be the beasts of burden.

Blackbeard shouted and gestured toward the blocks, ropes, and rollers. "Bastard," said Gideon.

Garza followed the others over. They were shouldering harnesses lined with palm fiber pads. Another man adjusted a net of ropes around a block. Garza, Gideon, and Imogen all took up harnesses alongside the others.

With a shout, Blackbeard waved his coiled whip, then gave it a crack. The group strained against their harnesses and the block inched forward. They slacked, then pulled again, then slacked off, in a rhythm punctuated by Blackbeard's periodic cracks of the whip.

After an hour of backbreaking work they had finally inched the block to the top of the ramp and fitted it into place. Blackbeard now roared orders to get started on the next block. Garza's shoulders were already aching from the rough fiber pads.

"Now we *know* we're slaves," Gideon said as they walked back down the ramp. "Do you suppose this is some kind of promotion for good behavior? I preferred digging ditches."

"This is how the great pyramids were built," said Imogen, slipping into a harness. "Hasn't changed in three thousand years."

"Who do you think it's for?" Garza asked, gesturing at the half-finished structure.

"Who else but the chief?" said Gideon. "He's not exactly a spring chicken."

Blackbeard roared at them, swinging his whip for silence.

"This is getting old really fast," murmured Gideon as he adjusted his harness.

The whip cracked and they began pulling up another block.

They spent the morning inching blocks up the hill. Finally, with the sun almost at the meridian, Blackbeard called for a rest. A lunch of chickpeas with boiled goat meat was served: far better than their usual fare. Blackbeard retired to a rectangle of shade under a hanging rock and sat down, playing idly with his bracelet of human teeth, which he seemed inordinately fond of. Maybe, Garza speculated idly, it was some symbol of status in the tribe. It wasn't long before the man went to sleep, snoring loudly. The other guards settled down, resting and watching over their charges.

Garza ate lunch with Gideon and Imogen. They were so tired they hardly spoke. After lunch, Gideon and Imogen dozed under an overhang. Garza, meanwhile, retired to a shady spot with a stray piece of rope and some sticks he'd collected from a pile of discarded rollers. He looked around the flinty ground, found a sharp rock, struck it hard along the edge with another stone, and knapped it to a sharp blade. He unraveled the discarded piece of rope into its individual strands and used them to lash the twigs together, creating a scaffolding. Using the sharp stone, he then carved a crude pulley wheel from rounds cut out of a broken pole lying in the nearby dust, cored it, slid it onto the twigs, and then lashed it to the scaffolding.

"What are you doing?" came a feminine voice. Imogen and

Gideon had wandered over and were watching him work. "Haven't you already slaved enough in the Home of the Dead?"

"The what?"

"The Home of the Dead. That's what the other coolies call this place."

"Yeah? Well, I don't know about the rest of you Israelites, but I'm tired of dragging those fucking blocks up a ramp."

"So what's this?"

"A demonstration model."

"Of what?"

"Of how to do it better. I've been thinking about it all morning."

Gideon shook his head. "Once an engineer, always an engineer."

"Instead of the smart comments, how about some help?"

Garza set them both to work carving more pulley wheels with sharp flakes he knapped out from the flint, which he in turn mounted in series on the scaffolding. He fashioned a crude crane out of sticks that could rotate using two strands of rope. Finally, he passed another strand of rope through the crane and tied it to a sling, threaded it through the pulleys, and attached it to a swatch of headcloth. Into that he put a rock.

"Now pull the string," Garza said to Gideon. "Carefully."

Gideon pulled the strand and the pulley apparatus lifted the rock, held in place by the scaffolding and crane.

"Now watch." Garza maneuvered the crane and it swiveled on its fixed base, carrying the rock.

"Now ease the string down."

Gideon let the thread slide through his fingers, lowering the rock into a new spot, atop a small mound of sand Garza scraped up.

"You get it?" Garza asked. "Each pulley wheel provides a mechanical advantage. Four wheels reduce the force required to lift something to one-quarter."

"Physics?" Imogen asked.

"Physics. With a four-wheel pulley system, a thousand-pound block of stone can be lifted with only two hundred fifty pounds of force. No more damn dragging."

"Yeah, but can we get them to try it?" Gideon asked dubiously.

"Hence the demonstration model."

From their resting places, the guards had idly watched Garza build the model. There had been no comprehension in their eyes, but it was obvious they were curious.

Now Garza motioned to them to come over. With gestures and broken phrases, he demonstrated the model by lifting and moving the rock several times. Now some of the other workers came over, gaping.

Garza gestured at one of the more alert-looking workers. "You try it. Try it."

The worker stepped forward and knelt, taking the strand of rope in his hand. He pulled it gingerly, lifting the stone, pushed the swiveling scaffold, and placed it on the small hill of sand. A smile appeared on his face and he nodded, realizing that the stone did indeed move more easily.

Garza gestured at a guard. "You. Try."

The guard came forward and, looking nervously around, tried it—again with an expression of amazement at this seemingly magical contrivance.

Garza launched into a broken exhortation of words and gestures, explaining that they should built a larger version of the apparatus over the pyramid using the poles and rope lying around to construct the scaffolding, pulleys, and wheels.

Suddenly a roar came from the worksite and the guards

jumped as if struck. Blackbeard came swaggering down, his whip out. With a curse he lashed Garza across the shoulder so violently that it knocked him to his knees. Blackbeard brought his massive foot down on the model, stomping and grinding it into the sand and reducing it to a mass of broken sticks.

Garza, seeing his model destroyed, blood streaming from the lash on his shoulder, rose with a furious cry and ran at Blackbeard, who was still occupied in destroying the model. He took a swing and caught the overseer by surprise with a blow to the head; the man went down but quickly surged up in a fury, drawing his dagger and slashing at Garza.

Jumping back, Garza just missed being cut. Blackbeard rushed him, stabbing and slicing while Garza stumbled back, trying to keep out of the way of the blade. Gideon and Imogen immediately tried to come to his aide but the guards turned on them, knocking Gideon down and pinning Imogen, holding them at spearpoint.

Blackbeard drove Garza up against the cliff wall, blocking further retreat. Seeing that his quarry was trapped, a cruel smile broke over his face. He stepped forward and placed the dagger on Garza's throat, still scabbed from the previous cut. He pressed the point slowly in, and Garza could once again feel the blade bite into his skin. Blackbeard's breath, reeking of mutton, washed over his face.

"*Aghat mu!*" the man yelled, pushing the point deeper into Garza's throat—when a voice rang out.

Blackbeard ignored it. The blood was running more freely now and Garza could feel the blade digging toward his windpipe. The sadist was going to make it slow.

The voice rang out again, much sharper. It was the chief, being carried down the trail in a litter. The bearers stopped at the worksite and the chief stepped out, swept his robes around his shoulder, and spoke angrily a third time to Blackbeard. This time the man hesitated, and then Garza felt the pressure on the knife lessening. Finally, it ceased altogether.

Breathing hard, his face creased with wrath, Blackbeard stepped back. The guards released Gideon and Imogen. With obvious effort, the chieftain came over and, ignoring Blackbeard's scowling face, spoke to Garza, gesturing with his staff at the ruined pile of sticks. It became evident that the chief had been watching the entire scene play out from the trail overhead. He'd seen the model from a distance, but had no idea why it had generated so much excitement. Now, it seemed, he wanted Garza to rebuild it. The chief pantomimed his way through a long explanation that Garza did not understand, but assumed it meant that he was very old and wanted his tomb completed in a hurry—and judging by the man's wan and sallow appearance, Garza wasn't surprised.

Sweating and inwardly cursing his own temper, Garza wiped away the blood from the wound in his neck. He nodded in agreement and went to work building another model as quickly as he could. When Gideon and Imogen went to help the chief waved them off, the gold watch glittering on his bony wrist, leaving Garza to construct it alone.

In forty minutes it was done. Garza demonstrated with the small rock, and then the chief knelt and tried the apparatus himself, raising and lowering the rock by the thread. The delight and amazement on his face were evident. He stood and, with a loud voice, ordered the workers and guards to construct a working version of the pulley. To Garza's surprise, the chief put him in charge of the detail.

With the slaves all working together, and the sharp bronze daggers of the guards to carve pulley wheels, and the fashioning of bronze pins to act as pulley axles, the work proceeded quickly. As they erected the scaffolding over the half-built pyra-mid and its adjacent pile of cut blocks, Garza could see Black-beard standing off to one side, motionless, hand on his dagger, staring at him with an expression of pure hatred on his face.

"You better watch out for that one," Gideon said quietly.

"You're not kidding. The bastard's tried to cut my throat three times now."

By late afternoon, as the alpenglow painted the surrounding peaks, the contraption was finished and ready to be tested. Garza realized he was nervous. Normally, as with any engineer-ing project, he would have done the math, run the bearing loads and structural members through computer programs to make sure everything would hold. In this case he'd been forced to make do with estimates. The most critical component, he knew, was the weight of the blocks. He'd measured them at roughly two feet by two by six, making twenty-four cubic feet of sand-stone. Stone, as any building engineer knew, weighed about a hundred fifty pounds per square foot, which gave each block a mass of thirty-six hundred pounds. His six-pulley, three-rope block-and-tackle system meant that two hundred pounds of lift would need to be applied on a rope manned by two workers. With this design, it would only take six men to raise a thirty-six-hundred-pound block of stone. Or so he calculated. Because of poor tolerances and lousy building materials, friction would add a few hundred more pounds, for a total load of two tons. He was pretty sure of the ropes—they were well made and strong. The big question was whether the jerry-rigged scaffolding and crane would hold up.

But the moment of truth had come. The chief, standing nearby, was leaning on his staff and waiting with an eager ex-pression. Garza now directed the workers to fix a net of ropes around a block, preparing to lift it. Additional ropes were threaded through the pulley apparatus, and still more were attached to a lever arm built to swing the dangling block into position over the pyramid.

Gideon stood next to him. "You sure this is going to work?"

"No."

"They'll probably cut off our heads if it doesn't," said Imogen.

"Anything's better than dragging those stones the rest of our lives," Garza said.

He took a deep breath and gestured for the six workers to pull. They had practiced with the rebuilt model and knew what to do. With a creaking sound and a flexing of the scaffolding, the stone block rose into the air. The chief watched intently.

When the block was at the right height, dangling free, Garza waved his arm and the workers controlling the crane swiveled it above the pyramid. With another order, Garza called for the workers to let it down carefully, watching as it was slowly adjusted into place.

It worked perfectly.

"*Khehat! Khehat!*" The chief came over excitedly and grasped Garza's shoulders, enveloping him in a bear hug. "*Khehat!*"

When he was finally released, Garza leaned over to Imogen and murmured: "What does *khehat* mean? Builder? Friend? Man of genius?"

"I think it means 'undertaker.'"

29

Gɪᴅᴇᴏɴ sᴛᴇᴘᴘᴇᴅ ɪɴᴛᴏ the tent, walked over to the ragged bundle of skins that served as his bed, and collapsed on it with a sigh. His fingernails were encrusted with mud, and his fingertips were greasy from handling goat meat—his hosts had not yet discovered such amenities as knives and forks—but he was too tired to care. He'd do his ablutions after he'd rested.

The past several days had passed in a blur—a backbreaking blur. After Garza's success with his pulley apparatus, the chieftain had elevated him to what was essentially foreman of the job, a development that had annoyed Blackbeard no end. As a further reward, the three had been moved from their cage to this roomier and far more pleasant tent. Their security had also been relaxed, although Gideon noticed their tent was situated on the far side of the settlement, away from the ravine that alone led out to freedom. They had been given free movement, with two warnings: They were not to go back to the mist oasis on the eastern side of the mountain, and they were warned away from a valley some miles to the west, which seemed to be a "place of demons" or some claptrap along those lines.

He sat up now and began rubbing his back. While the tribe was apparently an autocracy—the chieftain ruled with an iron fist; the crone was his Rasputin; and the young woman, perhaps the chief's wife, was a very powerful and respected adviser in her own right—there was a complex system of merit- and seniority-based layers to it that he was still figuring out. Age was held in great reverence, and everyone moved aside when an older person came down a trail. This was especially true of the crone and the four old priests in white or saffron robes that she commanded. Men and women were treated equally, it seemed: the best hunters went out daily with spears to hunt game, regardless of gender. Everyone worked at something, and there was obviously an attempt to assign members of the tribe duties to which they were best suited. Imogen, for example—after offering some suggestions on how soil cultivation could be improved—had now been assigned gardening duties. But she also spent a fair amount of time with the crone. Imogen was a quick study when it came to language, and the old woman peppered her with questions about the outside world and the almost mythical "English" she was apparently enamored of. These last few days, Imogen could often be seen sitting by the old woman's side, on the chief's ledge overlooking the settlement, conversing in a halted fashion. This had helped the three of them learn a little more about how the tribe functioned and what rules it lived by. It had also ultimately explained the mystery of how the crone—who, Imogen had told them, was named Lillaya—learned her fragments of English. As a child, she had wandered away from a scouting party, gotten lost in the desert, and was ultimately picked up by nomadic Arab bandits. For several months she had traveled with them as a slave, until a young English adventurer—or so Imogen understood—who'd been accompanying the band took pity on her. He'd speak to her in the evenings and try to communicate. One night, when their travels had taken them near the mountains, he pretended to have an epileptic fit, creating a diversionary uproar and allowing her to escape and find her way home. Hence her fragments of English; hence her fascination with the world beyond the canyon—and hence Garza's magical Rolex, which the chieftain always wore proudly. The Englishman had owned an identical watch. This unlikely combination was apparently what had saved them from the pit.

Now Gideon moved over to an earthen pot half filled with water and began washing his hands. And himself? He was no engineer like Garza. He didn't have a green thumb. He was a decent shot with the tribe's rudimentary bows, but it seemed there were no openings among the hunting packs—or maybe they simply didn't trust him enough. And he lagged behind in learning the language. So he'd been put back to work at the job he seemed best suited for and which required few linguistic skills: digging latrines.

The flap of the tent shifted and Garza stepped in. While they all ate communally, the lower-ranked members were served first and expected to leave the area of the central plaza before their betters settled in for a meal. Garza, now higher in social status than Gideon, was served later, and Imogen later still.

Garza walked over to his area of the tent and began shrugging off his outerwear, covered in sand and dust from the quarry. "Have a nice day?" he asked.

"Oh, great. Digging ditches is loads of fun."

"Nice to see you've found your niche at last." Garza sank heavily onto his own bundle of skins.

For a moment, neither spoke. Gideon dried his hands and stepped away from the bowl.

"You know, I've been thinking," he said.

"Not again."

"It's high time we began planning our escape."

Garza rolled his eyes. "We've talked about this already. We need to lie low until the tribe accepts us. Lets down their guard a little more. I mean, we just got an upgrade: from cage one point oh to tent one point one."

"It's been ten days. Just how much more do you think they're going to accept us than they already have? That big lummox Mugdol is never going to cozy up to you." Mugdol, they had learned, was Blackbeard's name—or as close as they could come to its pronunciation.

"Look. If we escape and get captured again, there won't be a reprieve—it'll be the pit. Best thing is to keep a low profile—do nothing. Be cool. Build up more trust."

A twinge shot through Gideon's aching back. Garza had always been the one eager to press on, and he was a little surprised by this hesitation. "What's wrong?" he asked. "Starting to enjoy your position in senior management?"

An angry look crossed Garza's face and Gideon realized that hadn't been fair. "Sorry," he said. "It's just that...well, unlike you, I'm on a clock."

The look on Garza's face softened a little. "I know."

"I'm not saying that we need to break out of here tonight. But we should be looking for opportunities to secretly scout out the Phaistos location. We need to at least see what's there. Then we can make a break."

"We'll only get one shot at escape."

Gideon nodded. "Yes. And to that end, we'll need weapons. Better weapons than what they have."

Garza looked skeptical. "Like what?"

"Don't forget, I *was* a weapons designer."

"Right. So what do you plan to do—build us a nuke?"

"In a manner of speaking. We need something that trumps their daggers and spears."

"Such as?"

Gideon summoned to mind the inventory of ancient weapons he'd been mulling over while digging ditches. "Atlatl?"

"Too unwieldy. And too difficult to learn how to throw."

"Rungu?"

"Hmm. Not exactly better than a spear."

"Meteor hammer?"

"A what?"

"It's like a flail with a round head. Very fast. You whip it around your head until you build up velocity, and then launch it at your opponent."

"Sounds good against one enemy. What about the other five who are aiming their spears at you?"

They fell into silence, each looking down at his hands.

"Bow and arrow?" Garza ventured. "It's amazing they don't seem to have that."

"No," Gideon said suddenly. "*Crossbow.*"

Garza looked up at him.

"A crossbow's got velocity and power. It doesn't require the skill of a regular bow. It reloads fast. Sights and fires its arrows like a gun. It would have shock value, too—none of these people have seen anything like it."

"A crossbow," Garza repeated. "That might work. All the necessary materials are lying around this camp. I could pocket the bronze we'll need for the bolt heads from the rock quarry tomorrow. And we can use a twisted rawhide strip from one of these pelts for the string." Then he paused. "But we need a way to generate the necessary force. You know, to pull the bowstring back and cock the device."

"The crossbows I've seen use some kind of winch or crank."

"Too difficult to make." After a moment, Garza snapped his fingers. "We could rig up a kind of lever system. With a hinge to increase pressure on the bowstring. If I can figure out the right measurements, the lever could also act as a trigger." He stood up and made for the tent flap.

"Where are you going?"

"Where do you think? We'll need a solid piece of wood for the stock, and some kind of flexible sapling for the bow. I can't very well do my shopping in daylight, can I? Meanwhile—" he gestured toward a bundle of sticks in a far corner—"pick out half a dozen of the straightest pieces you can find and get to work fashioning the arrows—which, by the way, are called bolts. If we can get one of these to work, and figure out where to hide it, maybe I'll consider making two more for you and Imogen." And with that he disappeared into the darkness.

Gideon sat for a moment, still rubbing his back. He was just about to reach for the pile of sticks when the tent flap stirred again and Imogen entered.

"Hi," she said, crossing over to her area of the tent. They had divided their living space into four quarters: three sleeping nooks and a common area.

"What kept you?" Gideon asked mischievously. "Dining on petits fours and caviar again with Her Majesty?"

"Very funny. I've been learning more of their language. Now I'm sure it's some kind of Coptic. Think about it: these people have led almost totally insular lives, cut off from civilization, for maybe thousands of years. Who knows what kind of tribal memories they might retain? From what I've gathered about their myths and rituals, their beliefs might very well date back to the time of the Egyptians. They seem to worship some sort of embodiment of the sun."

"Have those tribal memories given you any idea as to where your gold mines of the Middle Kingdom might be?"

"Gideon, you're treating this like a joke. It's the learning experience of a lifetime."

"Easy for you to say when you're not digging ditches from dawn until dusk."

"Maybe I can put in a word for you."

"You mean, get me a transfer? I'd appreciate it." He lay back on his goatskins. "Don't get me wrong. I can see how all this might interest you. But it's not exactly in my line. Geoarchaeologist." He chuckled. "Sorry, but it sounds like a mixture of the two most boring subjects imaginable."

"That's where you and everybody else are wrong. It's *fascinating*. The past is the greatest mystery we'll ever know. And it's the key to understanding ourselves—who we've become, where we've gotten to today. For example, when people think of ancient Egypt, all they think about is mummies and horror movies. And that's a shame. Because the Egyptian culture was incredibly rich—*and* advanced. Did you know their kingdom once covered an area stretching from Sudan to the Mediterranean? Or that their religion was as complex and multifaceted as any practiced today? The ancient Egyptians were obsessed with death. Outwitting death, overcoming the unknown, lay behind the mummies and the pyramids and the iconography and the Book of the Dead, the treasures left in the tombs, and everything else. Were you aware that the original idea of monotheism—a single god—was born in ancient Egypt?"

As she had spoken, her eyes began to glitter and her face flushed slightly in the reflected firelight. There was no doubt, Gideon thought, that this was in fact her real love. "I had no idea," he said honestly.

"It's true. Monotheism grew out of Egyptian religion, specifically through the Pharaoh Akhenaten, also known as Amenhotep the Fourth. He decreed the elimination of the many gods and declared that henceforth Egyptians would worship one god only, Aten."

"Who was Aten?"

"Nobody is sure, but he seems to be some aspect of the sun. But the effort failed, and after Akhenaten died the Egyptians went back to worshipping their many gods. But he was the first to introduce that revolutionary idea—which would lead to Judaism and Christianity. The idea that there was only one god—which seems so normal to us now—was incredibly radical back then. There are even scholars who claim that the Old Testament God of Judaism had His origin during the captivity in Egypt. Aten in fact may have been the basis of the Hebrew word *ha'Adon*, or *Adonai*, meaning 'the Lord'—"

At this point the tent flap rustled again. Imogen stopped in mid-sentence as Garza slipped in. He glanced back out through an opening in the flap, then pulled from beneath his garments a solid chunk of wood, a few sturdy saplings, some rawhide leather string, and a few bits of bronze, lining everything up on the dirt floor.

"What's all that?" Imogen asked.

Garza looked from Imogen to Gideon and back again. "Ask Gideon. It was his idea." Then he turned back to Gideon. "Haven't you gotten started on making those bolts yet?"

"Sorry." Gideon motioned to Imogen. "Come on. I'll explain as we go."

30

Garza jerked awake in a cold sweat, the night split by screams. He blinked the sleep out of his eyes. Surely it hadn't been more than five minutes since he'd dozed off? But suddenly it seemed as if the entire encampment had exploded into hysteria.

"What the hell—?" Gideon and Imogen came out of their sleeping corners, while Garza rose, threw on his robe, and lifted the flap of the tent to see what was happening. Burning firebrands were being lit, casting a lurid glow over the scene. A tent next to the chief's had been partially torn open. People in hysterics were running about carrying brands, collecting spears, and shouting. Amid the hubbub he could hear a woman's terrified screams again, off in the darkness.

Gideon and Imogen joined him in peering out.

"That tent up there has been slashed open by some animal," said Imogen.

The chief had now appeared in the midst of the crowd. He was panic-stricken as well, waving his arms and crying out, gesturing with his staff toward a ravine above the rear of the encampment, from which the woman's screams seemed to be coming.

Imogen listened intently to the babble. "It sounds like someone was dragged off by that one-eyed demon leopard they keep talking about."

Garza stared at the scene. "Why the hell aren't they pursuing it? Christ, if they don't get to her right away, she's dead."

"They're terrified of it," said Imogen. "They won't follow."

And Garza could see it was true. The men were making a terrific racket, arming themselves and lighting torches, and the chief was hollering and gesturing at them—but nobody, not even Blackbeard, was actually running toward the ravine.

"Screw this." Garza threw back the goatskin and grabbed the crossbow and the small bundle of handmade bolts.

"You just made that tonight!" Imogen protested. "You haven't even tested it yet!"

Ignoring her, Garza sprinted from the tent and headed toward the mouth of the ravine. Along the way he yanked a planted torch from the ground to light his way and, he hoped, drive off the beast. He could hear a lot of unintelligible shouting behind him, but no one followed.

The mouth of the ravine was not far, just a few hundred yards. On the sandy floor of the wash he could see drag marks and blood. The marks were easy to follow, and they led to a big pile of broken boulders a hundred feet inside the ravine. The screaming had ceased and Garza realized the cat, or whatever it was, must have dragged the woman up into the rocks.

"*Hah!*" he screamed and picked up a rock, flinging it toward the pile. "Come out of there, you bastard!"

He heard an answering growl. Then an immense leopard appeared on the topmost rock, staring down at him with one luminous eye. In place of the other eye was an ugly, puckered scar that ran from ear to snout. It crouched, still growling.

Garza waved the torch. This was the demon cat the whole tribe was scared of. And he'd decided to run after it. *Nice one, Manuel.*

There were only two choices: either drive it off or get close enough to shoot it with the crossbow. And the cat didn't seem to be going anywhere. That meant ascending the rock pile, with the beast crouched above. As he circled, trying to find a defensible route up, the leopard made deep coughing sounds, moving to keep Garza in view, tensing its muscles.

Using the crude lever, Garza cocked the crossbow, set a bolt into the groove, and aimed it—but the only exposed target was the animal's head, and it was too far away to be penetrated by a bolt unless he scored a hit on the eye, which was highly improbable. He'd grabbed for the crossbow instinctually as he ran from the tent, and now he recalled Imogen's warning: they hadn't even tested the thing yet. Its aim might be out of whack…or it might not work at all.

He yelled at the creature and waved the torch again, trying to drive it off. It snarled again, baring its teeth.

"Hyah!" He threw another rock, which missed.

The leopard gave an answering roar, shaking its head at him. The sound echoed mightily off the canyon walls before dying away.

At least it's distracted from eating, Garza thought.

Garza hoisted himself up one boulder. The leopard slid back a bit and growled again. He scrambled up another boulder, waving the torch ahead of him, hoping that fear of fire would drive it off. But the creature stood its ground, growling fiercely.

"Get away, you son of a bitch!" He hoisted himself up onto the next boulder. Now the leopard was less than twenty feet above him: not a good thing. At least it wouldn't leap on him as long as he held the burning torch—or would it?

From this vantage point he could see, just behind the animal, the tuft of a robe: a girl. The leopard was evidently standing guard over its victim. She was probably already dead, but there was a chance she might still be alive. After all, he hadn't given the beast much time to begin its meal.

Garza yelled again and waved the torch. The leopard rose up slightly, its one good eye reflecting the flickering orange torchlight, its glossy fur rippling with musculature. Garza took aim, but all he could see was the animal's head and neck. What he needed was the chest. Why had he brought along an untested weapon, anyway?

He rose further and jabbed the torch at the snarling animal, shouting at the top of his lungs: "Go away! Get lost!"

The animal backed up and Garza had the sudden hope it would turn and flee. He yelled, jabbed again—and then the leopard leapt at him from above, descending with its great claws unsheathed. Garza managed to fire the crossbow just as the animal fell on him.

It was like being hit by a car. He was thrown backward from the boulder, the leopard tumbling with him, issuing a terrifying screech as the two landed on the sand, swiping at him with a massive paw, catching the side of his face and raking the flesh. Blood was suddenly everywhere, a fountain of it, as the animal—now on its back—thrashed and bit at the bolt buried in its chest. Garza tried to scramble backward, but the animal pinned his leg even as it clawed at itself. And then, with one convulsive growl, it shuddered and ceased moving.

Blood pouring down his face, Garza managed to pull his leg from under the dead animal. Abandoning the torch and crossbow, he struggled up the heap of rocks to the top.

In the faint starlight, he could see the young woman was lying on her back. He recognized her immediately as the chief's young wife. Her shoulder was bloody and marked with punctures—evidently from being dragged. But otherwise she appeared untouched. He scooped her up and carefully picked his way down the rock pile to the sandy wash. Reaching it, he staggered slowly toward the mouth of the ravine, shaking his head to clear the blood from his eyes. His face was on fire and he felt his legs grow weaker by the second. Finally, at the mouth of the canyon, he sank to his knees, unable to carry his burden any farther.

Still on his knees, he was surrounded by a shouting frenzy of people. Someone—Gideon—picked up the girl and she instantly vanished. Garza felt dizzy, unable to maintain his focus. He was being congratulated, it seemed; hands were touching him, grasping him. And there was Imogen, forcing her way to the front, coming to his aid, trying to help him rise, but then the world folded in on itself and he collapsed.

31

GARZA FELT COOL water on his face and slowly opened his eyes. A boy was carefully dabbing at his cheek with a damp cloth. Gideon and Imogen were hovering nearby, staring down at him with concern. He was in a small, elegant tent. Some kind of hubbub was taking place outside.

"We told them you needed rest and quiet," Gideon said.

"The chief's wife?" Garza asked, raising his head to speak.

"Alive. Her shoulder's a bit chewed up, apparently, but the rest of her is fine."

Garza lowered his throbbing head. "And my face?"

A silence. "The cuts are superficial," Gideon said. "You're damn lucky it missed your auricular artery."

Imogen leaned toward him. "I think you're the bravest man I've ever met. Even if you are a nob some of the time."

"Nobody was doing anything. I couldn't let her just be eaten."

"The reason they weren't doing anything," she said, "is because they thought that leopard was an invincible demon. It's been killing them for years."

"I just got lucky with my shot." A thought struck him. "What did they do when they saw the crossbow?"

"We had some fancy explaining to do," Gideon said. "We told the chief we were making it for him as a surprise. I'm not sure he believed it, but he kept the crossbow for himself. And decreed that no others should be made, on pain of death."

Garza shook his head.

At that moment they heard a fresh commotion outside and the tent flap was thrust aside. The chief himself stepped in and spread his arms. He started speaking effusively and came over, embracing Garza once again.

"I think," said Imogen, "he's thanking you."

"I figured that much out."

More embraces. Garza saw that the old man's eyes were full of tears. Then the chief rose and spoke.

"What's he saying now?"

Imogen leaned forward. The chief slowed down, and she nodded. Her eyes went wide. She nodded again.

"He wants to know if you are well enough to walk."

"Why?"

"It seems he wants to make some kind of announcement."

Garza raised his head again. The world spun around him. "Christ. Do I have to?"

"If you can. Whatever it is, it seems pretty important."

Helped by Gideon and Imogen, Garza managed to get to his feet. He put one arm over each of their shoulders, and the three of them ducked out of the tent and into the early-morning sunlight. The tent was in the high-rent district, only a few steps behind the chief's own dwelling. And the chief was now standing on the little promontory of rock he used for important speeches, staff in hand, looking at Garza and smiling. The crone stood a few paces behind him. A crowd was gathering below—

the entire tribe, from what Garza could make out—and there were smiles and approving nods all around. Then the world spun again and he paused to clear his head.

More slowly now, they approached the chief. The old man bowed. As Gideon and Imogen released their holds, Garza managed to return the gesture without collapsing to the ground.

The chief began speaking in a stentorian voice, now facing the crowd below, now turning to face Garza. He gestured several times. There were gasps from the assembled throng. The chief continued speaking, his frail body animated, his movements full of passion. Then he turned toward Garza expectantly.

Garza, who had understood little of what had just transpired, glanced questioningly at Imogen. The look on her face startled him.

"Um," she began, "I don't know quite how to tell you this."

"Spit it out. How bad can it be?"

The chief looked from one to the other, waiting.

"It's not bad, exactly. It's . . ." She paused again.

"What?"

She took a deep breath. "It turns out the young woman you rescued isn't the chief's wife, after all."

"No? She wields an awful lot of influence for a concubine."

"She's not a concubine. She's his *daughter*. Her name is Jelena. And . . ." Her face reddened. "In return for saving her life, he will permit you to marry her."

"Oh for God's sake . . ."

"Manuel?" said Gideon quickly.

"What? This is absurd—"

"Stop for just a moment and try to look honored. You'll offend the chief."

And as Garza glanced back at the chief, he in fact saw a growing expression of displeasure. Lillaya, the crone, was beginning to frown as well. He did his best to put on a big smile, then said sotto voce to Imogen: "Can you tell him thank you, but I've got a girlfriend, or that I'm cherishing the memory of my dead wife, or some damn thing along those lines?"

Once again it was Gideon who replied. "We need to proceed very carefully here. He has no male heir, and he seems to consider you worthy of being his son-in-law. This is obviously a tremendous honor. If you refuse it...I think the offense might be great."

"You can't expect me to marry her!"

"We've come a long way, thanks to you," said Imogen. "Gideon's right. This is as much a danger as an opportunity."

Before Garza could protest, the chief launched into another long speech, which Imogen listened to, her brow furrowed with concentration.

"What now?" asked Garza.

"He pronounced that the wedding will take place in a week's time. I think he's already assumed you'll accept."

"A *week*?" Garza sat up. "Wait a minute, I'm not doing this."

"Keep smiling," said Gideon. "Just keep smiling while we talk."

"Hard pass." Garza grinned broadly over clenched teeth. "No fucking way. Not gonna do it."

Gideon leaned in. "Why not? This will get us in good with the tribe, solidify our position here. Make it easier to continue our search. And who knows? It might be fun."

"*Fun?* What a pig."

"When in Rome, and all that."

"My God." Garza turned to Imogen. "This is not right, on so many levels."

Imogen leaned toward him. "Manuel? I don't think you understand. *This isn't the kind of invitation you can refuse.*"

She turned to the chief and, haltingly, fumbled out a couple of sentences. The chief beamed with pleasure, and once more came over and embraced Garza. "*Samu! Samu!*"

When the chief had stepped back, Garza looked at Imogen. "What's *samu?*"

"It means 'son.'"

"You told him I *accepted?*"

"Of course. Would you rather I told him you refused—and get our heads impaled on those stakes for sure?"

Garza hesitated. "I guess not."

"Then just remember it's for a good cause—our survival. Now keep smiling!"

Then, just as the chief seemed about to launch into another speech, there was a hubbub in the gathering below. Garza, his vision still a little blurry, blinked downward. He could just make out Mugdol—Blackbeard—pushing his way through the crowd until he was standing alone before them. An incensed look on his face, he made a fist; pounded it twice against his chest; and then—with a few angry words—pointed it at Garza. There was another gasp from the crowd.

As with one voice, the chief and Lillaya spoke to Blackbeard. There was a brief, heated exchange. Then, almost reluctantly, the old man nodded. He turned to Garza, spread his hands, and spoke several sentences. Garza gestured to show that he did not understand. Then Lillaya came forward and conferred at some length with Imogen.

"Well?" Garza asked as she turned toward him. The crowd, too, was still looking up, great anticipation on their faces.

"There's, um, there's a problem." A grave look was on her face.

"I won't marry her. Then there's no problem."

She waved this away. "Because you saved his daughter's life, you deserve to have her hand in marriage. But our friend down there—" she gestured toward Mugdol, who was now standing, arms folded, legs apart, glaring up at them—"protests that, as the lead warrior of the tribe, she is already promised to him."

"Fine. Let *them* get married."

"It's not that simple. The chief has already given his consent to your marriage. And according to custom, there is only one way to settle this."

Garza's headache suddenly grew worse. "I don't think I want to know what it is."

Imogen paused a moment before continuing. "You've been challenged to a fight—a fight to the death."

Garza simply groaned.

Several of the tribal elders came forward, and now there was a brief conclave between them and the chief. At length, the chief spoke to the crone, who in turn spoke to the three.

"It seems there's no way out," Imogen said. "You can't refuse the chief's invitation, and you can't refuse the fight. The chief has allowed you two days to recover. Whoever survives the combat will marry his daughter in one week—just as he already decreed."

"Great." Garza grasped hold of Gideon as dizziness returned. "If this is what the engagement is like, I can't wait for the honeymoon."

32

For Gideon, the next two days and nights passed in a kind of nightmarish blur. He saw little of Garza, who spent most of his time in their tent, resting and—Gideon assumed—mentally preparing himself for the ordeal to come. He was clearly not in the mood for conversation and had barely said a word to either Gideon or Imogen.

Gideon felt an odd, desperate hopelessness. The way the villagers and even the chief acted—going about their business as usual, treating the three newcomers as if nothing had changed, as if his friend wasn't about to live or die in combat—was unnerving. He'd racked his brain for a way out but had come up with nothing: they had yet to put together a detailed plan of escape, and he could not challenge the chief's edict without all three of them putting their lives at risk. At his urging, Imogen had approached the crone, asking as diplomatically as she could if there wasn't some other way this could be resolved, but the answer was ironclad: it was ritual, it was custom. Nothing could be done.

And so it was early on the morning of the third day that

Gideon, along with Imogen and the silent Garza, stepped out of their tent to find the four white-bearded priests standing there, waiting for them. Behind the priests stood several guards. The priests began leading the way toward the far end of the valley, and the three followed. The guards swung into place behind and, over his shoulder, Gideon could see the rest of the tribe following. The guards were all armed with spears, their faces expressionless. The culture shock was almost beyond Gideon's ability to parse: despite all they'd accomplished—in particular, despite Garza's improving work efficiency dramatically and saving the chief's daughter—it almost felt like the very first day again, when they'd been led to the pit of headless bodies. Ironically, this time around nobody except Blackbeard and a few of his henchmen bore them any ill will: Garza's fate was simply out of their hands and into those of the gods.

The priests led the long procession along a winding path, through the Home of the Dead, and then in a direction Gideon had not gone before. After marching perhaps another quarter mile, they made their way through a slot canyon into a bowl-like depression, surrounded on all sides by rock. Gideon looked around. The spot looked more like a small gladiatorial arena than anything else. The stony floor was littered with animal corpses in various stages of decay. There were human remains, as well, lying scattered here and there among the litter of boulders and sharp stones. Gideon didn't need a translation to understand the nature of this place—he could guess for himself. It was a place of combat; a place for the settling of differences—and, perhaps, for savage amusements as well.

The tribespeople fanned out around the circular edge of the bowl, their faces shining with anticipation. Gideon and Imogen were led to a rickety canopy, built of poles topped with sticks that were in turn overlain with palm leaves. It was apparently a place of honor, next to the chief, his daughter Jelena, the crone, and the four priests. The men with spears now took up positions on both sides of the structure, like an honor guard. The rest of the onlookers stood in the bright morning sun.

Garza and Mugdol were escorted to the center of the arena by two warriors. The crone Lillaya stepped forward and began another wailing chant, which echoed off the surrounding peaks. After several minutes, the chanting stopped and the chief himself stepped forward. Speaking in a raspy voice, he went on for what seemed to Gideon like ages, gesturing at both Garza and Mugdol in turn. At last, clearly exhausted by his speech, the chief returned to the makeshift canopy. Blackbeard removed his robe, exposing a bronzed physique. The crowd cheered as he strode around, flexing his muscles, primarily it seemed for Jelena's benefit. The two warriors gestured at Garza and he reluctantly removed his own robes, exposing a pale torso. Gideon's heart sank. Garza was pretty damn fit, well muscled and tough, but next to Blackbeard—a six-foot-six ripped monster at least a dozen years younger—the contrast was still extreme.

The combatants removed their headcloths and they were placed to one side, along with their robes. A silence fell and the audience parted as four more warriors came through, carrying a pallet on which were laid out an array of weapons. Gideon squinted. He could see variously shaped spears, bronze daggers, and even a few stone blades and hatchets, along with an open wooden box holding the giant, technologically advanced steel blade Mugdol had wielded earlier. Clearly the tribe had not fashioned it, Gideon reflected; it must have been taken off the dead body of some luckless trespasser. Blackbeard immediately seized the sword, eliciting a roar from the crowd as he again paraded around, swishing the sword through the air in various fancy moves.

Garza stared at the rather pathetic arrangement of remaining weapons. He scowled.

"This is unfair," he said loudly. "None of these weapons are equal to that sword!"

Lillaya the crone acted again as translator. "The Father say you must choose one."

"I'll choose that crossbow we made for him, thank you."

More translation and discussion. "The Father say crossbow not traditional." The old woman gestured. "You take one."

"That's unfair. I refuse."

When this was translated it caused an ugly stir in the crowd. To Gideon it seemed sentiment was already swinging against Garza.

"The Father say fight. Or die."

Garza stared at her in disbelief. Instinctively, Gideon stepped forward to intervene, but Imogen restrained him. "Don't," she murmured. "Or you'll be the next one in that ring."

"But he's going to get killed!"

"You know these people. There's nothing we can do about it."

"Christ, that's cold. After he saved the chief's daughter?"

"We have no choice but to let it play out."

Gideon watched as Garza picked up a spear, hefted it. It was a sad-looking thing, with a wooden shaft and spearpoint and tail of hammered bronze. After a brief examination of the weapon, Garza shrugged and nodded, and the warriors carried the pallet of weapons off the field.

Watching, Gideon had to admire Garza's pluck. For all his complaining, when push came to shove he was still the bravest man Gideon had ever met.

Now two additional warriors—evidently referees of some sort—took both contestants by the shoulders and walked them to opposite sides of the dirt arena. A roar rose from the waiting crowd.

"I can't watch this," said Gideon.

The referees walked to the edge of the fighting ground and planted their spears. The chief gave a shout that was evidently the signal to begin.

Blackbeard immediately came forward, sword extended laterally. Garza, tense, circled him, holding the spear defensively before him.

Mugdol casually walked closer while Garza backed up, then took a desultory swing that Garza parried. He took another swing, insolently slow, and Garza jumped back. There was a hiss of disapproval from the crowd.

At least he's quick, thought Gideon, heart in his throat.

Now Mugdol lunged with the sword, and Garza scrambled backward, this time just missing being gutted and almost losing his balance. This was more to the crowd's liking. Garza danced backward as Mugdol continued to stride forward, sword now low and to the side, and then he swung again at high speed, the weapon hissing through the air. Garza tried to parry, but the sword made contact with the bronze end of the spear and knocked it to one side. Before Garza could fully recover, Mugdol came lunging in again and his sword, slashing the air, nicked Garza's right forearm, raising a small mist of red.

Another roar came up from the crowd at this first sight of blood.

Garza skipped out of range and cocked the spear, bringing it above his shoulder. At this, Mugdol tensed and began moving more cautiously, sword held out in both hands.

They circled each other and then, with sudden force, Garza launched his spear.

Blackbeard's sword flashed down and, with a great cracking

sound, swatted the spear away. It flew off into the dirt, cut in half through its wooden shank.

Another great roar from the crowd.

Now Garza scrambled backward, looking left and right as if for a route of escape. The crowd was in a fever of excitement. He retreated behind a small boulder, then picked up one of the smaller rocks that were scattered around. Blood was streaming from the nick on his left arm.

Mugdol strode confidently forward, a relaxed look again on his face. He was in no hurry, evidently planning to enjoy the kill. Gideon wanted to turn away but somehow was unable to force himself.

Garza threw the rock hard, but Blackbeard dodged it. This was followed by another, also dodged. There were jeers and cat-calls from the crowd.

Now, picking up a smooth round stone, Garza retreated farther, to the edge of the fighting ground, where their robes and headcloths lay draped on a boulder. Garza snatched up his head-cloth and shook it out into a long strip of fabric as he continued to retreat, while Mugdol came at him at a slow walk, relishing the sport. Fumbling with the headcloth, Garza folded it around the rock, then swung it up, stone cradled in the middle, gave it a whirl—and then released one end, letting the rock fly.

It went wild, missing Mugdol by at least twenty feet—but it moved fast, much faster than if Garza had thrown it. Mugdol paused, gave a mocking grin, and marched on.

Still retreating in a circular motion around the edge of the arena, Garza picked up some more smooth stones, holstered one in the cloth, whipped it around in an underhand motion, and launched it. This time, his aim was better and the rock whizzed past Blackbeard, missing him by inches.

The crowd loved it. They began to cheer, a sort of high keening sound, and Gideon had the impression they were growing beguiled by Garza and his spunk.

At least, that's how Mugdol took it. He scowled and, instead of continuing his leisurely chase, gave a roar of displeasure and charged, sword raised—just as Garza whirled the improvised sling again and released another stone.

Mugdol's charge was precisely the wrong strategy. Almost on top of Garza, he was so close that aim was no longer a factor and, with a sickening sound, the rock violently impacted his skull directly between the eyes. The huge figure stopped, swayed, then fell to the ground with a shuddering thump, sword flying. The high keening increased to a wail, led by Lillaya.

Garza leapt forward and seized the sword. A roar went up as he walked over to the unconscious body of his opponent. Planting his feet on either side of Mugdol's chest, Garza raised the sword in both hands and turned it point down, preparing to plunge it into his opponent's heart.

A hush suddenly fell over the crowd.

And then Garza hesitated.

The hush grew tense as the hesitation lengthened. Finally, Garza lowered the sword. "I can't kill a man who's down," he said simply.

Lillaya translated this and the hush turned to a dead silence—a silence, it seemed to Gideon, of disapproval. Garza then held up the sword and turned to the crone. "Tell everyone I'm keeping this. It's mine now and no one—*no one*—is to touch it."

When these words were translated, it was as if a dam broke. This, finally, was the right move. The crowd cheered, screamed, and stamped their feet, while Mugdol lay on the ground, moaning and thrashing feebly as consciousness returned. He struggled on the dirt, eyes rolling in his head, blood streaming from a deep gash between his eyes.

The crowd rushed into the fighting ground like fans after a game, reaching out noisily to touch Garza almost as if he were some kind of deity. His arm was now coated in blood from the sword wound. The gashes from the leopard were still healing, and he looked as if he might collapse at any moment.

"Get me out of here," he murmured as Gideon pushed his way up to him.

With a shout, Gideon raised his arm and, supporting Garza with the other, led his friend through the parting crowd, the sword of triumph held tightly in Garza's bloody fist.

33

GIDEON WOKE TO the heat of midday, still weary from Garza's wedding ceremony the previous night. He lay on his goatskin pallet, mind wandering back to the quaint and at times odd rituals that had made up the extended ceremony. Most of it was incomprehensible, conducted in a language he could still scarcely understand, but impressive nevertheless. The chief, looking more frail than usual, had been content to sit back and let the elders orchestrate most of the formalities. Garza had looked nervous and uncomfortable throughout, but went along gamely and managed to muddle through the various rituals. Following the combat with Mugdol five days before, he now seemed more resigned than anything else. At last the bride arrived, riding a camel and draped in long, shimmering robes, coming into a circle of light cast by the large bonfire, with the crowd chanting and a group of musicians playing stringed instruments that, though simple, nevertheless made a haunting, almost human sound that echoed off the cliffs. She had looked beautiful, her brown eyes rimmed with kohl, heavy mahogany hair braided with gold ribbons. Clearly aware of the gravity of the moment, she bore a self-assured air that was both regal and dignified, and looked every inch the princess she was. Upon seeing her, poor Garza had just about collapsed in discomfiture and amazement. That, Gideon thought, had been a truly spectacular moment.

He looked over at Imogen's sleeping nook and saw she was already gone. He rose, pulled on his robe, wound up his headcloth—the actions had become almost automatic—and went into the front part of the tent to splash water on his face from the well bucket that was always there. The wedding had culminated close to dawn when Garza, called upon to speak, told a story that he said had been passed down from his ancestors. He proceeded to relate the tale of David and Goliath, translated by Lillaya to the great entertainment of the crowd. Blackbeard was nowhere to be seen, and Gideon hoped that after his humiliation he'd gone away for good. Maybe he'd even been banished by the chief.

"Halloo! Breakfast!" Imogen returned, carrying two wooden bowls of dates and roasted camel meat kebabs: leftovers from the wedding feast. She sat down cross-legged on the rug and placed a bowl in front of Gideon.

"Thanks," he said. "That was one hell of a shindig."

"Too bloody right."

"The only thing missing was an ice-cold bottle of champagne," said Gideon as he tucked into the chunks of breakfast camel. He had grown used to the meat, and as long as he didn't think about where it came from he found it quite delicious: tender and not too gamy.

"By the way, Lillaya tells me we're moving," said Imogen.

"Really?"

"Because we are friends of the great and powerful Garza, defeater of the man-eating demon leopard and new son-in-law to the chief, our status has gone up another notch. It seems they're giving us a fancy tent with separate sleeping areas."

"Nice."

"And you're no longer on ditch-digging detail. In fact, thanks to Garza's status, we three are to form a new hunting party. Looking for antelope, rabbits, that sort of thing. You know, like the other warriors."

"Hunt with what? Spears?"

"As a special gift, the chief had crossbows and arrows made for us—copied from the original, apparently. I left them outside the tent. We're free to roam in search of game—except back through the canyon that leads to the mist oasis. That's the only way out of here, apparently, and they don't want us scarpering."

"We're free to go anywhere else?"

"It seems so. Except some riddle of canyons a ways west of here, where, it seems, the demon leopards live."

"But that's *fantastic*! It means—" Gideon suddenly realized what he was about to say and stopped himself abruptly.

"It means what?"

In his excitement, he had forgotten that Imogen was not one of them—that she was not privy to their secret. "It means," he said, "we can search for an escape route."

She leaned toward him with narrowed eyes. "That's utter tosh."

Gideon stared at her. "What do you mean?"

"*Please*. I know you've got some secret agenda. When are you going to finally tell me what's going on? I've leveled with you lot. How about leveling with me?"

Gideon faltered. She'd been with them almost from the beginning; they had been through hell; and she'd told them the truth and saved their lives. Twice, at least. If they let her in on their secret, she could be a most useful partner, knowing more about the country than they did. *What the hell*, he thought. *She's earned it.*

"Okay," he said.

Imogen crossed her arms. "I'm listening."

"It started in New York City, at a company called Effective Engineering Solutions."

Imogen listened while Gideon launched into the story: about Eli Glinn; their previous mission to the South Atlantic; the abrupt dissolving of EES that followed; how he and Garza had then stolen the translation of the Phaistos Disk, and why; and how it led them here. Imogen listened in silence, her blue eyes conveying intense interest.

When he was done, she said simply: "Incredible."

She was silent for a few moments. Then she asked: "So where exactly is the Phaistos location?"

"I figure no more than five miles west of here."

"And you really have no idea what's there?"

"None."

"But you must have speculated."

"Of course. Maybe a tomb. Or maybe it's King Solomon's Mines or an ancient library. Whatever it is, it was important enough to be inscribed on that Disk and sent up the Red Sea and then halfway across the Mediterranean to the island of Crete—the center of the Minoan civilization."

She shook her head. "It's a remarkable story. Thank you for being honest."

"It was high time we were. Now we can go there and check it out—under the guise of hunting, of course." He rose. "Let's go get Garza."

"He's still in his wedding tent." A smile played about Imogen's lips. "I imagine he's busy."

"Not so busy that we can't go find what we came all this way for. It's close to noon and we don't have much time left if we're to get there and back before dark."

Gideon emerged into the sunlight with Imogen following. The three new crossbows were leaning up against the side of the tent. He picked one up and examined it.

"Looks like it might actually work," he said.

"I tested one. It's rather like firing a gun—you cock it, put in a bolt, aim, and pull the trigger. Simple, crudely made, but effective."

Gideon slung his crossbow over his shoulder, picked up another one, and followed Imogen toward a large gray enclosure set up apart from the village—the wedding tent. As they walked through the encampment, people glanced at them and let them pass. Gideon had the sense that, at long last, they'd finally been accepted.

As they approached the tent, Gideon cupped his hands. "Hey, Manuel! Can we come over?"

No answer. He took a few steps forward. "Manuel?"

"Hold on," came a muffled voice from within.

Imogen glanced at Gideon.

After a minute Garza appeared, looking haggard, pulling his robe about him. "Look, I'm kind of tied up right now," he said.

Gideon raised his eyebrows. "Really? Because I'm going hunting, if you get my drift—"

"Yes. Well, we can hunt tomorrow." With no more ceremony he ducked back into the tent, closing the flap behind him.

Imogen and Gideon exchanged a look. "Told you," said Imogen, with that same wry smile.

"Let's you and I go."

Gideon laid Garza's crossbow against the wedding tent, then the two set off along the trail that led westward to the tomb field. Nobody seemed to pay much attention. They followed the well-trodden path into the valley and soon arrived at the tomb of the current chieftain—still under construction but now almost finished. Nobody was working on it; the day following the wedding seemed to be a general holiday.

At the far end of the valley, they reached the central trail that led, among other places, to the pit of the headless, and to the arena. The trail split, then split again, and each time Gideon was careful to keep heading westward. This new trail, which he had not been on before, eventually narrowed and halted at a seemingly impassable rockfall. But a barely discernible path led upward to a high ridge beyond, and they followed it, switchbacking across a series of ledges and cliffs. Reaching the crest, the trail ran along the ridgeline for a mile before coming to a fork at an overlook. To the right, the trail led on for at least half a mile before dipping below the ridgeline. To the left, there was no trail—only a labyrinth of nasty canyons far below, all running into a long winding wash. A weathered human skull, badly mauled and missing its lower jaw, lay beside the fork like a grim marker.

They paused.

"If I remember correctly from the aerial maps," Gideon said, "that wash to the left should lead to a place where three washes come together—and that's the Phaistos location. I'd say another mile or two." Catching the look on Imogen's face, he said: "What's the matter?"

"That way is forbidden."

"Excuse me?"

"Remember I told you we could hunt anywhere except the mist oasis and the place where the demon leopards live? Well, as far as I can tell, those canyons down there are their home."

Gideon licked his lips. "Who told you this again?"

"Lillaya."

"Did she say the way was forbidden, or did she simply say it was too dangerous?"

Imogen shrugged. "I don't speak the language well enough to tell you that."

Gideon turned his head slowly, taking in the vista. "We've come this far. We've got weapons. I vote we go on. If we find evidence of leopards, demon or otherwise, we'll head back and talk over our options with Manuel. What do you say?"

After a moment, she nodded.

They began moving forward with caution—a caution inspired by more than just the slippery terrain. As they began descending toward the wash, Imogen said: "Look. A mountain goat."

About a hundred feet away, to one side and a little below them, a mother goat and its kid were working their way along a tiny ledge, nibbling grass.

"Would they be feeding near a nest of leopards?" Gideon asked.

"Let's bag it. It'll be perfect cover."

Gideon felt impatient at the delay, but he recognized the sense of Imogen's suggestion. "All right. It'll give me a chance to acquaint myself with a crossbow. You stay here in case I flush them this way. And keep an eye out for leopards and vipers. I'll stalk from above."

Gideon cocked the crossbow, nocked in a bolt, and crept onto the ledge above, watching for predators at the same time he made sure he remained out of sight of the goats. The animals were upwind, and he moved cautiously so as not to make the slightest noise. He would have to get a lot closer with a crossbow than a gun. Gripping the crossbow in one hand, he moved around the swell of the cliff, staying out of sight, and crept up to a fin of rock. Peering over the top, he could see the animals about fifty feet below him. He wasn't sure just how accurate the crossbow was, but he felt close enough to at least get in a sporting shot. With infinite care he leveled the weapon at the kid, aimed through the crude sights, and—feeling a slight twinge of guilt—slowly squeezed the trigger lever.

With a sharp twang the crossbow let fly; the short, heavy bolt struck the kid in the side with tremendous force, the momentum knocking it off the ledge. It fell into the valley below with a high-pitched bleating cry. The mother goat, terrified, bounded away and was instantly gone.

Gideon glanced around quickly, but there was no sign that the racket had roused any man-eating leopards. Filled with pride, he went back to where Imogen was waiting. "Bull's-eye."

"Where is it?"

"At the bottom of the cliff. We have to go down there anyway."

With great difficulty they made their way down by the same faint trail and skirted the base of the cliffs. They soon found the kid, lying dead on some rocks. The bolt had gone almost completely through it.

"That crossbow packs a hell of a punch," said Imogen.

"We've got to gut it," said Gideon.

"Can't we do that when we get it back?"

"The meat will go bad and we'll look like idiots. Anyway, it'll make it a lot lighter."

With Imogen's assistance, Gideon used his dagger to cut open its belly, remove the guts and organs, and cut out the bolt. He draped the carcass over a rock. "We can pick it up on the return trip."

"If a pack of demon leopards doesn't get it first."

They set off down the winding, sinister-looking canyon. The sun lowered in the sky, the shadows grew longer, and they soon found themselves in a maze of stone. Gideon continued following what he hoped was the main wash, but it was hard to tell, given the side washes that came in at odd angles. Now and again they stopped to check for any sign—a low grunt, the shifting of a pebble—that might indicate a predator. But there was nothing. After a while his heart began to sink; they should have already reached the confluence of three canyons.

"We'd better turn around," he said. "And come back earlier tomorrow. With Garza riding shotgun this time."

"Let's go a little farther," said Imogen. "I'll bet it's just around the bend."

It wasn't just around the bend, but Imogen kept urging them on. Gideon was surprised at how quickly she seemed to have caught the Phaistos bug—the almost clinical attitude of scientific detachment she'd exhibited at times had fallen away. But then he recalled why she herself had braved the desert: to establish a name for herself, prove her worth as both a researcher and an explorer. Whatever the Phaistos Disk was leading them to might well do that.

Within thirty minutes or so they came around a sharp turn, and the canyon suddenly broadened into a natural fortress formed by the junction of three other canyons: sheer cliffs of basalt on all sides, unbroken save for a narrow open corridor to the west. No living thing was visible. The air was filling with the light of evening.

And there, on the opposite cliff face, was a rectangle. As the last rays of the setting sun gilded the stony wall, he could see that the rectangle was actually a massive portal, clearly human-made, with what looked like leaden seals hammered across one side, stamped with hieroglyphics.

And then the sun fell below the level of the cliffs and the light vanished.

"My God," Imogen breathed. "It *is* a tomb! With unbroken seals!"

While he'd always believed they would find something, now that it had happened, Gideon felt a sense of utter unreality. It couldn't be. It was too good to be true. But there it was. It certainly did *look* like a tomb, and—given the size of its entryway—an important one.

But the light was dying fast. He turned to Imogen, noticing the look of awe and wonder on her face. "What do you think?"

"A pharaoh's tomb, I would say," she said. "Unlooted. Untouched. And bigger than King Tut's. I want to take a look at those hieroglyphs."

Gideon hesitated. The light was dying fast and they had some rough ground to cover on the way back. He laid a hand on her shoulder and found it trembling with excitement. "Let's retrieve the goat and get back to camp," he said. "We can come back later... at our leisure. And with Garza."

For a moment, it was as if she hadn't heard him. Then with an obvious effort she pulled herself away and they headed back cautiously into the dark warren of canyons.

34

They returned in the dark, Gideon carrying the kid on an improvised pole he had slung over one shoulder. As they entered the broad valley, the evening's cooking fires were lit and the fragrance of wood smoke mingled with roasting meat. Small boys were driving flocks of goats into their pens, bells tinkling, and the tents were lit from the inside with oil lamps. The numerous camels were all bedded down for the night in a kind of natural corral made from a break in the valley wall, as usual neither tethered nor shut in—clearly, the communal tribe did not steal from each other, and anyway the camels were distinctive enough that everybody knew which ones belonged to whom.

"Looks almost idyllic," said Imogen, pausing to survey the scene.

"You know, despite all our troubles and misunderstandings, these are good people. They're just trying to protect their way of life."

"How quickly you forget they almost killed us—twice."

"I haven't forgotten." Gideon shifted the kid from one shoulder to the other. "Feel like barbecued kid tonight?"

"With a spicy rub? I'm famished."

They proceeded through the settlement to their new tent, which stood on a small rise, with other larger tents and greater distances between them. As they passed through, their kid aroused interest, and they received smiles and gestures of congratulations. A baby goat was considered a true delicacy.

Arriving at their tent, Gideon hung the kid on a tripod fashioned out of branches, skinned it with his stone dagger, and cut off the head and feet. As he worked, Imogen built a fire from a pile of desert hardwood that was stacked beside their tent. Their new quarters had, it seemed, been provided with all the necessities: in addition to wood for fuel, there were a variety of crude implements and utensils, a water barrel, cooking spices, a greenwood roasting pole with forked supports, extra skins for blankets, and their own camel saddles.

When the carcass was dressed and seasoned from the bags of spices, Gideon affixed it to the roasting pole and set it above the bed of coals. He turned the kid from time to time, the meat sizzling and giving off a heavenly aroma.

"I can't wait to get inside that tomb," said Imogen as she came up, her eyes shining.

"I was thinking the same thing. I was also thinking about the old crone's warning."

"You mean, about the forbidden path and the demon leopards?"

"Yup. Do you suppose that's just a story to keep curious tribesmen away?"

"It's possible. In fact, it's probable. Somebody *has* to know about it. It may well be a secret, known only to the priests and the chief. Or maybe just Lillaya. I mean, look at her critical role in the tribe—higher even than the priests. She might be the living repository of their cultural history, their sacred knowledge."

Gideon gave the kid another turn. "Sounds like an old H. Rider Haggard novel. You know, with that crone descended from a long line of priestesses, all sworn to guard and protect the sacred tomb."

"It's not as unlikely as you might think." Imogen stared into the fire. "How else can you explain its still being intact? Did you know that only *one* pharaoh's tomb has ever been found unlooted—and that just happened to belong to someone named Tutankhamen?" She let out a sigh. "He was just a second-tier teenage king. Imagine what *this* might contain."

Gideon basted the kid with drippings. "Any idea which pharaoh?"

"It's strange that an important tomb would be so far removed from the Valley of the Kings or the other ancient tomb fields. If I had to guess, I'd say it might be connected to the heretic Pharaoh Akhenaten."

"Heretic?"

"Yes." She squatted beside him. "Akhenaten, as I explained, tried to impose monotheism on Egypt. But after he died, the people revolted and restored the many ancient gods. They smashed his monuments and statues and chiseled his name from inscriptions. Forever after they referred to him not by name, but as 'that criminal.' Scholars have never identified his tomb for certain."

"So it's possible Akhenaten's followers hid his tomb way out here to protect it."

"It's certainly a possibility. Remember, during his life Ahkenaten was incredibly powerful. His queen was Nefertiti, and he was probably King Tut's father. If this really is his undisturbed tomb, it would be the biggest discovery in Egypt since the Rosetta Stone."

"So why record its location on the Phaistos Disk and send it to Crete?"

She shook her head. "Hard to know. Maybe his followers created a bunch of those disks and secretly distributed them to like-minded followers around the ancient world, so the location would never be forgotten."

Gideon turned the goat again and used his dagger to cut into it. A dribble of clear juices fell sizzling into the fire. "Looks done."

"Perfect timing!" Garza's voice came from the darkness as he stepped into the firelight. He rubbed his hands together. "Damn, I'm hungry."

"Sure you've got enough energy left to eat?" Gideon asked.

"Where's Jelena?" Imogen asked.

Garza flushed. Then he grinned. "Sleeping." He glanced at the fire, clearly eager to change the subject. "So where'd you get the goat?"

"I shot it," said Gideon, with no little pride. "The chief gave each of us a crossbow as a gift. Knockoffs of your, ah, present to him."

"I saw the one outside my tent. Well done."

Imogen passed around clay plates while Gideon hacked off cuts of meat and served them. He caught Imogen's eye. *It has to be said*, he realized; *there's no point hemming and hawing.*

He looked over. "Manuel?"

"Mmm?" Garza responded, biting into a haunch.

"We went to the Phaistos location today."

Garza paused, then put down the cut, looking from Gideon to Imogen and back. "You ... *told* her?"

"Yes. I felt it was about time."

Garza flushed again, this time from anger rather than embarrassment. "We had an agreement!" he said loudly, then—

looking around the encampment—lowered his voice. "All we've been through, and you didn't even have the decency to ask me first?"

"You're the one who wouldn't come out of your tent this morning—remember?"

"That's got nothing to do with it! Whatever's there is ours. We risked our lives for it several times over: remember *that*?"

"Of course. And who saved us, most of those times?"

Abruptly, Imogen cut in. "Don't throw a wobbly," she told Garza. "I'm not interested in whatever's inside that tomb. Not in any treasure *you'd* understand, at least." She paused. "I'd have thought by now you'd come to trust me."

There was a long silence. And then, to Gideon's surprise, the expression on Garza's face softened. "Fair enough," he said. "But I hope you don't blame me for being suspicious." He held out his hand. "Friends?"

"Friends," she said, taking it.

There was a brief, slightly awkward silence while the three ate their dinner.

Glancing furtively over his shoulder, Garza leaned in toward them. "For God's sake," he murmured, "what did you find?"

"Under the guise of a hunting trip, we headed west and found this spot where three canyons come together in a valley, surrounded by cliffs—just as we'd hoped. Set into the far cliff was a large stone door. It was set with lead seals—unbroken. Embossed in hieroglyphics."

Even in the firelight, Garza's face lit up with excitement. "And?"

"We just saw it at a distance. It was getting dark."

"But it's a tomb?"

"We think so," Imogen said. "An important one."

"A pharaoh?"

"Probably."

"Christ. When do we go back?"

Gideon leaned forward, too. "It's only five miles or so, but we have to be very careful: the path to the tomb is rough and, on top of that, forbidden. They say it's because of the demons that live there, but I think that may be just to keep people away. We figure at least some of the tribe must know about the tomb. It's likely they've been guarding it for centuries."

"I'd guess about thirty-five centuries, give or take," Imogen said.

"That's a long time," Gideon continued. "Stands to reason they'd take grave exception—so to speak—to our breaking in."

"So what's the plan?" Garza asked.

"All the hunting parties go out on the night of the full moon," Gideon said. "Seems to be a tradition. That's the night after next. We'll simply form a band of our own—like we did today—and head in that direction. The moonlight will help us get there unobserved."

Garza nodded. "Okay."

"I have a question," said Imogen. "Once we're inside the tomb—what's the goal? I mean, are you planning to document it?"

There was a silence. Then Gideon shook his head. "No, no. We're going to rob it."

Imogen stared at him. "You're going to *loot* it?"

"Damn right," said Garza. "Didn't Gideon tell you that part? We're here to make our fortunes. Are you really so naive? We've worked it out—how we're going to smuggle it out of Egypt, get it into the States, everything."

"I think that's horrible. You're nothing but thieves."

"Exactly. We're thieves, criminals—and proud of it. Listen: the company we used to work for was unique. We've toppled dictators, stolen nuclear reactors so they won't get weaponized. We've spent our whole lives working for others. *We* saved the world. Now this is for *us*. Besides, what do you care? You just said you weren't interested in any treasure for yourself."

"I'm not—in gold and jewels, at least. But I'm a geoarchaeologist. Looting and desecrating a tomb goes against everything I believe in."

Garza looked at Gideon with an expression that said: *You got us into this. Now get us out.*

"If you're not interested in treasure," Gideon asked Imogen quickly, "what exactly are you interested in?"

"History. Knowledge."

"Such as?"

"There might—there probably are—documents inside. Papyri, stone tablets, scrolls. That's the *real* treasure. Who knows what kind of light they might shed on ancient Egyptian history?"

"I don't give a damn about old scraps of paper," Garza said. "I want something I can convert into hard cash—quickly. While you *document* it, we *plunder* it. And then we ride hell-for-leather back out through the mist oasis."

"And supposing you succeed. Just how are you planning to smuggle a tomb's worth of loot out of Egypt? It's not only unethical, it's crazy. I won't let you try."

"Like I said, we've worked it out," said Garza. "What are you going to do? Raise the alarm? Get us all killed?"

"Wait a moment," Gideon said, interrupting the rising argument. "Imogen's right—we don't want to do anything that would wreck the historical record. But Manuel's right, too. We're the ones who made this discovery. We deserve to get something out of it." He looked at Imogen. "Besides, if we don't take at least a few pieces, who's going to believe us? It's not like we have any cameras."

A brief silence settled over the three as the fire flickered and danced.

"What's your proposal, then?" Imogen asked at last.

"We've got crossbows, waterskins, and food," Gideon replied. "But most important, we've got freedom of movement. We steal a couple of camels, load them down with food and water, and take off. We enter the tomb, Manuel and I will take what we want, and you'll have time to record the find, document everything you can. And here's the best part: we don't need to ride back through the camp and the mist oasis."

Garza frowned. "But that's the only way out."

"So we were told. But, Imogen, do you remember that cut we saw in the far side of the demon canyon? It led westward, to the other side of the mountains and open desert. That's our back door—and I'll bet it's kept secret even from most of the tribe. From there it's less than a hundred miles to the Nile River. We could avoid running a murderous gauntlet through camp...*and* make the journey in four, five days."

"You saw this back door yourself?" Garza asked.

"Hell, yes. And—"

"Hold on a minute, you lot," Imogen interrupted. "In all this excitement, aren't you getting a little ahead of yourselves?"

"What do you mean?" asked Garza.

"You're planning to just waltz in, steal the treasure, and ride off, like Bob's your uncle?"

Garza nodded. "That was the general idea, yes."

"Well then, allow me to make a couple of observations. First, that door isn't just going to open itself. Remember, it was made to resist penetration. You don't know how long it will take to get inside—especially given the tools at hand."

Gideon and Garza exchanged looks.

"Second, we have no idea what's inside. You're hoping for a tomb full of treasure. I'm hoping for a tomb full of unknown history. We could all be right—or wrong. Maybe there's nothing in there. Maybe it's full of statuary too heavy to lift. Until you know, how can you figure out the best method to cart it all away?"

There was a silence. Then Garza murmured, "Damn."

"This is what we'll do," Gideon said abruptly. "We'll go out on the full moon, as planned. But it will only be a recon expedition. We'll break in, or at least try to, and ascertain what's inside. That way, we'll know what to plan for."

"It might take more than one night to break in," Imogen said.

"Fine," Garza said. "Then we'll go out 'hunting' two nights in a row. And we'll plan the actual loot-'n'-leave for the next full moon."

"The *next* full moon?" Gideon echoed. "That's a month away."

"Like Imogen said, there are unknown variables to consider here. We need to plan this carefully. If we find something unexpected, it might take us additional weeks to prepare, and…"

As he was speaking, Garza caught the expression on Gideon's face. Recalling immediately that Gideon was on a clock—the *ultimate* clock—he added hastily, "On the other hand, delaying too long has its own set of unexpected variables. So let's plan to leave a week after the initial recon. That gives us seven days to get inside, take an inventory, and figure out how best to effect our escape."

Imogen considered for a moment. "Well, I still think you're both rotten to loot the tomb."

"But you're going to live with it," Garza said.

"What choice do I have? But assuming we find anything, you'll take only small stuff—gold, jewelry, and the like. No unique works of art. And especially no written documents or historically important artifacts. Agreed?"

Gideon nodded. Then—after a hesitation—Garza did as well.

35

GIDEON HAD NEVER seen a full moon as bright as the one that rose two nights later above the peak of Gebel Umm, the Mother of Mountains, casting a brilliant light into the valley. Outside, hunting parties were gathering in small groups and getting ready to venture into the rugged landscape. On this particular night, hunters stalked the curious nocturnal boar of southern Egypt, a reclusive animal that came out in small groups to root about for grubs and insects.

Gideon had an entirely different kind of hunt on his mind.

Although it was getting close to midnight, the fires were still lit, and the hunters gathered around them holding their spears, their long shadows flickering and wavering over the ground. There was a low murmur of conversation and the gentle clang and rasp of weapons being sharpened and assembled.

Garza, arriving from his tent with crossbow and bolts, came and stood next to him, silently contemplating the impressive scene. They had already worked out their plans; there was nothing left but to execute them. Imogen soon joined them. Each had a waterskin slung over a shoulder for the night hunt.

Soon the parties were departing in small groups, disappearing into the rugged ravines and ridges that surrounded the great grassy bowl of their encampment.

"Let's go," said Garza.

Gideon led the way. They had decided to head out in a different direction than the tomb, so as not to arouse suspicion, and then circle around to what they'd begun calling the Demon Valley. This proved more difficult than first anticipated: most paths they tried ended either in unclimbable rock faces or else abrupt, vertiginous cliffs. At last they found a barely discernible trail that wound its way up a rocky slope to a ridge, then down into a dry wash. Promisingly, the wash led northward, at a slight angle to the trail they'd taken on the earlier day but paralleling it. After a few miles they came to a headland, dropped down into an adjacent canyon, followed that at a different angle for another mile, and then paused to rest.

"All this circling around has wreaked hell with my dead reckoning," said Gideon. "But I'm pretty sure the trail we want is just one canyon over."

After a quick rest they climbed the next ridge, which topped out on a knife-edge of rock, sticking into the air like a broken blade. Picking their way through the vertical layers of stone, they at last reached an overlook down into the next canyon. Gideon paused to scan the landscape and check for other hunting parties, but they appeared to be alone. One again, there was no sign of leopards.

"Is that the canyon?" asked Garza.

"Hard to tell. I hope so."

Another steep descent brought them to the gentle, gravelly bed of the canyon bottom, pale silver in the bright moonlight. Walking more quickly now, they continued down the canyon, which wound its way among dark walls of basalt.

"All these damn canyons look the same," Garza muttered.

Just when it seemed to Gideon that he'd been mistaken and they must be on the wrong path, the defile widened and they reached the peculiar confluence of three canyons—and there, across a broad sandy wash, he could see the outline of the tomb door, illuminated by moonlight.

Garza stopped to stare. Then, with some difficulty, he swallowed. "Jesus."

"We've no time to waste," said Gideon. "Let's go."

They hurried across the canyon floor and within minutes stood in front of the door. It was about eight feet high and four across, carved of the same dark basalt, and recessed into the cliff face, which itself had been carved into a rectangular shape. Egyptian hieroglyphs decorated the lintels, and the leaden seals Gideon had only seen from a distance were affixed to the door, about head height, stamped with hieroglyphs.

Gideon reached out and touched one of them, pitted and whitened with oxidation. "You're right," he told Imogen. "It's unbroken."

Imogen scrutinized the seals. "Yes. And also cursed."

"Naturally," said Garza. "What's a tomb without a curse?"

She ran her fingers along the embossed glyphs. "It says, *You who enter here…*" She paused. "Hmmm. It's a little obscure. *You who enter here, may Aten the One God…set your bowels afire.*"

"Ouch," said Garza.

"Lillaya's cooking has accomplished that already," said Gideon.

"It's written in New Kingdom hieroglyphics of the Eighteenth Dynasty. And this—*Aten the One God*—means it comes from the reign of Akhenaten." She took a step back. "More evidence this is Akhenaten's tomb, and it's intact…my God." Then she took a sharp breath, as if thinking of something. "Wait a minute. It's possible his wife is buried here, too."

"Nefertiti?" Gideon asked.

Imogen nodded.

"The tomb of Akhenaten and Nefertiti," Gideon said almost reverently.

"If we don't get this door open," said Garza, "we'll never know who's inside." He turned to Imogen. "Got any tricks up your sleeve?"

A silence. "There is no trick," she said. "No secret button, if that's what you mean. It's like I warned you: tomb doors were deliberately made out of massive stone slabs that could only be moved by many men."

Gideon stared at the door. "It must weigh twenty tons. So how are we going to shift it?"

A long silence ensued as they stared at the ponderous slab before them.

Imogen finally spoke. "I hate to say I told you so, but it looks as if you fellows came thousands of miles only to be stopped by a door."

Garza stepped forward, then crouched, running his fingers along the bottom edge and up the sides. "We can use leverage." He pointed at a narrow fissure. "Wedge a lever in this crack, and if it's long enough it'll force the door ajar."

"So where's the lever?" Gideon asked.

Silence.

"And even if we did find a lever," Gideon continued, "it wouldn't be strong enough. It'll break. Even our bronze spears will bend like putty trying to force open that thing."

Garza examined the door more closely, this time going over it inch by inch. Minutes passed. Gideon stared up anxiously at the moon. Time was wasting. He racked his brains, but the answer seemed obvious: they were not going to move that stone slab without heavy machinery or explosives—and, as

Imogen had pointed out a few nights earlier, they possessed neither.

"What are these parallel drill holes?" Garza pointed to a line of small openings that ran diagonally from one side of the slab to the other.

"You see those on almost any massive blocks moved by the ancient Egyptians," Imogen told him. "They'd insert bronze pegs and attach ropes, pulled by a hundred slaves."

Garza grunted as he continued to examine the door. He found a twig and probed inside one of the drilled holes, testing its depth.

"Face it," said Imogen. "We're not going to move that door."

Gideon was growing increasingly frustrated. Here they were, mere feet away from the thing they'd been searching for at such great cost—and they were thwarted by a piece of stone. "You think this is funny," he said to Imogen.

"It's hilarious! Look, I'm just as curious as you to see what's inside—probably more so. But I can't say I'm sorry you won't be getting your grubby hands on it."

"Screw you."

"Sod off."

"Hey," said Garza. "Put a sock in it." He left off examining the door. Now he started wandering around the floor of the canyon, examining dead thornbushes. Taking out his dagger, he cut a slender branch off one of them. He stripped off the dead bark and began whittling it.

"What the heck is he doing?" Imogen asked.

Gideon, who'd been struggling mightily to push away the mounting feeling of defeat, shook his head. "Beats me."

Now Garza cut the branch into several pieces, which he carefully whittled into sharpened pegs. He did this with another dead bush, then another, until he had a dozen seven- to eight-inch pegs. He carried them to the door and, hunting around for a rock, placed a peg in one of the drilled holes and used the rock to hammer it in. Six inches of the peg disappeared, leaving an inch of wood exposed. He repeated the process until the entire line of drilled holes was bristling with exposed peg ends.

Gideon, who'd been watching, shifted from one foot to the other. "Manuel, I hate to tell you, but those pegs aren't going to hold—even if we had ropes to attach to them and those hundred slaves to pull."

Garza glanced over and then—to Gideon's vast surprise—flashed a grin. "Just watch."

He took his headcloth, unwound it, and tore it into short pieces. Then he soaked each piece with the waterskin. Next, taking the sopping pieces of cloth, he wrapped each one around an exposed stub of wood. When this was done, he carefully poured a little water on each rag-bundled stub, soaking it further.

"What's this?" said Gideon. "Magic?"

"In a way. The magic of capillary action. The dry wood takes the water in through the capillaries and the pegs swell up. Presto—the rock splits."

"You've gone barmy," Imogen said.

"Think so? This was a tried-and-true method of splitting rock for hundreds of years, in New England and elsewhere. It's called water wedging. I estimate it will take two hours, maybe more."

"Two hours?" Gideon asked, looking at the moon again. "We won't have any time left for exploration!"

"O ye of little faith."

"Even if this works," said Imogen, "and the door splits open, you realize the guards or whoever keeps watch on the valley are going to see it's been entered."

"That assumes it's actively patrolled," Garza told her. "You speculated they've been protecting this tomb for thirty-five centuries—and that its location is probably sacred and secret, known only to a few. I'll bet they only check up on it once or twice a year. Why else would they maintain that fiction about a Demon Valley? And just look at the sandy ground around here: if they were constantly patrolling, we'd see a trail, or at least footprints other than our own. I'll bet at most only a few elders know about it—maybe just Lillaya and the chief. Otherwise, people would realize there's a second way out of their valley."

It was a reasonable argument, Gideon thought. "But that door is basalt. One of the hardest rocks there is."

"Hard, yes. But brittle."

They sat cross-legged in the sand and fell into silence. A distant owl began to hoot: a low, mournful sound that seemed to shift about in the maze of canyons. Every twenty minutes or so, Garza would rise and pour a little more water on the rags. An hour went by, then two.

Gideon again glanced skyward as the minutes crawled by. The full moon had been gradually making its way across the sky, the shadows moving with it. They'd left around midnight, and with the hike in they'd arrived here around two thirty AM. Now it had to be at least four thirty. The sun would rise at six.

He rose. "Forget the possibility of bagging any game. If we don't leave now, we won't even get back to camp before dawn. People are going to wonder where we are."

In that moment, they heard a sudden *kak!* It wasn't overly loud, but it cut through the stillness of the night air like the crack of a whip. A fresh diagonal split had formed across the door, running through the line of pegs. A moment later the abrupt cracking noise was followed by another, this time hollow and mysterious. The stone slab began shifting, its two halves grinding against each other, under the irresistible pressure of their own massive weight—and then they fell atop one another in a kind of slow motion, hitting the ground with a shuddering boom and raising a huge cloud of dust.

Gideon waited for the dust to settle and the boom to stop echoing across the canyon walls. He looked around to make sure the noise hadn't been overheard, then he stared back into the dark maw of the tomb. Garza was already taking out three small pitch torches he had brought along. He pulled out a little fire drill he'd fashioned, produced a small flame, lit the torches, and passed them out.

"Let's go," he said.

They approached the door, the yellow lights faintly illuminating a long stone corridor.

"Are there likely to be booby traps?" Gideon asked Imogen.

"Only in the movies," she said. "If there's any trap here, it would be a well: a deep pit directly inside the door. But..." She advanced, holding her torch before her. "There doesn't seem to be any well at all. How odd."

The corridor, cut out of the living rock, sloped downward into the mountain at a gentle grade. They proceeded cautiously. Colorful paintings decorated the incised and plastered walls, a great procession of people in the Egyptian style, surrounded by panels of hieroglyphics.

A little farther along the corridor, Gideon saw that it came to an end in another door. But this was of wood, not stone, with a tiny second door built into it. The wood had once been gilded, and bits and pieces of gold leaf shone in the torchlight. The image of a golden chariot was carved into the door, with a pharaoh standing in it, holding the reins of four horses, surrounded by more hieroglyphics.

"What does all that say?" Gideon asked.

"I don't want to wait to decipher it," Imogen said breathlessly.

Despite herself, she was tremendously excited. "Let's see what's inside first."

Garza knelt and examined what appeared to be a bronze locking mechanism on the small wooden door. As he fiddled with it, the lock came apart in his hand, the wood crumbling to dust. With a low creak, the door inched ajar.

They all looked at each other.

"Who's first?" asked Imogen.

"Garza," said Gideon. "He got us in here."

"No," said Garza. "Imogen's the Egyptologist. She should go first."

There was no further discussion. Eyes shining, Imogen got down on her hands and knees and, holding the torch before her, crawled through the opening. The flickering light streamed back toward Gideon and Garza, wavering this way and that.

"What do you see?" Gideon asked.

There was a long silence. And then: "My God. Things. *Amazing things.*"

Gideon couldn't stand it any longer. He dropped to his knees. "I'm coming in."

He crawled through and Garza followed. They stood up and, in the flickering torchlight, found themselves in a surprisingly small chamber, perhaps fifteen by fifteen feet square. The walls were covered with paintings and hieroglyphics, and the barreled ceiling was painted a deep azure, decorated with golden stars and a silver moon. In the center of the chamber was a great granite plinth supporting an upright cabinet made entirely of chased and beaten gold. The cabinet doors were shut and sealed with lead tapes.

Gideon turned slowly, struck dumb, moving the torch this way and that in order to see better. Set on the stone floor surrounding the cabinet were a great many things, and it took

Gideon several moments to take them in. There was an alabaster bowl, filled with heavy gold nuggets; a slate tray covered with polished pieces of lapis lazuli and turquoise; and another tray of gold amulets inlaid with precious stones. There were gorgeous hand-carved bowls and elaborate vases of snow-white alabaster; solid gold slippers; daggers of fine workmanship with handles of ivory and sheaths of gold; scepters and crooks of gold, silver, and lapis; an entire bowl filled with gold rings and necklaces . . . and another filled with cut gemstones—diamonds such as Gideon had never seen or even heard of before, the color of the golden sun. Nearby lay the head of a leopard in beaten silver, a jackal in ebony . . . the array of treasures went on and on.

And the walls. One held a magnificent, life-size painting of a pharaoh mounted in a golden chariot, whip in one hand and reins in the other, driving a team of richly caparisoned stallions across a landscape. The other wall depicted an immense battle scene.

Gideon finally tore his eyes away. Imogen was pale, her face a sheen of perspiration. For what seemed forever, no one spoke.

And then Imogen said: "It's incredible. Almost unbelievable. But it's not a tomb."

Gideon stared at her. "What do you mean?"

"Where's the sarcophagus? Where are the canopic jars and ushabtis? And it's so small. Even King Tut's tomb had half a dozen rooms."

Gideon looked around. There were no other doors leading out. This was the only chamber.

"If it's not a tomb, what is it?" Garza asked.

"I don't know. These things on the ground—all these treasures—they look like . . . well, like offerings."

"But to what?"

"I assume to whatever's in that golden cabinet."

Another silence ensued. Then Imogen slid out her dagger and touched one of the cabinet's lead seals. "Should I?"

"Hell, yes," said Gideon.

Gently, carefully, Imogen cut the lead tapes holding the gold doors of the cabinet closed: first one, then the other. She slid off the clasp and gently opened the doors.

Gideon stared at what lay within. Whatever he'd been expecting, this wasn't it. The cabinet only held a black slab of stone, rough along the edges, with its polished face containing lines of hieroglyphic writing.

"A rock," Garza said. "Amid all these riches, a piece of rock."

Imogen stared at it, moving the torch closer, her eyes narrowing.

"What is it?" asked Gideon. "The pharaoh's laundry list?"

"It's what this tomb—this shrine—was built to contain." She continued scrutinizing it. "Clearly, it must be of the greatest importance."

"The secret rites of the Shriners?" Gideon asked.

"What *does* it say?" Garza pressed.

"Hang on a moment. It says: *As I am everywhere and always . . . I am your only God. Reject others and take me as your one true God.*"

She paused, brows contracting. "The second line reads: *Though I am formless to eyes such as yours, do not make . . . a carving.* No, that last bit's not quite right. *Make no carven image of me to worship.*"

"Sounds like the Ten Commandments." said Gideon.

"Yes—yes. Or maybe . . . a *draft* of them." She stared, her brow furrowed in concentration as she puzzled through the symbols. And then she straightened up, looking at the two of them silently, inexpressible surprise in her eyes.

36

They managed to make it back just before sunrise, dusty and exhausted. As they passed through camp—with no game to show for their nocturnal efforts—they endured a certain degree of ribbing from the other hunters. It seemed other hunts had been more successful: many small boars, gutted and strung from poles, were hung about the camp or were being skinned and dismembered, the haunches salted, ribs and chops smoking over the fires.

Garza hustled back to the tent he shared with his wife as the sky turned red in the east. Jelena was already up and putting on her special robes, long dark hair swinging as she worked. Instead of scolding him for the failure of their hunt, she indicated to him—with the gestures and pidgin talk they used to communicate—that he was to hurry up, cast off his filthy garments, and get dressed for some event, the nature of which he couldn't quite understand but seemed to involve her father, the chief. To his alarm, it also seemed to involve him, and if he understood Jelena correctly would be another kind of important announcement.

As he put on fresh robes—now familiar garments that had once felt so foreign to him—his head was still brimming with the images of what he'd seen in the treasure chamber. He had no idea of the meaning, or importance, of what Imogen had found inside the golden cabinet—they'd been so rushed scampering back to camp that they hadn't had time to talk.

As the sky brightened, Garza followed his wife up the path to the chief's tent. People were streaming out into the sunshine, dressed in whatever passed as their finery. Something big was clearly up, but try as he might, Garza could still only understand bits and pieces of Jelena's speech.

As they approached, two men carrying spears came and escorted them around the growing crowd to a small area in front of the chief's tent, beside the promontory where the old man made his pronouncements. They took their place next to Lillaya, who, nodding and smiling, gave him a friendly welcome in her broken English. Looking about, Garza saw Imogen and Gideon among the assembled multitudes.

A moment later, a hush fell. The chief's tent flap was drawn aside and the chief himself came out, moving slowly, staff in hand, his face lined with care, supported by a single soldier. He advanced to the promontory, then extended his hands, palms upward. A gong was struck to mark sunrise, and as the first rays of golden light streamed into the valley, he began to speak.

His voice was low, and because he spoke more slowly and haltingly than usual, Garza was able to follow the gist of his words. The chief began with a flowery gesture toward Garza. He told the story of how Garza saved his daughter's life. As Garza listened, he began to feel awkward and not a little guilty—given where they'd just returned from—and wondered where his new father-in-law was going with all this. The chief then went on to extol how Garza had brilliantly accelerated work on his tomb, so that when the end came he would not suffer any wait in reaching the afterlife.

The chief paused often to recover his breath, gasping a little between sentences, and he looked weaker than he had during the wedding ceremony. But still he continued, gamely heaping praise on Garza and speaking about how he had proved himself a valiant warrior as well as an inventor of new weaponry to help keep the citizenry safe. At this, Garza looked around nervously for Mugdol, but the man and a scattering of his most loyal cronies were nowhere to be seen, thank God. Maybe he'd decided that self-imposed exile was preferable to humiliation.

Still the chief went on, now shifting to the subject of his daughter. Based on Jelena's blushes, he was extolling her virtues, as well. Garza found himself growing increasingly worried—about not only where this speech was heading, but also the chief's increasing difficulty in speaking. Apparently the audience had noticed it, as well, because Garza could hear low murmurings of concern among them.

The chief halted again, but this time the silence stretched on...and on. The murmur from the crowd grew.

And then, quite suddenly, the chief keeled over. As the guards rushed to his side, he hit the stony ground, rolled over once, then lay still.

A huge outcry went up and Jelena rushed to her father with a shriek, Garza at her heels. The uproar continued as the crowd surged forward. The guards were trying to raise the chief, but Garza gestured sharply to them to leave him. He knelt and, alone, took the chief in his arms, supporting him gently, while the man stared up at him, lips moving silently.

"Water," said Garza. "He needs water." He racked his brains for the word. *"Soah! Soah!"*

Water was quickly proffered and Garza held the cup to the

old man's lips. He took a sip, then winced, dropping the cup and clutching at his chest in pain.

"*Samu*," he said in a whisper, raising his hand from his chest so that he could lay it on Garza's own. "*Samu*."

At this the crowd fell silent. *Samu*, Garza knew, was the word for "son."

"*Epourou!*" the chief cried, and with his remaining strength he struck Garza forcefully on the chest.

And then, with a convulsive spasm, his body sagged, his arm slipped to the ground, and he died.

The crowd, which had gone abruptly silent, now just as abruptly began to speak again. *Epourou*, they began to repeat: *Epourou, epourou*. Garza, still cradling the dead chief, dazed by this sudden development, looked around. Everyone was staring at him, repeating the same word over and over: *Epourou*. Even Jelena, though clearly distraught, was looking at him rather than her father.

And now here was the crone, leaning toward him on her two canes, an odd, approving smile creasing her ancient face, a claw-like hand reaching out to grasp his own.

"What...what does *epourou* mean?" he asked.

"*Epourou*," she said. "It means...'chief.' It means you."

37

Garza stood in the half-light of the wedding tent, staring mutely at the young woman with her back turned toward him. He could tell, from the shaking of her shoulders, that she was quietly crying. He began to advance toward her through the striped shadows, then stopped. Normally, he was a man who acted quickly, without excessive deliberation or self-doubt. But now he felt uncharacteristically at a loss. It was not, he realized, because of the language barrier between them, although that was of course partly the reason. It was more the speed at which his life had changed. So many things had happened, in such quick succession, that he realized he was completely unprepared for the role that had been thrust upon him: a chief-to-be in this strange distant land, comforting his bride of only a few days, who possessed a language he barely spoke and a culture he only remotely comprehended. The engineer in him would have taken one look at this problem; calculated the probability of finding a solution; and then given it a wide berth.

But gazing upon this weeping woman—who had, in her own way, taught him as much or more in just a few days as he'd taught the entire tribe since his arrival—Garza did not feel like an engineer.

He did not know what he felt, exactly—except for pity. Pity, and the certainty he could not let this woman grow dependent on him; after all, he'd be leaving in one week. It was a horrible thing to do to her, but he could see no way out.

But now her shoulders shook more violently and, instinctively, Garza stepped forward and gently put his hands out to still them. Immediately, Jelena turned toward him, kohl-colored tears running in dark rivulets down her cheeks, and buried her face in his chest.

"*Malagdaya,*" Garza said, slowly and awkwardly. "*Malagdaya, samu Jelena pinishti, rak...rak'shona.*"

For a while they held each other, and then Jelena slowly disengaged herself from him, collected herself, and dried her tears. She looked gravely into his eyes. Extending her arm, she placed her hand on his chest. "*Epourou,*" she said quietly, with a commanding dignity. And then she placed the same hand on her own chest and repeated the word—*Epourou.*

Her meaning was clear.

* * *

Gideon tightened the leather belt that held the dagger to his chest as he hurried out of their tent, Imogen at his side. They were late for the funeral ceremony—at least, that's what he assumed it was. The entire encampment was turning out in their finest: saffron robes edged in bright blue, with necklaces of bronze coins; festooned daggers and spears; hair greased with goat fat. A quarter mile away, at the trailhead for the path leading to the Home of the Dead, a group of bearers stood, supporting a litter that carried the body of the chief, which was covered with a shroud and surrounded by sprigs of fragrant herbs. It was midafternoon, the sunlight filling the valley and glinting off the freshly polished weaponry and jewelry of the gathering crowd.

"A funeral cortege," said Imogen.

"That was my guess," said Gideon. "You have to bury them fast in this heat."

As they hurried down the path, Gideon spied Garza near the head of the assembling throng, next to the litter and surrounded by various tribesmen. He looked troubled. They politely but firmly worked their way through the crowd.

Gideon touched Garza's arm. "Manuel," he said, his voice low. "This is an awful development. But you realize what this means—right? I've taken advantage of the distraction to get the last of the saddlebags. We just need to finalize a plan—*and* a backup."

Garza shook his head. "Can we talk later, please?"

"Like when? We can't take a chance on—"

"It's a *funeral*," Garza interrupted. "Do you mind?" Somebody was pulling at his sleeve and Garza turned toward the man, then disappeared. Already, it seemed the tribespeople were beginning to treat him with the deference befitting a chief.

Gideon felt Imogen pull him back. "Can't you see he's grieving? If not for himself, then for his wife. Give him a little space."

Her whisper was cut off by a high-pitched chant from the crone, her withered arms raised to the sun. She was flanked by the four priests in white robes, with long, grizzled, forked beards. They were each wearing a curious garment that looked like an apron. Their heads were bowed.

Lillaya spoke something—instructions to the crowd, as far as Gideon could tell—and the people began to fall in line, gathering for a procession to the tomb. Garza reappeared with Jelena and joined the front of the procession. Another singsong cry from the crone started the crowd moving. Several warriors then helped Lillaya into a sedan chair and she joined the slow-moving procession, directly behind the four bearded priests.

Soon a mysterious music rose up. He could hear what sounded like lutes, wooden flutes, rattles, and voices swelling in doleful song, all to the mournful cadence of a drum.

"Those lutes," whispered Imogen excitedly, glancing back at a group of musicians. "Identical to ones found in King Tut's tomb. And that sistrum—again, exactly like one in Tut's tomb. Incredible! This whole scene seems frozen in time from the days of the pharaohs."

The procession moved forward, at an agonizing shuffle, down the trail into the shadowy ravine leading to the Home of the Dead. The cavalcade strung out along the narrow way, and it took nearly an hour to reach the valley that contained the tomb they had helped build for the dead chief. The litter carrying the body, trailed by Garza, Jelena, Lillaya, and the priests, came to a halt before the peculiar raised table Gideon had noticed on his first visit to the valley. The stone table had long, narrow grooves carved along its edges. Apparently, it was going to serve as the stage for part of the coming ritual.

The crowd encircled the table at a distance. The wizened priests came forward while two workers transferred the dead chief to the table. The priests surrounded the body and began to lay out a series of bronze tools alongside it, many of them resembling crude surgical instruments. Meanwhile, the musicians continued playing, the sound of their ancient music filling the canyon and echoing off the cliffs.

A priest picked up one of the tools and held it toward the sun, his forked beard wagging as he intoned some sort of prayer in time to the dirge-like melody. The tool was a long hook, with a thin, sharp, spatula-like blade at the end. He heard Imogen draw in her breath.

Now the priest approached the corpse and gently propped its head on a wooden cradle. Another apron-clad priest came up beside him with an alabaster jar and knelt down. With a ritualistic motion, the first priest inserted the hook into the dead chief's nose, sliding it in until it encountered resistance, and then—with a sharp blow—he jammed it through the cribriform plate and deep into the brain. He gave it several deft twists. As the kneeling man held the jar below the corpse's nose, the priest withdrew the hook, making additional twisting motions that caused a portion of the corpse's brain to gush out in semi-liquid form, which the second priest neatly caught in the jar.

"Nice," Gideon murmured.

"Shh," said Imogen, watching with fixed attention.

With several additional insertions of the hook, the priest scraped out the rest of the brain into the jar, and it was set aside with a protective lid.

Now the priest picked up a curved bronze knife and made a deep cut along the left side of the chief's abdomen. A dark liquid immediately began to flow out, running down the grooves of the table and into a catchment basin below. The priest reached deep into the body cavity, knife in one hand, and much to Gideon's disgust he appeared to rummage about inside, making a series of cuts as he did so. Finally, he withdrew his gory arms, cradling the chief's heart in his hands, and carefully placed it on the stone table. He then removed the other internal organs—the stomach, intestines, liver, kidneys, spleen—which he meticulously arrayed around the body.

The haunting music and the endless booming of the drum continued unabated.

When the body cavity was empty, two long-robed women

approached the table, each carrying a tall clay amphora. One poured a dark liquid from her amphora into the cavity—Gideon caught the scent of wine—and the priests used linen cloths soaked in the same perfumed liquid to wash out the inside of the corpse. With more rolls of white linen, they carefully dried the body cavity, then proceeded to cleanse and wash the corpse with scented water from the second jar. The two women removed the amphorae, then returned with a series of bowls heaped with dried, ground spices of various bright colors, which the priests used to dust the inside of the body.

They then performed the same process on the heart, washing it with wine and carefully covering it with spices.

A priest now held the heart skyward; the music ceased; and in the resulting silence the priest intoned a prayer. He wrapped the heart in a linen sheet and placed it back in the chest cavity. Two men carrying long, coffin-like boxes came over and set the boxes down on either side of the corpse.

As the music swelled once again, all four priests removed the box lids to expose a white, crystallized substance. Using brass trowels, they first shoveled the loose material into the corpse, packing it well, then piled it over and around the body, heaping it up and pressing it firmly in place until the dead chief was entirely covered with a snowy heap of crystals.

Finally, with great deliberation, the four priests went around the table, washing the internal organs with wine and packing them in more of the white crystals. The music died away, the head priest offered another long prayer, and the ceremony came to an end just as the sun sank below the surrounding cliffs.

Imogen leaned toward Gideon. "What you just saw," she said, her voice trembling with excitement, "was the ancient Egyptian ritual of mummification. That white stuff is natron. What an incredible thing to witness in the twenty-first century."

In that moment a harsh voice from above split the air. The entire crowd looked toward it. Gideon frowned; this interruption was clearly not part of the ceremony. There, standing on top of the ridge at the head of the valley, flanked by a band of heavily armed warriors, was Mugdol, astride a camel. He made his way slowly down the path, his warriors following, and came to a stop on a small rise about twenty feet from the assembly. Lillaya spoke sharply, but he overrode her with a gesture and a sneer of disrespect. There was a murmur of displeasure from the assembled multitudes, but Blackbeard's forces stepped forward, raising their spears and daggers menacingly, and the voices subsided.

Mugdol opened his powerful arms wide, as if to embrace the tribe, and silence fell. He began to speak, slowly, distinctly, in a powerful voice that echoed the length of the valley, shaking his weapons as he did so.

"What's he saying?" Gideon asked Imogen.

"I think he's telling them he's the rightful chief; that Garza's a usurper, an outsider."

"Uh-oh."

Mugdol continued to speak and gesture, finally pointing a powerful arm at Garza, accusatory finger trembling with rage. The crone shouted again and a restlessness gripped the crowd. Now Jelena cried out sharply to Garza, and the cry was taken up by some—but not all—of the assembly.

"Jelena is urging Garza to stand up to Mugdol on her father's behalf," said Imogen. "Most of the villagers want him to as well. But a few . . . seem to agree with Mugdol."

Gideon looked at Garza. He was still standing in the forefront of the procession, Jelena at his side, confusion and anger on his face.

More shouts as those near Garza surged around him protectively. Blackbeard dismounted, drew his dagger, and came forward menacingly.

"He's announcing that he's the chief now," Imogen explained to Gideon.

The hubbub grew. Some people drew their daggers as if to block Blackbeard's path. Garza seemed paralyzed, as if uncertain how to respond to this development. Some in the crowd, led by Lillaya and Jelena, were now calling to Garza, clearly urging him to meet the challenge.

But Gideon knew that Mugdol and his men were too heavily armed. It would be suicide. He caught Garza's eye and shook his head. *No, no, no.*

That did it. Garza brusquely turned away and made a backhanded gesture of dismissal at everyone, Blackbeard and the villagers alike. He strode away, the crowd parting, and climbed the trail out of the valley.

With a great laugh of contempt, Mugdol waved his dagger at Garza's retreating form, shouting insults. His warriors followed suit, shaking their spears and jeering. Garza ignored it and vanished over the ridge. His sudden disappearance seemed to demoralize the assembled multitudes. Voices were raised in surprise and bewilderment. Jelena looked stricken.

Mugdol raised his hands again. *"Ti saji pinishti en ouroh! Empear moshi alla heamsi!"*

"I am now the Father," Imogen translated. "Death to the coward usurper."

As Mugdol continued the harangue, his warriors fanned out to contain the restless crowd. It was looking ugly—very ugly.

"I've seen enough," said Gideon, grasping Imogen by the arm and hurrying her along through the seething crowd. "We need to find Garza and get the hell out of here—before our heads really do end up on spikes."

38

Beyond the crowd they broke into a jog, trying to catch up with Garza on the trail, but he had either outpaced them or gone via some other route, and as deep twilight settled over the valley they arrived at an empty encampment.

They headed directly to their tent, and there Gideon paused.

"Are the supplies ready?" Imogen asked.

"The saddles are outside the tent, and I gathered the last of the saddlebags just before the ceremony."

"Good. You assemble everything while I grab the camels."

"And Garza?"

"He knows what this means. He'll show up."

She went off while Gideon went into the back of the tent, to the corner where he'd been stealthily assembling getaway supplies. He threw back a coverlet, exposing goatskins he'd filled with water the day before, along with some dried meat and dates in leather sacks. He carried the waterskins and food to a sheltered area outside the tent, then fetched the three crossbows and all the bolts they had fashioned. Imogen was right: whatever was happening in the Home of the Dead wasn't going to last long. Violence was brewing. They had to be gone before the populace returned.

Suddenly Garza appeared at the tent, exhausted and covered with dust.

"Where have you been?"

"I...I had to think. This is so sudden. We were planning to wait a week—"

"The time for waiting is over. Imogen's getting the camels. Help me with the last of these supplies."

A strange look came over Garza's face. "Gideon, you saw those people—they don't want Blackbeard to lead them. He's a tyrant!"

"None of our business."

"Yes, but..." Garza seemed reluctant to say more. "What if Jelena—and that hulking bastard...?" His voice trailed off.

Gideon could hardly believe this. *What a time for Garza to grow a conscience*, he thought. "Now that she's been married, Blackbeard isn't going to bother her. Besides, she's the daughter of the dead chief. She's still a princess."

"She stood up for me. You heard her. I've never run away from anything, I'll look like a coward—"

"You *had* to marry her. Remember? As I recall, you weren't too keen on the idea."

Garza didn't reply. He just shook his head.

"Look," Gideon said, his voice softening. "I get it. I can understand why you feel guilty. Maybe you're even a bit fond of her. But all we're doing is moving up our plans a little—plans that we'd already agreed on. You don't *really* want to stay here— you just don't want to look like a coward. And face it: you don't know the first thing about leading this tribe. These people have centuries of experience in this harsh environment. For better or worse, Blackbeard shares that experience—the beliefs, the rituals, that collective memory. The hard truth is that these people will be better off without us. And you know it. We don't belong here. If we stay, all we'll do is start a civil war. Your wife will die—and so will a lot of innocent people. If you go, they'll settle their differences and all will be well."

"Until they find the tomb's been looted, you mean."

"For God's sake, Manuel! Will you put your pride aside and listen to me? They're going to blame *us* for that—and by the time they find out, we'll be far away. This is all happening too fast and you're not thinking clearly. Remember: this whole thing was *your* idea. 'If it has value, we're gonna *steal* it'—your words to me, back at that bar on Thirteenth Street. We've come halfway around the world to realize *your* ambition. Now you can resurrect that Duesenberg factory, live that dream. You've got years—I have *weeks*. If I thought you were going to wimp out at the last minute, do you think I would have spent my last months on earth digging ditches and dying of thirst?"

He stopped, breathing hard. Garza's face was twisted in an agony of indecision. They had both raised their voices, and now silence fell. Gideon made an effort to calm himself, to gather his thoughts. Then he said, quietly: "Manuel, loyalty is both your greatest strength and your greatest weakness. You were loyal to Eli—and he screwed you. Now you feel loyalty to your wife of four days. To a dead chief whose language you barely speak. How about being loyal to *yourself* for a change? Your future is out there, just a few canyons away." He laid a hand on Garza's shoulder. "We've been through so much. Don't throw it all away now, partner—please."

In the silence that followed, Gideon saw Garza's face lose its indecisive look and become an expressionless mask. He drew a long, shuddering breath. And then he shook his head.

"You're right," he said. "Me and my misguided sense of

morality. I don't belong here—even when I'm with Jelena, *especially* when I'm with Jelena. I understand that. Eli owes me a debt, and I intend to collect…or die trying." He took Gideon's hand from his shoulder and grasped it firmly just as Imogen arrived with the camels out of the gathering dark.

"Bonding time, boys?" she asked as she expertly couched the four animals in the dirt before the tent.

"Just agreeing how much we're going to miss this paradise." Gideon hefted a saddle pad, threw it on the back of one of the camels. "Let's load up and get out of here."

39

Tʜᴇʏ ʟᴇꜰᴛ ᴛʜᴇ encampment via a route they hoped would make it look as if they'd escaped through the fog oasis. Then, at the eastern head of the valley, they turned and climbed a ridge until they were out of sight, at last circling back toward the westward trails leading to the Demon Valley and, ultimately, the treasure chamber. They trotted the camels as fast as they dared over the rugged terrain, the animals' long strides eating up the ground. The stars were out in all their glory, the moon not yet having risen. Imogen led the way, trailing the camel with the empty packsaddle on it, ready to be filled with treasure. Gideon brought up the rear. There were no hunting parties out. The ravines and ridges were sunken in darkness, the only light the feeblest glow of Jupiter, hanging in the west. But Gideon knew the moon, so recently full, would rise over the mountains in a few hours. For the time being it was a black night, making good cover; the three of them knew the way, while the camels, with their excellent night vision, knew where to put their feet.

They proceeded cautiously and in two hours had reached their objective. Nobody had spoken, and a silence like death reigned in the sunken valley. As they approached the vault door, Gideon saw it lying split on the ground, just as they had left it: two great slabs of stone. There was no sign of anyone else's presence. The torches they'd used were still propped up against it.

They dismounted, staking the camels in the sand. Gideon led the pack camel to the entrance of the vault and couched it there. He removed the leather bags hung on either side of the packsaddle, as well as the top pack, and opened them, ready to receive the treasure.

Using his fire drill, Garza lit three torches, placing one outside. They proceeded down the long passageway to the treasure chamber, where Garza affixed a second torch to light the corridor, placing the third inside the chamber itself. The feeble firelight glinted off the gold and jewels arrayed in rich splendor around the golden cabinet atop its plinth of stone.

"You take the left side," Gideon said to Garza, "I'll take the other. Imogen—"

"I'm not helping you loot," she interrupted. "I'm going to transcribe the text I found on that tablet."

"Fair enough."

"Don't break anything," she said. "Be respectful, please. Just take the gold and gems—not the fragile artifacts. And remember: nothing with writing."

Many of the offerings were heaped in alabaster bowls or contained in desiccated leather sacks and withered baskets. Gideon seized the closest bowl and carried it out into the night, emptying it into one of the panniers. Garza did the same. Back in the chamber, he realized they were only going to be able to take a small fraction of what was there, and that it would be smart to be selective. He picked up a leather sack, untied the brittle strings, which came off in his hands, and looked inside. In the dim light he could see that the sack was bulging with jewels. As he carried it out, however, the sack burst and the stones went skittering and bouncing over the stone floor—gorgeous golden diamonds of that same unique color, flashing with internal flecks of fire. Gideon dropped to his knees, gathering them up and stuffing them into his pocket.

"Forget that shit," said Garza.

"But these diamonds are—"

"A waste of time! There's tons more back there."

Gideon reluctantly abandoned his effort to retrieve the stones. He headed back to the chamber and grabbed another sackful of gems, this time cradling it on the way out before slipping it into one of the panniers.

As they went to and fro, lugging out the loot, Gideon was relieved to see that Garza was working quickly, even eagerly. Just the sight of the stupendous riches in the chamber had chased off his doubts. The heavy gold objects, the gems and semiprecious stones, the jewelry and necklaces and finely inlaid objects, were enough to incite a kind of delirium in them both.

"Don't take that!" Imogen said sharply, as Garza went to pick up a pair of gold jackals inlaid with lapis.

"Or *that!*"

Gideon sheepishly put down the golden scarab he was about to stuff into a sack. Imogen, crouching before the open cabinet, was staring at the inscribed stone within and scribbling notes in a notebook fashioned out of old cloth, occasionally barking at one or the other of them not to touch something that—obviously or not—she deemed particularly valuable or unusual. But Gideon didn't mind: there was so much stuff, such a superabundance of gold, silver, cut and uncut gemstones, that it hardly made a difference. Even after filling the panniers with millions of dollars' worth of plunder, they were hardly going to scratch the surface of the room's vast trove. He remembered her incredulous look when she'd first read what was on the tablet, and her allusion to the biblical commandments. But he was too busy now to ask questions—there'd be plenty of time for that later.

As they worked, the sky began to lighten in the east as the moon came up behind the jagged peak of Gebel Umm. As soon as it cleared the top, Gideon knew, it would become almost as light as day in the clear air of the desert. That light would be of great assistance in navigating the unfamiliar westward route through mountains and foothills to the far side of the range. If they pushed hard all the rest of the night, he figured, they would be well outside tribal territory by sunrise and therefore safe from pursuit. Once they reached the Nile, then they would face the additional challenge of smuggling the loot out of Egypt, but in quiet hours he and Garza had worked out what seemed like an almost foolproof scheme.

It was a matter of thirty minutes to fill the two panniers and the burlap top pack to bursting. The thief in Gideon felt rueful that they had taken so little, relatively speaking, and yet his conscience was glad that the vast majority of treasure would remain.

The eastern sky brightened as the moon rose behind the great outline of Gebel Umm. "Let's pack this on the camel and go," said Gideon.

"One more bag," gasped Garza, staggering up the corridor under the weight of an alabaster bowl full of golden necklaces, earrings, and heavy bracelets.

"The pack's too heavy already," said Gideon.

"Just this *one* more," Garza said, his face glistening with sweat.

Gideon shook his head. "Put it down. We can't risk laming the camel—then we'd lose everything."

With a muttered curse Garza left the bowl by the entrance.

The two men lifted the heavy panniers full of loot and hooked them, one at a time, on the packsaddle's metal rings. They hoisted the top pack in place and tied it down carefully with a linen cover. The camel groaned under the weight, its lips drawing back with displeasure, exposing its yellow teeth.

As they were about to mount up, Garza grabbed Gideon's hand. "Just one thing."

Gideon turned. "Yes?"

"What we talked about? Back there, in your tent?"

"What about it?"

"All that happened in the encampment—my marriage and the rest of it. Never bring that up again. What we're leaving behind, stays behind. That's past. It's like you said: my new life starts right now, with this treasure. So don't mention any of that again—to anyone. Ever."

"You've got my word."

Garza released his hand.

"Where's Imogen?" Gideon asked.

"Son of a bitch, she said she was coming right out." They dashed back into the chamber. Imogen was still crouched, notebook open, scribbling like mad with her improvised pencil, wisps of her hair escaping from beneath her head covering.

"Let's go!"

"Give me a damn moment!"

They waited, Gideon becoming increasingly exasperated. "Come on."

"I knew this was incredible, but...my God, I can hardly *believe*..." She mumbled to herself, her fingers flying over the pages as she copied the hieroglyphic symbols.

"Enough." Garza reached down and took her arm. "Up, *up*."

She tried to shake him off but he gently pulled her to her feet.

"Just one more line to copy."

They waited while she finished sketching a last few hieroglyphics.

"Haul ass!" Garza said, some steel in his voice this time.

They almost had to drag her out of the chamber. Back outside, the limn of the moon was just creeping above the jagged
top of Gebel Umm. They climbed onto their camels, the beasts
lurching to their feet with the usual roaring and bellowing of
complaint. The light of the moon now spilled into the valley,
bathing it in a crystalline silver glow, as they turned toward the
westward opening in the rock face and urged their camels forward.

Garza suddenly jerked to a stop. "Oh shit."

Gideon followed his gaze to see, arrayed along the rimrock to
the east, bathed in moonlight, a row of warriors astride camels.
The massive form of Mugdol was at the fore, sword at his side,
spear raised.

"*Rash a'urbouji!*" he yelled, stabbing the air with the spear as
he whipped his camel into a gallop along the ridge, heading toward the trail into the valley, followed by his howling mob of
warriors.

40

*G*o!" GIDEON CRIED, whacking his camel with the driving stick. The beasts hardly needed persuading, given the unholy shrieks of the horde on the ridgetop that filled the valley with blood-thirsty ululations. Gideon aimed his camel at the opening in the far rock wall and they galloped along the edge of the valley toward it. Looking over his shoulder, Gideon saw that Imogen was close behind, with Garza bringing up the rear, trailing the pack camel.

A galloping camel is more like a bucking bronco than anything else, and Gideon held on to the rings of his saddle for dear life as they went bounding and lurching across the sand. The pounding of the camels' pads on the ground was like the beating of drums, accompanying the whoops and cries of Blackbeard and his warriors.

They entered the narrow canyon and the walls quickly closed in on them. Its bottom was a floor of sand and gravel, almost flat, with steep hills of eroded sandstone on either side. Gideon whipped his camel again, feeling sorry for the creature but terrified about what would happen if they were caught. Imogen remained close behind but Garza, hauling the pack camel, was having trouble keeping up, the riderless beast showing reluctance to run as fast as the others. Gideon was glad they had taken care to tie the packs of treasure down tightly; the camel's motions were so violent, it seemed the panniers might fly off at any moment.

As they ran, bits of camel saliva flew back from the animal's rubbery lips, speckling Gideon's face and limbs. Their pursuers were now close to the bottom of the trail and would soon be chasing them on the flats—unfortunately, the carefully curated legends about the Valley of the Demons had obviously not deterred Mugdol from his revenge.

The narrow canyon made a gradual turn to the right, and then swung through a leftward arc. Thank God, Gideon thought, they had the moonlight to see by. But then again, every advantage they had, their pursuers had as well. If it became a flat-out race, they would lose. While Imogen had selected good camels, Blackbeard and his crew were far superior riders. They would inevitably catch up, and soon, and then the slaughter would commence.

Even as they raced along the canyon, Gideon's mind was furiously turning over the possibilities. They did have one advantage: crossbows. Blackbeard and his gang didn't even have simple bows—just spears and daggers. This would give them an edge as long as they weren't forced into fighting at close quarters. But better to avoid a fight at all.

"We can't outrun them!" Imogen cried from behind.

"I know—I'm thinking!"

"Think harder! They're gaining!"

But Gideon found it hard to think while filled with terror and being thrown up and down like a rag doll. The canyon made another turn and the wadi sloped ever so slightly downward. A side canyon entered from the right, and another from the left, then more and more as dry washes began joining the main wadi on both sides. Could they flee up one of these? But their tracks would be obvious, and besides none of them looked promising—they all seemed to box up, which would leave them trapped.

The crossbows. If they could take one of the side canyons and gain the tactical advantage of high ground, establishing a position where they could shoot down on their pursuers as they passed below, that might work. But they had to do it soon, while the warriors were still far enough behind.

"Just running is a losing strategy!" Garza yelled.

Ahead the main canyon narrowed once again, but to the right a twisting wadi seemed to form a path up and out, to a low saddle above the main canyon. It was just the setup Gideon was looking for. If they could get up there with their crossbows, they might be in time to fire down on Mugdol and his riders as they passed—and with total impunity, as the height was too great for thrown spears.

"On the right!" he called over his shoulder. "We're going up!"

Neither objected. As they galloped into the side-wadi, Gideon was forced to slow down so his camel could negotiate a bed strewn with rocks. He gave the camel its head and it picked its way through the boulder field. Now the wash mounted a narrow ravine, and the animals stumbled upward, heaving with exertion, between walls of stone. Soon they came to a tumble of boulders with very little room to pass.

"It's too hard on the camels," said Imogen. "We need to get off and walk."

They slid out of the saddles and led the animals by their halters through the tricky terrain. Up and up they went, until the wadi petered out in the depression Gideon had seen from below.

He turned his camel sharply to the right and they came out on the ridgetop overlooking the canyon. It was an excellent setup for an ambush. He could hear the cries of the warriors growing louder as they galloped down the canyon.

"Tie up the camels," he said, grabbing his crossbow. "We'll fire on my signal."

They wrapped the halter ropes around boulders and scrambled up the edge of the precipice to where it beetled over the canyon. The unholy din of the warriors grew still louder.

"When they come in sight," said Gideon, "don't aim for the men. Shoot their camels. They make a bigger target."

"Fuck that," said Garza. "First chance, I'm killing Blackbeard."

Gideon's reply was cut off by a swell of sound from below. He stared into the moonlight-drenched canyon and saw the first rider tearing around the bend—Blackbeard—followed by the others, robes flying.

Gideon notched a bolt, then cocked it. The others did the same. Their quivers stood beside them, each with a dozen bolts ready to go.

The group thundered down the canyon. Gideon took aim at the camel directly behind Blackbeard, tracked it, and waited for it to come into range.

"Fire!" Three crossbows snapped and the bronze-tipped darts shot downward.

With a bellowing screech, two camels went down, their riders flung off, robes gyrating. There was a moment of confusion, with the others reining in their camels, pulling spears out of scabbards and casting about. Mugdol, who was unhurt, wheeled about and cried out a command, pointing up toward their perch. Meanwhile, Gideon and the others had cocked their crossbows and nocked fresh darts. Gideon aimed at Mugdol's camel and fired, the other two quickly following.

"Keep firing!" he cried.

With another roared command, Blackbeard signaled for his warriors to ride past and get out of the line of fire. The riders whipped their camels forward and headed down the wash, angling toward the wadi that led up to their ambush place, abandoning the riders whose animals had been wounded.

"They're coming up after us," said Imogen.

"Fire again!"

Firing a third round into the rear guard of warriors, they managed to bring down another camel, but then the horde had gone past and there was no chance to fire a fourth.

"Time to run again," muttered Garza.

Slinging the crossbows and quivers over their shoulders, they jumped back on their camels and whacked them into motion. With more roaring and grumbling, the camels rose.

"Which way?" Imogen called.

"West. Along the top of the ridge."

As they accelerated to a gallop, Gideon could hear the clatter and shriek of their pursuers charging up the steep wadi. Soon their robed forms emerged at the top and the cries redoubled. With Blackbeard still in the lead, they charged along the ridge in furious pursuit.

"Where are we going?" Imogen yelled as they flew along.

"Who the hell knows?" Gideon yelled back.

41

THEIR CAMELS GALLOPED at terrifying speed, gravel flying in every direction from the leathery pads of their feet. Looking ahead, Gideon could see that the ridge ran forward in a straight downhill line. On either side were deep canyons, parallel ridges, and then still more canyons, all pitched at a descending angle. Far ahead, many miles away, the foothills smoothed out to a moonlit plain that seemed to stretch forever.

Glancing back, he saw Mugdol gaining, spear in one hand and reins in the other, with the rest of the warriors coming up behind. They were only about four hundred yards away now. Gideon redoubled his efforts, urging his camel forward.

"Faster!" Imogen cried. "We've got to go faster!"

But Garza had fallen behind again, struggling to drag the packed camel along with him.

Gideon reined back a little. "Manuel, go past me. I'll whip that sluggish thing's ass for you."

"Promises, promises."

Imogen and Garza rode past, and as they did so Gideon glanced behind again to see how quickly Blackbeard was catching up. He was startled to find that their pursuers appeared to have vanished.

"Where'd they go?" asked Imogen.

Gideon held up a hand for silence.

They halted. And now, in the quiet, they could make out the low thunder of galloping somewhere in the canyons below—apparently coming from both sides.

"They've divided," said Imogen as she strained to listen. "They're outrunning us—on either side—to cut us off in a pincer movement."

"Then we've got to do something unexpected," said Garza. "Like turn around."

"We're not going back," Gideon said.

"No, we're not. We turn around, go back up the ridge a ways, then drop down into a side canyon. Then we climb up one of these adjacent ridges and head westward again."

"It's a smart plan," said Imogen.

"Hell," said Gideon. "Fine."

They turned their camels and headed back up the ridge, Imogen riding ahead. This time they proceeded more slowly, trying to make as little noise as possible. After about a quarter of a mile they came to a slope leading into the right-hand canyon that, again, was too steep to ride down. The animals were exhausted anyway, their sides heaving, but they negotiated the rocky slope without further protests. The three soon reached the sandy bottom of the wadi, remounted, and went forward at a trot. Another quarter mile down the canyon, a slope on the right appeared to offer a way up the adjacent ridge. They turned out of the wash and climbed yet again, the camels struggling to find their footing. Halfway up, with their mounts blowing and grumbling, Gideon heard the telltale thud of camel pads somewhere below, echoing up the canyons.

He held up his hand. "Listen!"

The sound, surprisingly, was coming from *ahead* of them. Somehow, Mugdol had managed to cut off their escape route and was now coming back. Even as they listened, a silvery cloud of dust, illuminated in the bright moonlight, swept up from a nearby ridgeline, carried by the breeze. They were about to be cut off.

"Back!" Gideon cried. "Back into the canyon!"

Once again, they wheeled their camels around and sent them plunging back down the slope they had just climbed, the animals bucking in protest. Gideon grasped the front loop of his saddle with both hands, trying to stay mounted. At the steepest part of the ridge, Gideon heard a scream: Imogen's camel had lost its footing and was plunging forward, the animal skidding on loose rock. Twisting sideways, it came down on one shoulder. Imogen leapt off at the last moment, barely escaping having the animal fall on her. The camel cartwheeled, screaming in fear, gangly legs churning the air before at last finding the ground.

Gideon reined in his own camel and, holding its halter rope, jumped off the uphill side of the slope and raced over to Imogen, pulling his camel behind him. She lay on a sandy slope, dazed and filthy. Above, Blackbeard had appeared on the top of the ridge not three hundred yards away. With a roar of triumph, he urged his own camel toward them at a breakneck pace, a dozen warriors still mounted behind.

Garza had reined in his own camel just above Gideon's. He now pulled the crossbow off his shoulder and cocked it, fitting a bolt in the slot and aiming uphill. He fired. The shot was followed by a scream, and a camel went crashing to the earth.

"Are you all right?" Gideon asked, kneeling over Imogen.

"Shaken." She tried to rise, winced. "Help me up."

He grasped her around the shoulders, helping her to her feet. She had cut her forehead, and a thin stream of blood was running toward her temple. He dabbed it away with his robe.

She pushed it aside. "Get me back on the camel," she said, staggering a little.

Pulling his own beast behind him, trying to shut out the sound of the screaming horde, Gideon helped her over to where her camel was struggling to rise. Miraculously, the animal was a little skinned up but otherwise still sound. Garza unleashed another shot, and then another, briefly curbing the downward charge.

"Grab his lead rope," Imogen gasped. "Give it an upward pull."

Gideon did so and the camel, with a furious roar, regained its feet. Gideon heaved her into the saddle.

"Let's go!" she cried.

Gideon turned in time to see Garza's final shot flash through the air and bury itself in the neck of Mugdol's camel. The animal reared up with a furious squeal, then fell sideways, sending its rider somersaulting through the air. Without waiting to see more, Gideon grabbed his own saddle and hauled himself up, dangling and swinging even as his camel bolted after the others. They reached the bottom of the canyon and headed westward. But their pursuers had been only temporarily checked and Mugdol, apparently unhurt, was now riding another camel in hot pursuit. He was less than a hundred yards behind and catching up fast. Ahead, Gideon could see no escape—just a long, narrowing canyon with sheer sides. Over his shoulder, the yelling reached a triumphant crescendo as the band realized they were about to catch their quarry.

As they raced along the sandy wash, the ravine grew ever narrower, the sides pressing in, sheer black cliffs of stone. There was no escape either up or out—they could only continue forward. It was a race they would soon lose. The war cries of their pursuers echoed chillingly between the canyon walls. Blackbeard and his men were now virtually upon them.

Gideon heard a camel scream and glanced over to see Garza's mount going down, a spear sticking from its side. Gideon reined in his own camel and turned it around, unshouldering his crossbow, and Imogen did the same.

Garza scrambled up from the fall, grabbed the pack-camel's lead rope, swung up—then pulled the staggering animal around to face their attackers.

"Keep going!" he yelled at Gideon as he pulled out his crossbow, cocked it, and let fly a bolt at the approaching horde. He was almost out of ammunition.

"What are you doing?"

"I'm saving your ass!" Garza unleashed another bolt into the wall of riders piling down upon him, jostling into each other as they were forced together by the tightening cliff walls.

"You can't fight them all!" Gideon protested in disbelief.

"The hell I can't! Now *go!*" Garza, somehow managing to let fly the last of his bolts, was suddenly in the thick of the fight as the lead warriors reached him, some colliding with his mount amid a clash of spears, the savage roaring of camels, and the shrill ululating of the men. Abruptly, as Gideon stared in horror, he saw his friend surrounded by a strange coruscating light, flashing and winking in brilliant yellows, reds, blues, and greens: it was the gold and gems they had dreamed of and worked for so long, had labored so hard to take from the treasure chamber— erupting upward and outward into the air from burst saddlebags, obscuring Garza in a curtain of incalculable value as the camel thrashed and bucked, the ruptured bags spraying arcs of glittering stones.

"Garza!"

But the man and his glittering halo were obscured as a vast cloud of dust rolled down and covered the scene of battle. The last glimpse Gideon had was of Garza being thrown from his camel, crossbow in hand, his body blocking the constricted pass, like King Leonidas at the Battle of Thermopylae, amid a boiling turmoil of warriors.

"*Garzaaa!*" he cried.

"Gideon!" Imogen yelled. "If we don't go now we're *all* finished. Can't you see he's doing this to save us?"

Gideon wheeled his camel around and followed Imogen as she lashed her camel to a furious pace, feeling the stinging wetness of tears on his cheeks. They had lost Garza, lost the treasure, lost everything but their lives. As they barreled down the narrow canyon, the clash of battle receded. Gradually the ravine began to open up. Still they loped on, the camels falling into a rhythm of mechanical exhaustion. It seemed like they rode at that pace for hours—and then, quite suddenly, it was as if they passed through a magic portal into a vast desert sweeping to an infinite horizon, the stars and moon far above, a cool breeze playing about. On their own, the camels slowed into a walk and then continued to plod on.

They had left the tribal territory behind. When Gideon at last forced himself to look back, all he could see was a seemingly impenetrable confusion of ravines, peaks, precipices, and massifs mounting up, layer upon layer, to the distant summit of Gebel Umm, silver in the moonlight. They continued eastward in silence, across the vast desert, toward the Nile River.

42

THE CRIMSON SUN declined behind a limp row of palm trees lining the western shore of the Nile as the old boat chugged northward, belching a stream of diesel smoke. Imogen and Gideon stood leaning on the rail, watching in silence as the scenery slipped by in the evening light. After escaping both the mountain and their pursuers, the trip became for them a nightmarish four-day journey across a scorching desert. They were so plagued by mirages of distant water that when they at last reached the shores of Lake Nasser, Gideon could scarcely believe it was real. A dirt road had led them to a dusty village on the shore opposite the tourist attraction of Abu Simbel. Their robes were so filthy, and their faces so sunburnt, more than one person had mistaken them for local beggars and tried to drive them away. In Abu Simbel, an eternally smiling man with a single gold tooth had good-naturedly swindled them out of their camels and saddles. They had been too tired to argue. He had then kindly helped them buy tickets for the boat journey to Cairo, arguing furiously with the ticket seller to bargain the man down to a price they could afford, given how little he'd paid them for the camels. Despite carrying the grand and ironic name of the *Queen Nefertiti*, the boat was a shabby tourist cruiser that had seen better times. They were booked for the three-day trip into two windowless cabins deep in the belly of the ship, close to the throbbing engines.

They had nothing—no passports, no money, and no Western clothes. Gideon figured that when they reached Cairo, he could get a new passport from the American embassy. Imogen had promised to wire for money and loan Gideon airfare back home to New Mexico.

Leaning against the rail, watching the swirling muddy waters of the Nile pass by, Gideon felt almost paralyzed with grief for his lost partner. Once again, he reflected that he'd never met a man with such rare courage. And not just in holding off their attackers at the end, but throughout the entire journey: saving children on the sinking ferry even though he couldn't swim; rescuing the chief's daughter from the leopard. It had been a horrible way to die, slashed to pieces by Blackbeard and his men. He hoped to God it had been quick: the idea that Garza might have been captured alive by Mugdol made him feel sick.

Imogen had remained almost silent the entire trip. They stood pensively watching as the sun disappeared below the horizon and the air turned from yellow to green to an unnatural desert mauve. He noticed that Imogen had her soiled notebook in hand, at the rail, turning its crude pages pensively.

"You know," Gideon said, thinking out loud, "if we hadn't stopped to rob the treasure chamber, if we'd only kept going, Manuel would still be alive. I can't escape the feeling it's my fault he's dead."

"You can't think that way. You'll just cheapen his sacrifice. Besides, you decided together to rob the treasure."

She hesitated for a moment, then turned toward him. "Listen to me, Gideon." She spoke quickly, the words tumbling out as if they'd been bottled up for days. "We've got to figure out what we're going to say about all this. I mean, what our story's going to be."

"What do you think we should do?"

"I...I think we should keep our mouths shut."

"About the treasure?"

"About everything."

"Why?"

Imogen was silent for a long time. "Remember what I first thought I'd discovered back in that chamber? An early formulation—a first draft, if you will—of the Ten Commandments. Inscribed by the Pharaoh Akhenaten."

"I remember."

"To me, it's more evidence that Akhenaten was the father of monotheism—and in being so he changed the world."

"But I thought it was Moses who received the Ten Commandments, on a mountaintop in the Sinai—directly from God."

"Makes a brilliant story, doesn't it? And a great way to legitimize a new religion. But what I found in the golden cabinet seems proof that the Ten Commandments were first formulated in Egypt by Akhenaten. When the Egyptians rejected monotheism after his death, a follower—most likely a follower named Moses—left Egypt with other adherents to this new religion."

"To found Israel."

"Yes."

"That's crazy."

"No, it's not. It's not even a new idea. Sigmund Freud, of all people, claimed in his book *Moses and Monotheism* that Moses was Egyptian. Some biblical researchers go so far as to say Akhenaten *was* Moses, chased out of Egypt with his followers."

"So what does this have to do with our not telling of the discovery?"

"I'm getting there. Those inscriptions I deciphered indicate there was a split among the monotheists. Afterward, Moses led one group—the main group—east to Israel. But another, much smaller group split away from them and went south to Gebel Umm. They were no doubt the ancestors of our little tribe. They carved the commandments into that tablet and placed it in that golden cabinet, their very own Ark...the location of which was recorded on the Phaistos Disk. They haven't exactly thrived over the centuries, as you know, but it's probable they started out as a far larger group—and as we've speculated, it's also possible several of those disks were carried by proselytizing adherents to other areas of the world."

"Why did the two groups split?"

"Well..." Her voice, which had been so urgent, trailed off. "Doctrinal differences."

"What do you mean?"

"The group that fled south had an Eleventh Commandment."

"*Eleven* commandments?" It sounded like a joke.

"Eleven is the most sacred number in Egyptian numerology. Having only ten would feel incomplete to an ancient Egyptian."

"What did this Eleventh Commandment say?"

Imogen shook her head.

"It's that bad?"

"It wasn't a commandment in the form we've come to know," she said. "It—well, it was more of a disturbing prophecy. *Proclamation* might be a better word. On the nature of the One God."

"So? Spill it. Stop being coy."

"It was so strange I'm not sure my translation is accurate. Besides, I...would hate to burden you."

"You're kidding, right? *Burden* me?"

She shook her head. "Trust me, you're better off not knowing. You and everyone else."

"Are *you* burdened by it?"

"Let me put it this way: I'd give almost anything not to have read it."

He couldn't help but laugh. "Don't tell me you believe it, whatever it is? You just said you're unsure of the translation. And it's not like we're talking about the literal word of God here: it's just some disaffected, heretical group of ancient Egyptians or something. False prophets weren't exactly a rare thing in that era."

She said nothing, turning over the notebook in her hands as if it were a sort of worry stone. "The main point is, we can't tell anyone about what we found. The tribe would be overrun and destroyed. All the secrets they've been guarding—and I believe they *have* been actively guarding them these many centuries—will end up in museums. The tribe itself will be relocated to government housing and eventually cease to exist. And the world will become a poorer place."

"What about Manuel's death? What do we tell his siblings?"

"That he was brave and saved our lives and died during an expedition in the desert." She glanced at him. "You didn't tell anyone else about your discovery, right? The secret of the Phaistos Disk?"

Gideon shook his head. "No. Not that anyone would believe us. All we have for evidence are those scribbled notes of yours."

"Oh, someone would believe us," Imogen said.

"How can you be so sure?"

"Because…" She hesitated, a faint tremor in her voice. "I know Eli Glinn will believe us."

Thunderstruck, Gideon stared at her. "You know Glinn?"

"I'm his niece."

Gideon went mute as he tried to process this.

She ran one hand along the rail. "Eli helped raise me when I was orphaned by a plane crash. He put me through Westminster School and Balliol. I stayed on at Oxford for graduate work. I've been freelancing as an archaeologist and Egyptologist in Cairo, and he called me up with an unexpected favor to ask—an assignment. He explained how he'd discovered that you and Manuel had stolen the Phaistos Disk translation and were apparently headed to the location it revealed. He'd managed to track you as far as Safaga. He asked me to talk my way onto your expedition and then report back to him what you found."

"And you said yes? Just like that?"

"I couldn't exactly refuse him. Besides..." She paused. "The Egyptian Middle Kingdom really is my area of expertise. And it wouldn't have been the first time I'd done work for EES."

Gideon felt like he'd been sucker-punched. He stared at her. "You dirty little liar!"

She shrugged. "We've been lying to each other all along."

"Maybe, but I finally told you the truth."

"And so have I."

Gideon gathered himself to retort, but to his surprise nothing came to mind. She was right. "So you're going to report back to Eli?"

"Of course."

"What are you going to say?"

"That we found nothing."

"Really? And why is that? Why agree to this mission, risk your life, if you weren't going to see it through to the end?"

"I'd always planned to see it through to the end. But after all that's happened... well, I just can't rat you out like that." She looked out toward the far bank. "Don't think it's easy for me. I know Eli and his ways even better than you do, but he was still a kind of surrogate father. At least, he tried to be."

"I can imagine."

She flared up. "He was very kind to me, and he did his best."

"So what will you tell *him* about Manuel? About the treasure chamber—and the tablet?"

"Oh, I'll make sure Eli has enough closure to content himself with. I'll inform him, through our private back channel, that Manuel died and was buried in the desert; that the expedition was a total bust; and that you went off, disappointed, to your cabin to..." Her voice trailed off as she seemed to catch herself.

"To what?"

She did not answer right away. "Eli also told me about your terminal condition."

"Of course he would." He could see her eyes fill up.

"Look. The more I got to know you two—especially after we reached the village—the more I realized I wanted to come down on your side, not Eli's. I wanted to be on your side particularly, Gideon, because..." She stopped, as if to consider her words carefully. "Anyway, I can't count the times I wanted to tell you all this, but I never seemed to find the right moment. I'm sorry."

Gideon shook his head. It was all too much. Losing the treasure, losing Manuel, and now this confession. Eli Glinn. A sect who believed in a mysterious and apparently frightening Eleventh Commandment. *There's so little time.* Of course she didn't want to fall in love with a dying man. None of it seemed real.

"The best thing," said Imogen in a firmer voice, "is for us to get our stories straight and make sure no one ever, *ever* finds out about that chamber. You understand? *Nobody* must know."

"As you said, I'm going back to my cabin. To die."

She flinched, as if in pain. She hesitated for a moment. And then—whether on impulse or premeditation he could not tell—she flung the notebook into the Nile, where it bobbed for a moment before sinking into the murky water.

"When the world is ready," she said, "the chamber will be opened. And the truth—if we choose to believe it—will be known."

Epilogue

THE SUN WAS hanging low in the sky when Gideon drove along the rutted road to his cabin, pulled up beside the shabby lean-to stacked with firewood, and killed the engine. He glanced out briefly at the surrounding scenery, gauging it with an appraising eye: summer would be early this year. Then he got out, whistling tunelessly under his breath and pulling a sheaf of mail and a small sack of groceries from the passenger seat as he did so. A long, narrow *pain d'epi* stuck up from the sack like a flagpole; while he considered himself a gourmet chef, the art of bread baking was a skill that had always eluded him. Besides, there was a place in Santa Fe that made the best French bread he'd tasted this side of the Rive Gauche.

He stepped up onto the porch, kicked open the screen door—this far up in the mountains and away from civilization, he never bothered to lock anything—and walked through the timbered living room into the kitchen alcove, where he dumped everything on the counter. Still whistling—the tuneless ditty had now morphed into Charlie Parker's "Confirmation"—he pushed the mail aside and plucked the groceries out of the bag:

bread, cheese, arugula, half a pound of Culatello di Zibello, and a few other delicacies, which he stored in their proper places. He rinsed his hands in the sink, dried them on a dish towel, then looked around. Was there anything he'd forgotten to do?

No. There was nothing.

The cabin was very quiet, with only the sigh of a breeze in the great ponderosa pines outside. As he listened to the whispering of the trees he realized what a strange feeling it was: to have done everything necessary. Not just paid his property taxes or finished that E. M. Forster novel on the bedside table or patched that elusive leak in the roof—but *everything*. He glanced around the cabin, his gaze falling on one treasured possession after another. It had taken him years to find them, collect them, even steal them—but he had taken only days to determine their ultimate fates. The paintings he owned would all go to the New Mexico Museum of Art. His treasured cookware—the copper pans and French rolling pins and the lovingly cured iron skillet he'd inherited from his grandmother—would go to a friend and fellow chef he knew in Los Alamos. And his pride and joy—an antique third-phase Red Mesa Navajo blanket that lay across his bed—would go to Alida Blaine...if she'd accept it. As for the rest, cabin included—it would remain unlocked and available to anyone who wanted to use it...until it was reclaimed by time and decay, which eventually took everything.

Gideon was well aware that, in the two weeks since he'd returned from Egypt, these periods of reflection had grown more persistent. While on the expedition, and especially while living with—and escaping from—the tribe, he'd been too busy to think much about his terminal situation. Now that he was home, however, and having—thankfully—heard nothing from Eli Glinn, the quietness and solitude had allowed him to dwell on just how short a time he had left.

The strange thing was, he felt fine. His health seemed to be excellent. The various ordeals in southern Egypt had left him physically unscarred. If anything, he was as fit now as he'd ever been in his life. What a supreme irony, then, that Glinn's words—words the man had uttered the very first time Gideon met him—came to mind now: *The end typically comes very fast, with little or no warning. You will live a normal life for about a year— and then you will die very, very quickly.*

About a year. There was a chance, small but definitely quantifiable, that he might last longer. The future was inherently unknowable, and miracles did happen. And who knew if the strange "lotus" he had ingested on the Lost Island, which had so benefited Glinn's own health, might somehow mitigate his condition? But it seemed unlikely, given what the neurosurgeon had said when he'd examined Gideon's latest cranial MRI: *The progress of the AVM has been textbook, unfortunately. So yes, I would say two months is a likely time frame.*

And that had been just over two months ago.

Gideon's whistling died away. Pulling his phone out of his pocket, he paired it with a Bose portable speaker, dialed up Spotify, and selected one of his jazz playlists: Charlie Parker could do a much better job with "Confirmation" than he could. The sounds of a tenor saxophone filled the cabin, and Gideon put down the phone; he marveled that gigabit broadband Internet could now reach even so remote an outpost as this. Even in his relatively short lifetime, the world had changed—and so fast.

Moving more purposefully now, energized by Bird's bebop riffs, he placed the *pain d'epi* on his Boos cutting board, pulled off two of its crusty ends and, cutting each in half lengthwise, quickly fashioned sandwiches from the cured ham, arugula, and ripe Camembert, topping the ingredients with a smear of the truffle aioli he'd whipped up the day before. A thin drizzle of

DOP balsamic vinegar was the finishing touch. He moved the two small sandwiches from the cutting board to a plate, tucked the mail under one arm, grabbed a bottle of Lagavulin and an empty glass, and then—balancing everything precariously— kicked the screen door open again, walked out onto the porch, and took a seat in one of two weather-beaten Adirondack chairs that were placed there.

Leaning back, he surveyed his surroundings. The Jemez Mountains rose up protectively around the bowl-like valley that cradled his house, their flanks studded with majestic ponderosa pines. Straight ahead, between the mountainsides, the valley fell away into distant foothills that graded into the stark red deserts of New Mexico. The sky was a pale blue, touched here and there by Japanese brushstrokes of cirrus clouds. Gideon poured himself a generous splash of scotch, closed his eyes, and took a long, reverent sip. He let the heavy, peaty single-malt linger in his mouth for a moment, then swallowed, opened his eyes again, and turned his attention to the mail.

There wasn't much of it: he'd always managed to stay off mailing lists. The day before he and Garza had departed for Egypt, he paid all his bills three months in advance. There was a letter from the HR department of Los Alamos National Laboratory; he chucked it away like he might a Frisbee. There was an invitation from the Yazzie Gallery in Albuquerque, admitting two persons to a special preview of their forthcoming exhibition of Georgia O'Keeffe's early Precisionist-style work. Ten years before, such an invitation might have aroused a strong interest in him—of a predatory and not entirely licit nature. But he'd given that kind of thing up. Besides, the preview was still over a month away.

Putting this aside, he arrived at the final piece of mail: a battered postcard depicting the Great Sphinx of Giza. He held it up, curious. It looked as if it must have traveled around the world a dozen times. Not only was it creased and soiled, but his address had been scrawled in almost indecipherable letters, abraded by travel. The postmark was from Cairo, dated a week earlier. Curiously, there was no message or note on the card. Instead, there was only a symbol, evidently scribbled in a hurry:

Gideon stared at it for a moment. It couldn't be. But then again, it must: the postcard could only be from one person: Garza. And it could only mean one thing—he'd survived.

Gideon felt a swelling of indescribable emotion. Garza had promised to let him know if, should they get separated during the expedition, he had managed to survive…and this was his fulfillment of that promise. It was incredible. Somehow, Garza had saved him and Imogen, allowed them to escape—and then on top of that he'd managed to survive Blackbeard and his vengeful horde, as well. How was it possible?

Gideon took another sip of scotch and stared at the dusty postcard, shaking his head, his emotions finally boiling over into a peal of laughter. He turned the card over in his hands. The man was resourcefulness personified, the ultimate survivor. It was just like the ferry sinking, with him showing up out of the blue, against all odds. No wonder Eli Glinn had selected him as his lieutenant. Garza was truly a cat with nine lives.

Had he somehow recovered the treasure? But no—that was too much to hope for. Just his surviving was more than enough. Besides, Garza would have used the postcard to let him know.

At the thought of that vast treasure, Gideon stirred. He

reached into the pocket of his faded jeans and pulled out a precious stone: a flawless diamond, perhaps five carats, of a deep saffron color. He held it up to the sun, now falling behind the fringe of pine trees, marveling at the way the light turned the jewel to liquid fire. This was the one—the only one—that had made it all the way home, unbeknownst to him, in the inner pocket of his filthy robe. He was, in fact, unpacking his stuff and getting ready to toss the shabby garment away when the stone dropped out.

He carefully placed the diamond on the wide red cedar arm of the chair, then raised the sandwich and took a bite. Munching contentedly, he began planning what he would do tomorrow. There was a particular hole about a mile up Chihuahueños Creek, which he had been saving for a long time, where a large rock had snagged a deadfall. In the deep scoop of water behind that obstruction, he knew in his bones there lurked a wily old battle-scarred cutthroat trout. He'd left that trout alone, waiting for something special. And now that something had arrived—in the form of a postcard. Tomorrow, *truite amandine* paired with a flinty Graves would do very nicely for his daily meal.

Finishing the sandwich, he glanced back at the small but exquisite diamond. Only one—but it was enough.

You know how much time is allotted you, the neurologist had told him. *Do something worthwhile with the time you have left.* And as he reflected on the events of the last two months—the triumphs, the letdowns, the surprises, the moments of beauty and fear and greed and compassion that had together made up their unraveling of the mystery of the Phaistos Disk—he realized that it was, in its own way, a microcosm of how he'd lived his entire adult life. That it had, in fact, been an adventure most eminently worthwhile.

And then there was the shock of its conclusion, and what they had found in the treasure chamber. Imogen had refused to tell him what it meant; what that last commandment—if it was a commandment at all—had been. *When the world is ready*, she had said, *the chamber will be opened. And the truth—if we choose to believe it—will be known.*

Gideon took another sip of scotch. He stretched, then settled himself more comfortably in the chair. That day, and that truth, he reflected, could wait until after he was gone. And with that, his thoughts dissolved into memories: of avenging the death and disgrace of his father; of grappling with a trained assassin atop a crumbling smokestack; of stealing a page from perhaps the world's most valuable manuscript, and getting away with it; of discovering a living, breathing creature the world had always consigned to myth and fable. He shook these and other memories away with a smile. He had tricked, talked, and fought his way through enough adventures to last a dozen lifetimes. Now the ultimate adventure was approaching. When that happened—tomorrow, the week after, the month after—it was a mystery he felt prepared for.

But right now, he had a more immediate concern: a certain fat trout, sleeping in the creek that sparkled along its course out of sight over the rise of land.

He stretched once more, then winked at the setting sun. And it was without surprise that he noticed it winked back at him.

New York City

Aʟᴍᴏsᴛ ᴛᴡᴏ ᴛʜᴏᴜsᴀɴᴅ miles to the northeast, the sun had set. In Lower Manhattan, evening was already in full swing. From the windows of his penthouse in the building on Little West 12th Street, Eli Glinn—a piece of paper in one hand—looked down at the Millennials and Generation Zs and slack-jawed tourists milling around outside the restaurants and bars below. While the Meatpacking District was no longer the hippest scene in Manhattan—that transitory claim currently belonged to the Lower East Side—weekends were still busy with the B&T crowd.

After several minutes during which nothing moved except his eyes, Glinn turned away from the window and faced the interior of his apartment. While all the equipment and mechanical contrivances once necessary for his physical limitations had been removed, very little furniture had been added, and the space retained a spare, Zen-like asceticism. The various computers, web intercept devices, and other surveillance and data-gathering equipment he'd retained after the dissolution of Effective Engineering Solutions had been relegated to the floor below. The rest of the building had been leased to an independent film production company, who'd been delighted to find such a vast soundstage—formerly the central laboratory of EES—near the southern tip of Manhattan.

Now Glinn walked slowly and thoughtfully forward, seated himself in one of two 1958-vintage Arne Jacobsen Egg Chairs, and returned his attention to the piece of paper. It was a letter, scrawled with a fountain pen in a confident hand. He re-read the final paragraphs.

There's nothing else to tell. Dr. Crew never suspected I was acting as your agent—as you'd predicted in the initial briefing, he was more interested in the romantic possibilities than in questioning my background. And while Manuel Garza seemed naturally suspicious of everyone, he never connected me to you. Dr. Crew and I went our separate ways in Cairo. He, not surprisingly, was headed back to his cabin in New Mexico.

We avoided speaking of the subject of Mr. Garza's death in the Eastern Desert. Without wishing to sound sentimental about it, my own belief is that the man died of heartbreak. He seemed overwhelmed by the rigors of the journey—and, particularly, by the disappointment of finding nothing at the end but broken dreams.

In truth, I have to admit my own role in this failed expedition has left me emotionally and spiritually exhausted. I am going away for a time, perhaps a long time, and will be out of reach even of you. I hope you'll understand, Uncle, that while I will always be thankful for your guidance and assistance over the years, I don't believe I will be able to accept any future assignments. Please always remember, though, that wherever I am I will think of you with affection.

The letter was unsigned, but Glinn knew the handwriting well and could mentally add the missing signature: Imogen Blackburn.

Even more slowly, he placed the letter on the cherry-and-glass Noguchi table before him. In addition to furnishing Imogen with a first-class education, Glinn had taught her numerous things not on the Oxford University curriculum: how to obtain a false identity; how to launder money; how to lie successfully under interrogation. When she wanted to, Imogen could be an excellent liar. That is why Glinn was surprised the lies in this letter were so patently false.

What was the reason? Had she fallen for the charming Gideon Crew? But no—Gideon had flown back to Albuquerque alone; Glinn had already checked the manifests. Had she been turned? Yet the individual facts in her letter rang true. Gideon had gone home without baggage. Garza had vanished from the radar; if he wasn't dead, he might as well be. Yes, the facts rang true—and yet he felt certain the letter, as a whole, was not.

Something had happened out there in the wastes of southern Egypt. If they had reached the location of the Phaistos Disk, which wasn't even clear, they had at least brought nothing back. But had they actually found something? Had he been deceived? While he was sure the letter was a tissue of lies, he had no idea where its germ of truth might be.

Glinn took in a deep breath, then slowly exhaled. As he did so, he was reminded of how much he'd grown used to having a fully functional body again. One that did as it was told. Strange that, after those years of crippling difficulty, he could forget so quickly.

There was something else he had realized, as he'd brooded over—no, that was not quite the correct term—*taken stock* of his life over the last several weeks. He realized his memory of Sally

Britton: the one and only love of his life, the woman he'd lost through his own damnable egotism...had, sadly, begun to fade. Captain Britton deserved far better than to be forgotten, even temporarily, in his delight at regaining use of his limbs.

Here was an ironic twist of fate that Glinn—master of irony—could readily appreciate. Quite by accident, in their successful scheme to distract him into lowering his guard, Gideon Crew and Manuel Garza had rewoken that memory. What Glinn had first believed to be anger at the two for humiliating him was, in reality, anger at his own forgetfulness. Seeing her on that grainy video, hearing her voice again, had driven this forcefully home. Providence had given him a new lease on life: and there was no better way for him to live it than by honoring Sally Britton's memory and never allowing himself to forget again.

What would she say, were she here now? *Let it go, Eli.*

Let it go. Gideon Crew: there was nothing Glinn could do that would make a difference to Gideon. Best leave him in peace. Manuel Garza—the man had been his loyal aide-de-camp, both in the military and for over a dozen years in private life. Dead or alive, this insurrection of his was long in coming, and it could be forgiven. And Imogen...Imogen had her own life to live, and Glinn no longer had a right to intrude upon it.

I don't know much about poetry, but what I know I could share with you. And I could love you, Eli...

Letter in hand, Glinn leaned over toward the one mechanical item he allowed in the room—a micro-cut paper shredder, with a security rating of P-6 as measured by the Deutsches Institut für Normung—and slipped the paper into it. With a whisper, it vanished into confetti.

Then he sat back again. His book of W. H. Auden poems was in the next room, but for the memory that came ghosting up to him now he didn't need it. It was when he'd first met Sally

Britton: in a leafy New Jersey suburb, outside a neat Georgian house. He had been waiting at the curb, and she'd approached him with all the authority, self-discipline, and confidence of the ship captain she was. And she was beautiful. On the spot, Glinn had offered her a job. And in return, she had smiled and quoted Auden. Closing his eyes and leaning back ever so slightly, Glinn's own lips formed the faintest of smiles as he remembered her words, as vividly now as if she had spoken them that very afternoon:

> All the little household gods
> Have started crying, but say
> Good-bye now, and put to sea.

Two Months Later

An unusual haze hung over the upper reaches of the Nile; the sun, rising sluggishly in the east, was slow to burn it off and expose the desolate region known as the Hala'ib Triangle. First to be illuminated were the miles of trackless desert sands, stretching to the west. Next, the light reached a slow upwelling of foothills, punctuated by dry washes: auguries of the mountains to come. Next came Gebel Umm itself, its stern peak turned to flame by the sun's ascent, the fire creeping down rugged flanks.

At last the sun, rising higher still, penetrated the deep green bowl of the hidden valley beyond the mist oasis. Like a curtain lifting, it revealed clusters of tents, flocks of goats, herds of somnolent camels resting beneath groves of trees, and—near the far end of the valley—long lines of irrigated fields: recently turned earth that had been sown with wheat or barley, judging from the green shoots just beginning to sprout from the manure-enriched soil. Moving on, the curtain of light illuminated an escarpment in the center of the valley, then fell on the large tent atop it—dyed a deep yellow, bordered with a geometric design in black—that belonged to the chieftain of the tribe.

At that precise moment, the flap of the tent was thrown open. This appeared to be a signal, because immediately afterward the flaps of all the tents in the village below opened as well and their occupants emerged: some alone, others holding the hands of children, spouses, or aged parents. With a single purpose, they came forward silently until they were gathered below the narrow promontory that jutted, like the bow of a ship, from the escarpment.

When they had gathered, a young woman emerged from the tent. She was tall and slender, with kohl-rimmed eyes, dressed in a simple yet beautiful robe of a flaxen material that shimmered in the light. The crowd, which had begun to murmur among themselves, fell silent. All eyes turned to the dark entrance of the tent.

A minute passed, then two. And then a warrior emerged: muscular, deeply tanned, with a luxuriant beard and tightly curled hair that reached almost to his shoulders. He was wearing an ankle-length robe the color of saffron, and he carried a tall staff—the symbol of leadership, to be wielded only by the Father of the tribe. In his leather belt was tucked, not a dagger, but the glittering steel sword that was the pride of the settlement. On one wrist the man wore a bracelet of human molars; on the other, a wristwatch made of eighteen-karat gold.

The chief stepped up to the young woman, then the two of them made their way to the edge of the narrow promontory—the place chieftains had used for centuries to address the people—and stood shoulder-to-shoulder. He looked down at the assembled multitude for a moment, and then—with a sudden movement—balled his hands into fists and held them out at shoulder level, raising his staff.

"*Ti saji manyechem!*" he said, his clarion voice ringing across the valley like a bell. *"Yor hagashna gron'alla samu heamsi epouroun!"*

At this, a cheer erupted from the crowd. *"Epouroun!"* they cried. *"Epouroun!"*

Now from one of a cluster of tents behind the chief's residence an ancient, hag-like woman emerged, her body bent from long years, dressed in goatskins and wearing a veil. Slowly, painfully, she approached the chief, supporting herself with canes fashioned from human bones. As she came up on his other side, the warrior was flanked simultaneously by extreme age and extreme beauty.

Slowly, the chief lowered his arms and let the point of his staff rest on the rocky ground. Chest swelling, he began again. *"Ti saji walikana korog wan…wan…"*

Over his shoulder, without turning his head, he murmured to the old crone: "What's the word for 'crops' again?"

"Susuman," she murmured back.

"Right, right. And 'good health'?"

This time, it was the young woman who replied. *"Kango douru."*

The man raised his staff again, shaking it to emphasize his point. *"Ti saji walikana korog wan susuman!"* he proclaimed. *"Wig walikana ne kango douru, epouroun!"*

Epouroun was the plural form of the tribe's word for "chief."

Another thunderous cheer erupted from the crowd at this promise of an end to seasonal hunger and malnutrition—thanks to the newly planted crops that would ensure a bountiful supply of grain, year-round, irrigated by a clever system devised by the new chief.

Now Garza paused to survey the clamoring people—*his* people—spread out below. He didn't like to admit it—after all, he'd always worked in the background, shunning the spotlight—but this daily address had become one of the highlights of his day. Whereas the previous chief, his father-in-law, had used this bully pulpit only for occasional proclamations or warnings, Garza and his wife Jelena, who ruled together, used it every morning. Not only did the daily speeches force him to learn the language, but he'd found that the people were more content if they were kept abreast of what was going on. And every morning Jelena or Lillaya related a story of the tribe's history and mythology that never failed to interest Garza. There was so much going on—the pulley system he'd improvised, while still equal parts prisoner and slave, had been only the tip of the iceberg. In addition to designing a new irrigation system, he'd also moved to design and build stronger fortifications and fashion better weapons. He had taken steps to block and camouflage the approaches more thoroughly. He sensed that someday, somehow, the outside world would inevitably intrude, but not—he was determined—for a very long time. Certainly there would be no more luckless adventurers stumbling into this little paradise; no more heads mounted on stakes around the decapitation pit.

With another deep breath, he launched into the next part of his speech—a part he'd memorized the night before with coaching from Lillaya. He told the gathering that, starting today, he was abolishing the tomb labor detail. There would be no hours wasted building a grand memorial in which to house his own remains—something he'd been unaware was in the offing until recently. Instead, the Home of the Dead would become a public graveyard for the entire tribe—a home of eternal rest for everyone, not just the chiefs. The goal he shared with Jelena was to preserve, as much as possible, the tribe's ancient way of life and heritage against the encroachments of the modern world. He had been able to bring about some welcome changes by applying his knowledge of engineering and medicine, but the last thing he wanted to do was "save" them in some way. The ancient and disciplined way of life enjoyed by these so-called primitive people was just as fulfilling and rich as anything offered by the modern world. For the first time in Garza's ambitious and striving life, he felt he had found his place.

As he finished his new pronouncement about the valley of the tombs, another cheer went up—and nobody cheered louder, he noticed, than those he recognized as his former fellow toilers in the tomb field.

After a hurried trip to Cairo to fulfill a promise to his partner, Garza had made sure that every last bit of treasure was returned to the chamber. When he assumed the chieftainship, Lillaya, the head priestess, and the four subpriests had divulged their knowledge of the sealed chamber and how they had protected its wonders over the centuries. But through cautious questioning he realized, with huge surprise, that they had lost all specific knowledge of its significance ages ago. Beyond the gold and gems he had returned, they had no knowledge of what lay within the chamber, nor had they any notion of how to read hieroglyphic writing. All that survived was a worship of the sun and a profound determination among the priesthood to protect the contents of the sealed vault... forever.

As the roars continued to echo across the valley, Garza, planting his staff firmly again in the dusty ground, took another look around. How strange life was, he reflected. For years he'd felt restless, unrewarded, and unfulfilled. To think he'd believed that looting the treasure chamber and becoming immensely rich would be the answer. What a fool he had been; *these* people, *this* life, and above all *this* woman next to him were the answer he'd been searching for.

It was, in a way, miraculous. His mind wandered back to that transformative moment when he wheeled to face Blackbeard and his onrushing horde of killers. He had pivoted his camel—carrying the bags of treasure—and charged headlong into the attackers, with Blackbeard at the fore. He was sure he would die, and hoped only to save his friends. As he'd fired his last bolt, the dust had come down like a curtain, and the clash of camels and slashing daggers had ruptured the bags, spilling gold and gems everywhere just as he was thrown from the saddle. And the world had gone black.

When he woke, only minutes later, all had changed. He lay on the ground amid a heap of gemstones and gold, covered with the same, and all around him the warriors had dismounted and stood in a circle, staring with fear and astonishment. As he struggled into consciousness, they began prostrating themselves, one by one. Blackbeard lay nearby, dead—Garza's final crossbow bolt buried in his heart. The abrupt death of Mugdol, combined with his own unexpected baptism in a treasure they had no idea he was carrying, had—he was to learn—given the warriors the notion he was a being endowed with supernatural power. This in turn had given Garza the opportunity, using a combination of gestures and broken phrases, to explain that the treasure belonged to the tribe; that he was returning it to its rightful place; and that henceforth he would be its protector. They had bundled him on a camel and gathered up the treasure, then carried him back into the village, proclaiming him chieftain in accordance with his father-in-law's wishes.

His mind returned to the present. As the echoes of the cheering continued to sound, Jelena stirred beside him and took his hand. He smiled at her. In this capable, accomplished woman, he had at last found a life's partner not only wise beyond her years, but loyal as well. How strange life was, indeed. Gideon had told him to be loyal to himself for a change, and how true that was. Standing here on this promontory of rock, co-leader of these ancient and worthy people, was surely the last thing he could have ever have imagined to be his fate. And yet it now felt like the one challenge he'd been preparing for his entire life.

"How's this for loyalty, partner?" he said under his breath.

He felt Jelena move his hand slowly until it rested on the center of her belly. He glanced at her again and saw the answer to his unvoiced question in her eyes. The tribe, noting the movement and its significance, redoubled their cheers. He passed the staff to her. Taking a deep breath, she began to tell a story, her voice rich and assured. He was able to get the gist of it, a fascinating tale that went back to the mythical founding of the tribe, explaining how everything that was to happen had begun in precisely this way: a woman with child.

When she was done, Jelena passed the staff back to Garza, and he raised it to signal that their morning oration was complete. And then, as a gong sounded and the entire group turned to acknowledge the rising of the life-giving sun, the valley reverberated with the echoes of a single word, repeated again and again: *Epouroun! Epouroun! Epouroun!*

ABOUT THE AUTHORS

The thrillers of **DOUGLAS PRESTON** and **LINCOLN CHILD** "stand head and shoulders above their rivals" (*Publishers Weekly*). Preston and Child's *Relic* and *The Cabinet of Curiosities* were chosen by readers in a National Public Radio poll as being among the one hundred greatest thrillers ever written, and *Relic* was made into a number one box office hit movie. They are coauthors of the famed Pendergast series, and their recent novels include *City of Endless Night*, *Beyond the Ice Limit*, *Blue Labyrinth*, *Crimson Shore*, and *The Obsidian Chamber*. In addition to his novels, Preston writes about archaeology for *The New Yorker* and *National Geographic* magazines. Lincoln Child is a Florida resident and former book editor who has published seven novels of his own, including the huge bestseller *Deep Storm*.

Readers can sign up for The Pendergast File, a "strangely entertaining" newsletter from the authors, at their website, PrestonChild.com. The authors welcome visitors to their alarmingly active Facebook page, where they post regularly.